WE ARE INSIDE THE MIND OF PROFESSOR CHARLES WATKINS . . .

He is doomed to spin endlessly on a raft in the currents of the Atlantic. He makes a landfall on a tropical shore. He discovers a ruined stone city, participates, moon-dazed, in bloody rituals in the paradisal forest, is caught in the swirling, savage war of the Rat-dogs, is borne on the back of the lordly White Bird across the sea of the dead . . .

Charles Watkins is having a mental breakdown.

Or is he?

BRIEFING FOR A DESCENT INTO HELL

An extraordinary voyage into inner space . . .

"Moving from freak-out to a status almost mythic, and enriching the mental life of the reader to an almost incalculable extent!"

—*Washington Post*

Bantam Books by Doris Lessing

BRIEFING FOR A DESCENT INTO HELL
THE FOUR-GATED CITY

BRIEFING FOR
A DESCENT
INTO HELL
DORIS LESSING

BANTAM BOOKS
TORONTO · NEW YORK · LONDON

BRIEFING FOR A DESCENT INTO HELL
A Bantam Book / published by arrangement with
Alfred A. Knopf, Inc.

PRINTING HISTORY
Knopf edition published March 1971
2nd printing......March 1971
Bantam edition published August 1972
2nd printing
3rd printing
4th printing

Bantam Books are published by Bantam Books, Inc., a National
General company. Its trade-mark, consisting of the words
"Bantam Books" and the portrayal of a bantam, is registered
in the United States Patent Office and in other countries. Marca
Registrada. Bantam Books, Inc., 666 Fifth Ave., N.Y., N.Y. 10019.

PRINTED IN THE UNITED STATES OF AMERICA

This is for my son John,
the sea-loving man.

If yonder raindrop should its heart disclose,
Behold therein a hundred seas displayed.
In every atom, if thou gaze aright,
Thousands of reasoning beings are contained.
The gnat in limbs doth match the elephant.
In name is yonder drop as Nile's broad flood.
In every grain a thousand harvests dwell.
The world within a grain of millet's heart.
The universe in the mosquito's wing contained.
Within that point in space the heavens roll.
Upon one little spot within the heart
Resteth the Lord and Master of the worlds.
Therein two worlds commingled may be seen . . .

> The Sage Mahmoud Shabistari,
> in the Fourteenth Century
> *(The Secret Garden)*

This minuscule world of the sand grains is also the world of inconceivably minute beings, which swim through the liquid film around a grain of sand as fish would swim through the ocean covering the sphere of the earth. Among this fauna and flora of the capillary water are single-celled animals and plants, water mites, shrimplike crustacea, insects, and the larvae of infinitely small worms —all living, dying, swimming, feeding, breathing, reproducing in a world so small that our human senses cannot grasp its scale, a world in which the microdroplet of water separating one grain of sand from another is like a vast, dark sea.

> Marine Biologist Rachel Carson,
> Twentieth Century
> *(The Edge of the Sea)*

CENTRAL INTAKE HOSPITAL

Friday 15th August 1969

ADMITTANCE SHEET

NAME: *Unknown*

SEX: *Male*

AGE: *Unknown*

ADDRESS: *Unknown*

GENERAL REMARKS: *At midnight the police found Patient wandering on the Embankment near Waterloo Bridge. They took him into the station thinking he was drunk or drugged. They describe him as Rambling, Confused, and Amenable. Brought him to us at 3 a.m. by ambulance. During admittance Patient attempted several times to lie down on the desk. He seemed to think it was a boat or a raft. Police are checking ports, ships, etc. Patient was well dressed but had not changed his clothes for some time. He did not seem very hungry or thirsty. He was wearing trousers and a sweater, but he had no papers or wallet or money or marks of identity. Police think he was robbed. He is an educated man. He was given two Libriums but did not sleep. He was talking loudly. Patient was moved into the small Observation ward as he was disturbing the other Patients.*

NIGHT NURSE. 6 A.M.

Patient has been awake all day, rambling, hallucinated, animated. Two Librium three-hourly. Police no information. Clothes sent for tracing, but unlikely to yield results: Chain-store sweater and shirt and underclothes. Trousers Italian. Patient still under the impression he is on some sort of voyage. Police say possibly an amateur or a yachtsman.

DOCTOR Y. 6 P.M.

I need a wind. A good strong wind. The air is stagnant. The current must be pounding along at a fair rate. Yes, but I can't feel it. Where's my compass? *That* went days ago, don't you remember? I need a wind, a good strong wind. I'll whistle for one. I would whistle for one if I had paid the piper. A wind from the East, hard on to my back, yes. Perhaps I am still too near the shore? After so many days at sea, too near the shore? But who knows, I might have drifted back again inshore. Oh no, no, I'll try rowing. The oars are gone, don't you remember, they went days ago. No, you must be nearer landfall

than you think. The Cape Verde Islands were to
starboard—when? Last week. Last *when?* That was
no weak, that was my wife. The sea is saltier here
than close in shore. A salt salt sea, the brine coming
flecked off the horses' jaws to mine. On my face,
thick crusts of salt. I can taste it. Tears, seawater. I
can taste salt from the sea. From the desert. The
deserted sea. Sea horses. Dunes. The wind flicks
sand from the crest of dunes, spins off the curl of
waves. Sand moves and sways and masses itself into
waves, but slower. Slow. The eye that would measure the pace of sand horses, as I watch the rolling
gallop of sea horses would be an eye indeed. Aye
Aye. I. I could catch a horse, perhaps and ride it,
but for me a sea horse, no horse of sand, since my
time is man-time and it is God for deserts. Some
ride dolphins. Plenty have testified. I may leave my
sinking raft and cling to the neck of a sea horse, all
the way to Jamaica and poor Charlie's Nancy, or, if
the current swings me South at last, to the coast
where the white bird is waiting.

Round and round and round I go, the Diamond
Coast, the Canary Isles, a dip across the Tropic of
Cancer and up and across with a shout at the West
Indies to port, where Nancy waits for her poor
Charlie, and around, giving the Sargasso Sea a miss
to starboard, with Florida florissant to port, and
around and around, in the swing of the Gulf Stream,
and around, with the Azores just outside the turn of
my elbow, and down, past the coasts of Portugal
where my Conchita waits for me, passing Madeira,
passing the Canaries, always *en passant*, to the Diamond Coast again, and so around, and so around
again and again, for ever and ever unless the current swings me South. But that current could never
take me South, no. A current is set in itself, inexor-
able as a bus route. The clockwise current of the
Northern seas must carry me, carry me, unless ...

yes. They may divert me a little, yes they will, steering me with a small feather from their white wings, steadying me South, holding me safe across the cross not to say furious currents about the Equator but then, held safe and sound, I'd find the South Equatorial at last, at last, and safe from all the Sargassoes, the Scillas and the Charibs, I'd swoop beautifully and lightly, drifting with the sweet currents of the South down the edge of the Brazilian Highlands to the Waters of Peace. But I need a wind. The salt is seaming on the timbers and the old raft is wallowing in the swells and I am sick. I am sick enough to die. So heave ho my hearties, heave— no, they are all gone, dead and gone, they tied me to a mast and a great wave swept them from me, and I am alone, caught and tied to the North Equatorial Current with no landfall that I could ever long for anywhere in the searoads of all that rocking sea.

> *Nothing from Police. No reports of any small boats yachts or swimmers unaccounted for. Patient continues talking aloud, singing, swinging back and forth in bed. He is excessively fatigued. Tomorrow: Sodium Amytal. I suggest a week's narcosis.*
>
> DOCTOR Y. 17TH AUGUST.

> *I disagree. Suggest shock therapy.*
> DOCTOR X. 18TH AUGUST.

Very hot. The current is swinging and rocking. Very fast. It is so hot that the water is melting. The water is thinner than usual, therefore a thin fast rocking. Like heatwaves. The shimmer is strong. Light. Different textures of light. There is the light we know. That is, the ordinary light let's say of a day with

cloud. Then, sunlight, which is a yellow dance
added to the first. Then the sparkling waves of heat,
heat waves, making light when light makes them.
Then, the inner light, the fast shimmer, like a suspended snow in the air. Shimmer even at night
when no moon or sun and no light. The shimmer of
the solar wind. Yes, that's it. Oh solar wind, blow
blow blow my love to me. It is very hot. The salt has
caked my face. If I rub, I'll scrub my face with pure
sea salt. I'm becalmed, on a light, lit, rocking, deliri-
ously delightful sea, for the water has gone thin and
slippery in the heat, light water instead of heavy
water. I need a wind. Oh solar wind, wind of the
sun. Sun. At the end of Ghosts he said the Sun, the
Sun, the Sun, the Sun, and at the end of When we
Dead Awaken, the Sun, into the arms of the Sun via
the solar wind, around, around, around, around . . .

> *Patient very disturbed. Asked his
> name: Jason. He is on a raft in the
> Atlantic. Three caps. Sodium Amy-
> tal tonight. Will see him tomorrow.*
>   DOCTOR Y.

DOCTOR Y: Did you sleep well?
PATIENT: I keep dropping off, but I mustn't, I must
not.
DOCTOR Y: But why not? I want you to.
PATIENT: I'd slide off into the deep sea swells.
DOCTOR Y: No you won't. That's a very comfortable
bed, and you're in a nice quiet room.
PATIENT: Bed of the sea. Deep sea bed.
DOCTOR Y: You aren't on a raft. You aren't on the sea.
You aren't a sailor.
PATIENT: I'm not a sailor?
DOCTOR Y: You are in Central Intake Hospital, in bed,
being looked after. You must rest. We want
you to sleep.

PATIENT: If I sleep I'll die.

DOCTOR Y: What's your name? Will you tell me?

PATIENT: Jonah.

DOCTOR Y: Yesterday it was Jason. You can't be either, you know.

PATIENT: We are all sailors.

DOCTOR Y: I am not. I'm a doctor in this hospital.

PATIENT: If I'm not a sailor, then you aren't a doctor.

DOCTOR Y: Very well. But you are making yourself very tired, rocking about like that. Lie down. Take a rest. Try not to talk so much.

PATIENT: I'm not talking to you, am I? Around and around and around and around and around and around and around and around and around and around and around and around and . . .

NURSE: You must be feeling giddy. You've been going around and around and around for hours now, did you know that?

PATIENT: Hours?

NURSE: I've been on duty since eight, and every time I drop in to see you, you are going round and round.

PATIENT: The duty watch.

NURSE: Around and around what? Where? There now, turn over.

PATIENT: It's very hot. I'm not far away from the Equator.

NURSE: You're still on the raft then?

PATIENT: *You* aren't!

NURSE: I can't say that I am.

PATIENT: Then how can you be talking to me?

NURSE: Do try to lie easy. We don't want you to get so terribly tired. We're worried about you, do you know that?

PATIENT: Well, it is in your hands, isn't it?

NURSE: My hands? How is that?

PATIENT: *You.* You said *We.* I know that We. It is the categorical collective. It would be so easy for you to do it.

NURSE: But what do you want me to do?

PATIENT: *You* as *we.* Not you as *you.* Lift me, lift me, lift me. It must be easy enough for you. Obviously. Just use your—force, or whatever it is. Blast me there.

NURSE: Where to?

PATIENT: You know very well. Tip me South with your white wing.

NURSE: My white wing! I like the sound of that.

PATIENT: You can't be one of them. If you were, you'd know. You are tricking me.

NURSE: I'm sorry that you think that.

PATIENT: Or perhaps you're testing me. Yes, that's a possibility.

NURSE: Perhaps that is it.

PATIENT: It's just a question of getting out of the North Equatorial Current into the South Equatorial Current, from clockwise to anticlockwise. The wise anticlocks.

NURSE: I see.

PATIENT: Well, why don't you?

NURSE: I don't know how.

PATIENT: Is it a question of some sort of a password? Who was that man who was here yesterday?

NURSE: Do you mean Doctor Y? He was in to see you.

PATIENT: He's behind this. He knows. A very kindly contumacious man.

NURSE: He's kind. But I wouldn't say contumacious.

PATIENT: I say it, so why shouldn't you?

NURSE: And Doctor X was in the day before that.

PATIENT: I don't remember any Doctor X.

NURSE: Doctor X will be in later this afternoon.
PATIENT: In what?
NURSE: Do try and lie still. Try and sleep.
PATIENT: If I do, I'm dead and done for. Surely you must know that, or you aren't a maid mariner.
NURSE: I'm Alice Kincaid. I told you that before. Do you remember? The night you came in?
PATIENT: Whatever your name, if you sleep you die.
NURSE: Well, never mind, hush. There, poor thing, you are in a state. Just lie and—there, there. Shhhhh, hush. No, lie still. Shhh . . . there, that's it, that's it, sleep. Sleeeeeeeep. Sle-e-ep.

> *Patient distressed, fatigued, anxious, deluded, hallucinated.*
> *Try Tofronil? Marplan? Tryptizol? Either that or Shock.*
> DOCTOR X. 21ST AUGUST.

DOCTOR Y: Well now, nurse tells me you are Sinbad today?
PATIENT: Sin bad.   Sin bad.   Bad sin.
DOCTOR Y: Tell me about it? What's it all about?
PATIENT: I'm not telling you.
DOCTOR Y: Why not?
PATIENT: You aren't one of Them.
DOCTOR Y: Who?
PATIENT: The Big Ones.
DOCTOR Y: No, I'm just an ordinary sort of size, I'm afraid.
PATIENT: Why are you afraid?
DOCTOR Y: Who are they, The Big Ones?
PATIENT: There were giants in those days.
DOCTOR Y: Would you tell them?
PATIENT: I wouldn't need to tell them.
DOCTOR Y: They know already?

PATIENT: Of course.

DOCTOR Y: I see. Well, would you tell Doctor X?

PATIENT: Who is Doctor X?

DOCTOR Y: He was in yesterday.

PATIENT: In and Out. In and Out. In and Out.

DOCTOR Y: We think it would help if you talked to someone. If I'm no use to you, there's Doctor X, if you like him better.

PATIENT: Like? Like what? I don't know him. I don't see him.

DOCTOR Y: Do you see me?

PATIENT: Of course. Because you are there.

DOCTOR Y: And Doctor X isn't here?

PATIENT: I keep telling you, I don't know who you mean.

DOCTOR Y: Very well then. How about Nurse? Would you like to talk to her? We think you should try and talk. You see, we must find out more about you. You could help if you talked. But try to talk more clearly and slowly, so that we can hear you properly.

PATIENT: Are you the secret police?

DOCTOR Y: No. I'm a doctor. This is the Central Intake Hospital. You have been here nearly a week. You can't tell us your name or where you live. We want to help you to remember.

PATIENT: There's no need. I don't need you. I need Them. When I meet Them they'll know my needs and there'll be no need to tell Them. You are not my need. I don't know who you are. A delusion, I expect. After so long on this raft and without real food and no sleep at all, I'm bound to be deluded. Voices. Visions.

DOCTOR Y: You feel that—there. That's my hand. Is that a delusion? It's a good solid hand.

PATIENT: Things aren't what they seem. Hands have

come up from the dark before and slid away again. Why not yours?

DOCTOR Y: Now listen carefully. Nurse is going to sit here with you. She is going to stay with you. She is going to listen while you talk. And I want you to talk, tell her who you are and where you are and about the raft and the sea and about the giants. But you must talk more loudly and clearly. Because when you mutter like that, we can't hear you. And it is very important that we hear what you are saying.

PATIENT: Important to you.

DOCTOR Y: Will you try?

PATIENT: If I remember.

DOCTOR Y: Good. Now here is Nurse Kincaid.

PATIENT: Yes, I know. I know her well. She fills me full of dark. She darks me. She takes away my mind.

DOCTOR Y: Nonsense. I'm sure she doesn't. But if you don't want Nurse Kincaid either, we'll simply leave a tape-recorder here. You know what a tape-recorder is, don't you?

PATIENT: I did try and use one once but I found it inhibiting.

DOCTOR Y: You did? What for?

PATIENT: Oh some damned silly lecture or other.

DOCTOR Y: You give lectures do you? What sort of lectures? What do you lecture about?

PATIENT: Sinbad the sailor man. The blind leading the blind. Around and around and around and around and around and . . .

DOCTOR Y: Stop it! Please. Don't start that again. Please.

PATIENT: Around and around and around and around and . . .

DOCTOR Y: Around what? You are going around what? Where?

PATIENT: I'm not going. I'm being taken. The cur-

rent. The North Equatorial, from the North
African Coast, across, past the West Indies
to the Florida Current, past Florida around
the Sargasso Sea and into the Gulf Stream
and around with the West Wind Drift to
the Canaries and around past the Cape Verde
Islands around and around and around and
around . . .

DOCTOR Y: Very well then. But how are you going to
get out?

PATIENT: They. They will.

DOCTOR Y: Go on now. Tell us about it. What happens
when you meet them? Try and tell us.

> *He gives lectures. Schools, universi-*
> *ties, radio, television, politics? So-*
> *cieties to do with? Exploration,*
> *archeology, zoology? Sinbad. "Bad*
> *sin." Suggest as a wild hypothesis*
> *that just this once patient may have*
> *committed a crime and this not just*
> *routine guilt?*
>
> DOCTOR Y.

> *Accept hypothesis. What crime?*
>
> DOCTOR X.

Setting off from the Diamond Coast, first there
is the Southerly coastal current to get out of. Not
once or twice or a dozen times, on leaving the
Diamond Coast, the shore-hugging current has
dragged us too far South and even within sight of
that African curve which rounded would lead us in
helpless to the Guinea current to who knows what
unwanted landfalls. But we have always managed
just in time to turn the ship out and pointing West
with Trinidad our next stop. That is, unless this time
we encountered Them. Around and Around. It is

not a cycle without ports we long to reach. Nancy waits for poor Charlie in Puerto Rico, George has his old friend John on Cape Canaveral, and I when the ship has swung far enough inshore wait to see Conchita sitting on her high black rock and to hear her sing her song for me. But when greetings and farewells have been made so many times, they as well as we want the end of it all. And when the songs have been heard so often, the singers no longer are Nancy, alone, poor Charlie alone, or any of us. The last few journeys past the garden where Nancy waits, she was joined by all the girls in her town, and they stood along the wall over the sea watching us sail past, and they sang together what had so often called poor Charlie and his crew in to them before.

> Under my hand
>   flesh of flowers
> Under my hand
>   warm landscape
> You have given me back my world,
> In you the earth breathes under my hand.

> My arms were full of charred branches,
> My arms were full of painful sand.
> Now I sway in rank forests,
> I dissolve in strong rivers,
> I am the bone the flowers in flesh.

> Oh now we reach it—
>   now, now!

> The whistling hub of the world.
> It's as if God had spun a whirlpool,

> Flung up a new continent.

But we men stood in a line all along the deck and we sang to them:

If birds still cried on the shore,
If there were horses galloping all night,
Love, I could turn to you and say
Make up the bed,
Put fire to the lamp.
All night long we would lie and hear
The waves beat in, beat in,
If there were still birds on the dunes,
If horses still ran wild along the shore.

And then we would wave each other out of sight, our tears lessening with each circuit, for we were set for our first sight of Them, and they, the women, were waiting with us, for on us their release depended, since they were prisoners on that island.

On this voyage there were twelve men on board, with myself as Captain. Last time I played deckhand, and George was Captain. We were four days out from shore, the current swinging us along fair and easy, the wind coming from the North on to our right cheeks, when Charles, who was lookout, called us forward and there it was. Or, there they were. Now if you ask how it is we knew, then you are without feeling for the sympathies of our imaginations in waiting for just this moment. And that must mean that you yourselves have not yet learned that in waiting for Them lies all your hope. No, it is not true that we had imagined it in just such a form. We had not said or thought, ever: They will be shaped like birds or be forms of light walking on the waves. But if you have ever known in your life a high expectation which is met at last, you will know that the expectation of a thing must meet with that thing—or, at least, that is, the form in which it must be seen by you. If you have shaped in your mind an eight-legged monster with saucer eyes then if there is such a creature in that sea you will not see anything less, or more—that is what you are set to see. Armies of angels could appear out of the waves, but if you are waiting for a one-eyed giant, you could sail right through them and not feel more than a freshening of the air. So while we had not determined a shape in our thoughts, we had not been waiting for evil or fright. Our expectations had been for aid, for explanation, for a heightening of our selves and of our thoughts. We had been set like barometers for Fair. We had known we would strike something that rang on a higher, keener note than ourselves, and that is why we knew at once that this was what we had been sailing to meet, around and around and around and around, for so many cycles that it might even be said that the waiting to meet up with Them had become a circuit in our minds as well as in the ocean.

We knew them first by the feeling in the air, a crystalline hush, and this was accompanied by a feeling of strain in ourselves, for we were not strung at the same pitch as that for which we had been waiting.

It was a smart choppy sea and the air was flying with spray. Hovering above these brisk waves, and a couple of hundred yards away, was a shining disc. It seemed as if it should have been transparent, since the eye took in first the shine, like that of glass, or crystal, but being led inwards, as with a glass full of water, to what was behind the glitter. But the shine was not a reflected one: the substance of the disc's walls was itself a kind of light. The day was racingly cloudy, the sky half cloud, half sun, and all the scene around us was this compound of tossing waves and foam, and flying spray, of moving light, everything changing as we watched. We were waiting for strangers to emerge from the disc and perhaps let down, using the ways of humanity, a dinghy or a boat of some kind so that we, standing along the deck's edge, grasping fast to ropes and spars, might watch Them approach and take their measure—and adjust our thoughts and manners for the time. But no one appeared. The disc came closer, though so unnoticeably, being part of the general restless movement of the blue and the white, that it was resting on the air just above the waves a few paces off before we understood by a sinking of our hearts that we were not to expect anything so comfortable as the opening of a door, the letting down of a ladder, a boat, and arms bending as oars swung. But we were still not expecting anything in particular when it was already on us. What? What we felt was a sensation first, all through our bodies. In a fever or a great strain of exhaustion, or in love, all the resources of the body stretch out and expand and vibrate higher than in ordinary life. Well, we were vibrating at a higher pitch, and this was accompanied by a high shrill note in the air, of the kind that can break glasses— or can probably break much more, if sustained. The disc that had been in our eyes' vision a few yards away, an object among others, though an object stronger than the others, more obliterating—seemed to come in and invade our eyes. I am describing the sensation, for I cannot say what was the fact. It was certain that this disc rose a little way up from the waves, so that it was level with our deck, and then passed over us, or through us. Yet when it was on us, it seemed no longer a disc, with a shape, but it was more a fast beating of the air, a vibration that was also a sound. It was intolerable while it lasted, as if two different substances were in conflict, with no doubt of the outcome—but it did not last more than a moment, and when my eyes had lost the feeling of being filled with a swift-beating light, or sound, and my whole body from having been stretched or expanded or invaded, as if light (or sound) had the capacity of passing through one's tissues, but in a shape as definite as one's own, then I looked to see if George, who stood nearest to me, was still alive. But he was gone, and when I turned in terror to see where he was, and where the others were, they weren't there. No one. Nothing. The disc, which had again become a crystal disc, hovering over the waves on the other side of the ship, was lifting into the sky. It had swept away or eaten up or absorbed my comrades and left me there alone. All the ship was empty. The decks were empty. I was in terror. And worse. For all these centuries I had been sailing around and around and around and around for no other reason than that one day I would meet Them, and now at last we had indeed inhabited the same space of air, but I had been left behind. I ran to the other rail of the ship and clung there and opened my mouth to shout. I might indeed have shouted a little, or made some feeble kind of sound, but to what or to whom was I shouting? A silvery shining disc that seemed, as it lifted up and away into the air, that it ought to be transparent but was not? It had no eyes to see me, no mouth to acknowledge my shouting with a sound of its own. Nothing. And inside were eleven men, my friends, who I knew better than I knew myself. Since we do know our friends better than we know ourselves. Then, as I stood there, gazing into the scene of blue and white and silver that tossed and sprayed and shook and danced and dazzled, sea and air all mixed together, I saw that I was looking at nothing. The disc had vanished, was no more than the shape of a cell on my retina. Nothing.

I was sickened with loss, with knowledge of an unforeseeable callousness on their part. To take them and to leave me? In all our voyagings we had never envisaged that we might simply be lifted up and taken away like a litter of puppies or kittens. We had wanted instructions, or aid, we needed to be told how to get off this endless cycling and into the Southern current. Now that this had not happened, and no instructions or information had been given, only a sort of kidnapping, then I wanted to scream against their coldness and cruelty, as one small kitten that has been hidden by a fold of a blanket in the bottom of a basket mews out in loneliness as it moves blindly about, feeling with its muzzle and its senses for its lost companions among the rapidly chilling folds of the blanket.

I stayed at the deck's edge. For while the ship needed steering and the sails setting, and for all I knew we had already swung about, I could not handle this ship by myself. I already knew that I must leave her, unless I was to choose to live on board her alone, on the small chance that the Disc would hover down again and discharge my companions in the same way it had taken them off. But I did not think this was likely to happen. And I was afraid to stay.

It was as if that Disc, or Crystal, in its swift passage across or through the ship, across or through me, had changed the atmosphere of the ship, changed me. I was shaking and shivering in a cold dread. I could hardly stand, but leaned clinging to a rope. When the shaking had seemed to stop, and I stood clenching my teeth and waiting for the puppy-warmth of life to come back, then the shaking began again, like a fit of malaria, though this was a sort of weakness, not a fever. Now everything in the ship was inimicable to me, as if the disc's breath had started a rot in its substance. To say that I had been terrified and was still terrified would be too much of an everyday statement. No, I had been struck with foreignness, I had taken a deep breath of an insupportable air. I was not at all myself, and my new loathing that was so much more than a fear of the ship was in itself an illness. Meanwhile the sails shook and flapped and bellied or hung idle above my head. Meanwhile the ship shuddered and swung to every new shift in the fitfully changing wind. Meanwhile she was a creature that had been assaulted and left to die.

I began making a raft, using timber from the carpenter's store. I worked feverishly, wanting to get away. It never crossed my mind to stay on her, so strong was my fear. Yet I knew that to set off by myself on a raft was more dangerous than staying. On the ship was water, food, some shelter, until it foundered or crashed on a rock. Until then, it would be my safety. But I could not stay. It was as if my having been ignored, left behind, out of all my old comrades, was in itself a kind of curse. I had been branded with my ship.

I worked for many hours and when daylight went, I lashed a storm lantern to a spar and worked on through the night. I made a raft about twelve by twelve of balsa wood poles. To this I lashed a locker full of rations, and a barrel of water. I fitted a sail on a mast in the middle of the raft. I took three pairs of oars, and lashed two spare pairs securely to the timbers of the raft. In the centre of the raft I made a platform of planks about four feet across. And all this time I worked in a deadly terror, a cold sick fear, attacked intermittently by the fits of shaking so that I had to double up as if in cramp, and hold on to a support for fear I'd shake myself to pieces.

By the dawn my raft was done. The sky reddened in my face as I stood looking forward with the ship's movement, so I saw that the ship had already swung about and was heading back in the grip of the Guinea Current to the Cameroons or the Congo. I had to leave it as quickly as I could, and trust that I could still row myself out of this deadly shore-going current and back into the Equatorial stream once again. I put on all the clothes I could find. I let the raft fall into the sea, where it floated like a cork. And with all the sky aflame with sunrise like the inside of a ripening peach, I swarmed down a rope and swung myself on to the raft just as it was about to bob right out of my reach. I reached the raft still dry, though already beginning to be well damped by spray, and at once began rowing with my back to the sunrise. I rowed as if I were making towards safety and a good dry ship instead of away from one. By the time the sun stood up in a clear summer-hazy sky three or four handsbreadths from the horizon, our ship's sails were a low swarm of white, like a cluster of butterflies settled on the waves, and well behind me, and I was heading West on my real right course. And when I turned my head to look again, it was hard to tell whether I was looking at the white of the sails or at foam on a distant swell. For the sea had changed, to my advantage, and was rolling and rocking, and no longer chopping and changing. And so I rowed all that day, and most of that following night. I rowed and rowed and rowed, until my arms seemed separate from myself, they worked on without my knowing I was ordering them to. Then one day—I think it was three days after I last saw the sails of my ship vanishing East—there was a sudden squally afternoon and my clothes got soaked, and I lost my spare oars. And two days after that, a heavy sea dragged my last oars from me and since then I've been trusting myself to the current that curves West and North. And now I have all the time in the world to reflect that I am still engaged in the same journey in the same current, round and round and round, with the West Indies my next landfall, and poor Charlie's Nancy and her song, just as if I had stayed on the ship with my comrades. And after the women's song, just as before, around and around, past the

Sargasso Sea, and around in the Gulf Stream, and around in the swing of the sea past the coasts of Portugal and Spain, and around and around. But now I am not in a tall ship with sails like white butterflies but on a small raft and alone, around and around. And everything is the same, around and around, with only a slight but worsening change in the shape of my hope: will They, or the Disc, or Crystal Thing, on its next descent, be able to see the speck of my raft on the sea? Will they see me and find the kindness to give me a hail or a shouting reply when I ask them, How may I leave this Current? Friends, set me fair for that other coast, I pray you.

Yes, I'll hail them, of course, though now a new coldness in my heart tells me of a fear I didn't have before. I had not thought once, not in all those cycles and circles and circuits, around and around, that they might simply not notice me, as a man might not notice a sleeping kitten or a blind puppy hidden under the fold of his smelly blanket. Why should they notice the speck of a raft on the wide sea? Yet there is nothing for it but to go on, oarless, rudderless, sleepless, exhausted. After all I know it would be a kindness to land on Nancy's coast and tell her that her Charlie has met up at last with— what? Them, I suppose, though that is all I can tell her, not even how he felt as he became absorbed into the substance of that shining Thing. Will she sing her song to me on my raft, drifting past, will the women line up along the walls of their summer gardens and sing, and shall I then sing back how the time is past for love? And then on I'll drift to George's friend and shout to him how George has—what? And where? And then on and on and on, until I see again my Conchita waiting, dressed in the habit of a nun, where all my wandering and sailing has put her.

Man like a great tree
Resents storms.
Arms, knees, hands,
Too stiff for love,
As a tree resists wind.
But slowly wakes,
And in the dark wood
Wind parts the leaves
And the black beast crashes from the cave.

My love, when you say:
"Here was the storm,
Here was she,
Here the fabulous beast,"
Will you say too
How first we kissed with shut lips, afraid,
And touched our hands, afraid,
As if a bird slept between them?
Will you say:
"It was the small white bird that snared me"?

And so she sings, each time I pass, around and
around, and on and on.

DOCTOR X: Well, how are you this afternoon?
PATIENT: Around and around and around . . .
DOCTOR X: I'd like you to know that I believe you
could snap out of this any time you want.
PATIENT: Around and around and around . . .
DOCTOR X: Doctor Y is not here this weekend. I'm go-
ing to give you a new drug. We'll see how
that does.
PATIENT: In and out, out and in. In and out, out and
in.
DOCTOR X: My name is Doctor X. What is your name?
PATIENT: Around and . . .

*I think he may very well have re-
verted to age eleven or twelve.*

> *That was the age I enjoyed sea
> stories. He is much worse in my
> opinion. The fact is, he never ac-
> knowledges my presence at all.
> Doctor Y claims he reacts to him.*
> DOCTOR X. 24TH AUGUST.

DOCTOR Y: What is your name today?

PATIENT: It could be Odysseus?

DOCTOR Y: The Atlantic was surely not his sea?

PATIENT: But it could be now, surely, couldn't it?

DOCTOR Y: Well now, what's next?

PATIENT: Perhaps Jamaica. I'm a bit further South than usual.

DOCTOR Y: You've been talking practically non-stop for days. Did you know that?

PATIENT: You told me to talk. I don't mind thinking instead.

DOCTOR Y: Well, whatever you do, remember this: you aren't on a raft on the Atlantic. You did not lose your friends into the arms of a flying saucer. You were never a sailor.

PATIENT: Then why do I think I'm one?

DOCTOR Y: What's your real name?

PATIENT: Crafty.

DOCTOR Y: Where do you live?

PATIENT: Here.

DOCTOR Y: What's your wife's name?

PATIENT: Have I got a wife? What is she called?

DOCTOR Y: Tell me, why don't you ever talk to Doctor X? He's rather hurt about it. I would be too.

PATIENT: I've told you already, I can't see him.

DOCTOR Y: Well, we are getting rather worried. We don't know what to do. It's nearly two weeks since you came in. The police don't know who you are. There's only one thing we are fairly certain about: and that is that you aren't any sort of a sailor, professional

or amateur. Tell me, did you read a lot of
sailing stories as a boy?

PATIENT: Man and boy.

DOCTOR Y: What's George's surname? And Charlie's
surname?

PATIENT: Funny, I can't think of them . . . yes of
course, we all had the same name. The name
of the ship.

DOCTOR Y: What was the name of the ship?

PATIENT: I can't remember. And she's foundered or
wrecked long ago. And the raft never had a
name. You don't call a raft as you call a
person.

DOCTOR Y: Why shouldn't you name the raft? Give
your raft a name now?

PATIENT: How can I name the raft when I don't know
my own name. I'm called . . . what? Who
calls me? What? Why? You are Doctor
Why, and I am called Why—that's it, it was
the good ship Why that foundered in the
Guinea Current, leaving Who on the slippery raft and . . .

DOCTOR Y: Just a minute. I'll be away for four or five
days. Doctor X will be looking after you
till I get back. I'll be in to see you the
moment I'm back again.

PATIENT: In and out, out and in, in and out . . .

*New treatment. Librium. 3 Tofro-
nil 3 t.a.d.*

DOCTOR X. 29TH AUGUST.

The sea is rougher than it was. As the raft tilts
up the side of a wave I see fishes curling above my
head, and when the wave comes crashing over me
fishes and weed slide slithering over my face, to
rejoin the sea. As my raft climbs up up up to the
crest the fishes look eye to eye with me out of the

wall of water. There's that air creature, they think, just before they go slop over my face and shoulders, while I think as they touch and slide, they are water creatures, they belong to wet. The wave curls and furls in its perfect whirls holding in it three deep sea fish that have come up to see the sky, a tiddler fit for ponds or jam jars, and the crispy sparkle of plankton, which is neither visible nor invisible, but a bright crunch in the imagination. If men are creatures of air, and fishes whether big or small creatures of sea, what then are the creatures of fire? Ah yes, I know, but you did not see me, you overlooked me, you snatched up my comrades and let me lie squeaking inside my fold of smelly blanket. Where are they, my friends? Administering justice, are they, from the folds of fire, looking at me eye to eye out of the silkily waving fronds of fire. Look, there's a man, that's an air creature, they think, breathing yellow flame as we breath H_2O. There's something about that gasping gape, they think—George? poor Charlie?—that merits recognition. But they are beyond air now, and the inhabitants of it. They are flame throwers. They are fire storms. You think justice is a kindly commodity? No, it razes, it throws down, it cuts swathes. The waves are so steep, they crash so fast and furious I'm more under than up. They are teaching men—men are teaching men—to have fishes' lungs, men learn to breathe water. If I take a deep breath of water will my lungs' tissues adapt in the space of a wave's fall and shout: Yes, yes, you up there, you, sailor, breathe deep and we'll carry you on water as we carried you on air? After all *They* must have had to teach my friends George and Charles and James and the rest to take deep lungfuls of fire. You're not telling me that when the Crystal swirl enveloped me with the others it was ordinary air we breathed then, no, it was a cool fire, sun's breath, the solar wind, but there are lungs attached to men that lie as dormant as those of a babe in the womb, and they are waiting for the solar wind to fill them like sails. Air lungs for air, but organs made of crystal sound, of singing light, for the solar wind that will blow my love to me. Or me onwards to my love. Oh the waves rear so tall, they pitch and grow and soar, I'm more under than up, my raft is a little cork on the draughty sea and I'm sick, oh I'm so sick, pitch and toss, toss and pitch, my poor poor head and my lungs, if I stay on this thick heavy slimy barnacled raft which is shrieking and straining as the great seas crash then I'll puke my heart out and fall fainting away into the deep sea swells. I'll leave the raft, then.

Oh no, no, no, I've shed my ship, the good ship Why, and I've clung like limpets to my new hard bed the raft and now how can I leave, to go spinning down into the forests of the sea like a sick bird. But if I found a rock or an islet? Silly, there are no rocks or isles or islands or ports of call in the middle of the wide Atlantic sea here at 45 degrees on the Equator. But the raft is breaking up. It breaks. There were only ordinary sea ropes to fasten the balsa poles side by side and across and through, and what ropes could I ever find that could hold this clumsy collection of cross rafters steady in this sea? It's a storm. It's a typhoon. The sky is thunder black and with a sick yellowish white at the cloud's edge and the waves are blue Stephen's black and higher than the church tower and all the world is wet and cold and my ears are singing like the ague. And there goes my raft, splitting apart under me like bits of straw in the eddy of a kitchen gutter. There it goes, and I'm afloat, reaching out for straws or even a fishbone. I'm all awash and drowning and I'm cold, oh I am so cold, I'm cold where all my own inside vital warmth should be held, there along my spine and in my belly but there it is cold cold as the

moon. Down and down, but the corky sea upsends
me to the light again, and there under my hand is
rock, a port in the storm, a little peaking black rock
that no main mariner has struck before me, nor map
ever charted, just a single black basalt rock, which is
the uppermost tip of a great mountain a mile or two
high, whose lower slopes are all great swaying forests through which the sea buffalo herd and graze.
And here I'll cling until the storm goes and the light
comes clear again. Here at last I can stay still, the
rock is still, having thrust up from the ocean floor a
million years ago and quite used to staking its claim
and holding fast in the Atlantic gales. Here is a long
cleft in the rock, a hollow, and in here I'll fit myself
till morning. Oh now I'm a land creature again, and
entitled to a sleep steady and easy. I and the rock
which is a mountain's tip are solid together and now
it is the sea that moves and pours. Steady now. Still.
The storm has gone and the sun is out on a flat calm
solid sea with its surface gently rocking and not
flying about all over the place as if the ocean wanted
to dash itself to pieces. A hot singing salty sea, pouring
Westwards past me to the Indies next stop, but pouring past me, fast on my rock. Fast Asleep. Fast. Asleep.

NURSE: Wake up. Wake up there's a dear. Come on,
no that's it. Sit up, all right I'm holding you.

PATIENT: Why? What for?

NURSE: You must have something to eat. All right
you can go back to sleep in a minute. But
you certainly can sleep, can't you?

PATIENT: Why make me sleep if you keep waking me
up?

NURSE: You aren't really supposed to be sleeping
quite so much. You are supposed to be relaxed and quiet, but you do sleep.

PATIENT: Who supposes? Who gave me the pills?

NURSE: Yes but—well never mind. Drink this.

PATIENT: That's foul.

NURSE: It's soup. Good hot soup.

PATIENT: Let me alone. You give me pills and then you keep waking me up.

NURSE: Keep waking you up? I don't. It's like trying to wake a rock. Are you warm?

PATIENT: The sun's out, the sun . . .

> Who has not lain hollowed in hot rock,
> Leaned to the loose and lazy sound of water,
> Sunk into sound as one who hears the boom
> Of tides pouring in a shell, or blood
> Along the inner caverns of the flesh,
> Yet clinging like sinking man to sight of sun,
> Clinging to distant sun or voices calling?

NURSE: A little more, please.

PATIENT: I'm not hungry. I've learned to breathe water. It's full of plankton you know. You can feed your lungs as you feed your stomach.

NURSE: Is that so dear? Well, don't go too far with it, you'll have to breathe air again.

PATIENT: I'm breathing air *now*. I'm on the rock you see.

> See him then as the bird might see
> Who rocks like pinioned ship on warm rough air,
> Coming from windspaced fields to ocean swells
> That rearing fling gigantic mass on mass
> Patient and slow against the stubborn land,
> Striving to achieve what strange reversal
> Of that monstrous birth when through long ages
> Labouring, appeared a weed-stained limb,

A head, at last the body of the land,
Fretted and worn for ever by a mothering
sea
A jealous sea that loves her ancient pain.

NURSE: Why don't you go and sit for a bit in the
day room? Aren't you tired of being in bed
all the time?
PATIENT: A jealousy that loves. Her pain.
NURSE: Have you got a pain? Where?
PATIENT: Not me. You. Jealously loving and nursing
pain.
NURSE: I haven't got a pain I assure you.

PATIENT: He floats on lazy wings down miles of foam,
And there, below, the small spreadeagled
shape
Clinging to black rock like drowning man,
Who feels the great bird overhead and
knows
That he may keep no voices, wings or winds
Who follows hypnotised down glassy gulfs,
His roaring ears extinguished by the flood.

NURSE: Take these pills dear, that's it.

PATIENT: Who has not sunk as drowned man sinks,
Through sunshot layers where still the
undercurve
Of lolling wave holds light like light in
glass,
Where still a jewelled fish slides by like
bird,
And then the middle depths where all is dim
Diffusing light like depths of forest floor.
He falls, he falls, past apprehensive arms
And spiny jaws and treacherous pools of
death,

Till finally he rests on ocean bed.

Here rocks are tufted with lit fern, and fish
Swim shimmering phosphorescent through
the weed,
And shoals of light float blinking past like
eyes,
Here all the curious logic of the night.
Is this sweet drowned woman floating in her
hair?

The sea-lice hop on pale rock scalp like
toads.
And this a gleam of opalescent flesh?
The great valves shut like white doors fold-
ing close.
Stretching and quavering like the face of
one
Enhanced through chloroform, the smiling
face
Of her long half-forgotten, her once loved,
Rises like thin moon through watery
swathes,
And passes wall-eyed as the long dead
moon.

He is armed with the indifference of deep-
sea sleep
And floats immune through searoots fed
with flesh,
Where skeletons are bunched against cave
roofs
Like swarms of bleaching spiders quivering,
While crouching engines crusted with pale
weed,
Their shafts and pistons rocking through
the green . . .

NURSE: Now do come on dear. Oh dear, you are upset, aren't you? Everybody has bad times, every one gets upset from time to time. I do myself. Think of it like that.

PATIENT: Not everyone has known these depths
The black uncalculated wells of sea,
Where any gleam of day dies far above,
And stagnant water slow and thick and foul . . .

NURSE: It's no good spitting your pills out.
PATIENT: Foul, fouled, fouling, all fouled up . . .
NURSE: One big swallow, that will do it, that's done it.
PATIENT: You wake me and you sleep me. You wake me and then you push me under. I'll wake up now. I want to wake.
NURSE: Sit up then.
PATIENT: But what is this stuff, what are these pills, how can I wake when you . . . who is that man who pushes me under, who makes me sink as drowned man sinks and . . .
NURSE: Doctor X thinks this treatment will do you good.
PATIENT: Where's the other, the fighting man?
NURSE: If you mean Doctor Y, he'll be back soon.
PATIENT: I must come up from the sea's floor. I must brave the surface of the sea, storms or no, because They will never find me down there. Bad enough to expect Them to come into our heavy air, all smoky and fouled as it is, but to expect them down at the bottom of the sea with all the drowned ships, no that's not reasonable. No I must come up and give them a chance to see me there, hollowed in hot rock.

NURSE: Yes, well, all right. But don't thrash about like that . . . for goodness' sake.

PATIENT: Goodness is another thing. I must wake up. I must. I must keep watch. Or I'll never get out and away.

NURSE: Well I don't know really. Perhaps that treatment isn't right for you? But you'd better lie down then. That's right. Turn over. Curl up. There. Hush. Hushhhhhhh. Shhhhhhhhhhhhhhhhhhhhh.

PATIENT: Hushabye baby
lulled by the storm
if you don't harm her
she'll do you no harm

I've been robbed of sense. I've been made without resource. I have become inflexible in a flux. When I was on the Good Ship Lollipop, I was held there by wind and sea. When I was on the raft, there was nobody there but me. On this rock I'm fast. Held. I can't do more than hold on. And wait. Or plunge like a diver to the ocean floor where it is as dark as a fish's gut and there's nowhere to go but up. But I do have an alternative, yes. I can beg a lift can't I? cling on to the coattails of a bird or a fish. If dogs are the friends of man, what are a sailor's friends? Porpoises. They love us. Like to like they say, though when has a porpoise killed a man, and we have killed so many and for curiosity, not even for food's or killing's sake. A porpoise will take me to my love. A sleek-backed singing shiny black porpoise with loving eyes and a long whistler's beak. Hold on there porpoise, poor porpoise in your poisoned sea, filled with stinking effluent from the bowels of man, and waste from the murderous mind of man, don't die yet, hold on, hold me, and take me out of this frozen grinding Northern circuit down and across into the tender Southern-running current and the longed-for shores. There now. Undersea if you have to, I can breathe wet if I must, but above sea if you can, in case I may hail a passing friend who has taken the shape of a shaft of fire or a dapple of light. There, porpoise, am I true weight? A kind creature? Kith and Kind? Just take me South, lead me to the warmer current, oh now it is rough, we toss and heave as it was in the Great Storm, when my raft fell apart like straw, but I know now this is a good cross patch, it is creative, oh what a frightful stress, what a strain, and now out, yes out, we're well out, and still swimming West, but South West, but anti-clock Wise, whereas before it was West with the clock and no destination but the West Indies and Florida and past the Sargasso Sea and the Gulf Stream and the West Wind Drift and the Canaries Current and around and around and around and around but now, oh porpoise, on this delicate soap bubble our earth, spinning all blue and green and iridescent, where Northwards air and water swirl in time's direction left to right, great spirals of breath and light and water, now oh porpoise, singing friend, we are on the other track, and I'll hold on, I'll clasp and clutch to the last breath of your patience, being patient, till you land me on that beach at last, for oh porpoise, you must be sure and take me there, you must land me fairly at last, you must not let me cycle South too far, dragging in the Brazil current of my mind, no, but let me gently step off your slippery back on to the silver sand of the Brazilian coast where, lifting your eyes, rise the blue and green heights of the Brazilian Highlands. There, there, is my true destination and my love, so, purpose, be sure to hold your course.

There now, there's the shore. And now more than ever we must hold our course to true. There are no rocks, shoals or reefs here porpoise, which could stub your delicate nose or take strips of blubber off your sleek black back, but there is the shining coast and of all the dangers of the Southern Current this one is worst, that if we keep our eyes on that pretty shore wishing we were on it, then the current will sweep us on in our cycle of forgetting around and around and around and around again back to the coasts of Africa with hummocks of Southern ice for company, so hold on now porpoise and keep your mind on your work, which is me, my landfall, but never let yourself dream of that silver sand and the deep forests there for if you do, your strength will ebb and you'll slide away southwards like a dead or a dying fish.

There. Yes. Here we are, close in, and the thunder of the surf is in us. But close your ears, porpoise, don't listen or look, let your thoughts be all of a strong purposeful haul. In. And in. With the wash of the southdragging current cold on your left flank. In. Yes, and I'm not looking either dear porpoise, for if I did not reach that shore now and if we did have to slide away falling South and around again and again and again then I think I'd ask you porpoise to treat me as men treat porpoises and carve me up for your curiosity. But there, closer. Yes, closer. We are so close now that the trees of the beach and the lifting land beyond the beach are hanging over us as trees hang over a tame inland river. And we're in. But will you come with me, splitting your soft fat black shining tail to make legs to walk on, strolling up with me to the Highlands that are there? No, well then, goodbye porpoise, goodbye, slide back to your playful sea and be happy there, live, breathe, until the poison man makes for all living creatures finds you and kills you as you swim. And now I roll off your friendly back, thank you, thank you kind fish, and I find my feet steady under me on a crunching sand with the tide's fringe washing cool about my ankles.

And now leaving the sea where I have been around and around for so many centuries my mind is ringed with Time like the deposits on shells or the fall of years on tree trunks, I step up on the dry salty sand, with a shake of my whole body like a wet dog.

————————————————————————

It must have been about ten in the morning. The sun was shining full on my back at midmorning position. The sky was cloudless, a full deep blue. I was standing on a wide beach of white sand that stretched on either side for a couple of miles before curving out of sight behind rocky headlands. Before me, a thick forest came down to the sand's edge. A light wind blew off the sea and kept the branches in a lively movement. The leaves sparkled. So did the sea. The sands glittered. It was a scene of great calm and plenty and reassurance, but at the same time, there was a confusion of light. I was pleased to step out of the sands' glare into the cool of the trees. The undergrowth was low, and it was easy to walk. From the beach I had seen that the land lifted fast to some heights that seemed as if they might be rock-fringed plateaux. I was looking for a path as I walked Westwards under the great trees, and at last I saw a sandy track that seemed to lead to the high land in front. It was a calm and soothing walk. The pounding of the surf made a heavy silence here. Above, the branches held a weight of silence that was sharpened by a thousand birds. And soon I heard in front of me a thundering as loud as the surf which was now three or four miles behind. I was on the banks of a river which cascaded down through rocks to crash into a lower wider stream which rolled glossily away to join the sea. The track ran upwards beside the stream, and became a narrow footpath between rocks by the cataract. I walked slowly, drenched by a spray that dissolved the bitter salt of the sea from my face. When I reached the top of the cascade and looked back, I was surveying a sharp sliding fall in the land all the way along the coast. The river, where it broadened out and became peaceful, after its long rocky descent, was a mile or even more below where I now stood. I could see North and South for miles over the roof of the forest I had passed through and, beyond the forest, the blue ocean that faded into the blue of the sky in a band of ruffling white cloud like celestial foam. Turning myself about, the headlands I had seen from the beach were still high in front of me, for this was an intermediate ridge only. And I was again in a forest, which was rather less tall and thick, and where the gorse and heather of the higher land was already beginning to intrude downwards. This forest had a more lively and a more intimate air than the lower one, for it was full of birds and the chattering of troops of monkeys. There was a heavy scent. It came from a tree I had not seen before. It was rather like a chestnut, but it had large mauveish-pink flowers, like magnolias, and the light breeze had spread this scent so that it seemed to come from every tree and bush. There was no feeling of hostility towards the intruder in this place. On the contrary, I felt welcome there, it was as if this was a country where hostility or dislike had not yet been born. And in a few moments, as I steadily climbed up the track, a large spotted animal like a leopard walked out of the clump of bamboo just off my course, turned to look reflectively at me, and then squatted by the side of the path, watching what I would do. Its face was alert, but benign, and its green eyes did not blink. It did not occur to me that

I should be frightened of it. I walked steadily on until I came level with it. It was about six paces away and seemed extremely large and powerful. Squatting, its head was no lower than mine. I looked into the beast's face with a variety of nod, since I did not think a smile would be signal enough, and then, like a housecat that wishes to acknowledge your presence, or your friendship, but is too lazy or too proud to move, this leopard or puma or whatever it was, simply half-closed its eyes and purred a little. I walked on. The beast watched me for a while, followed me for a few steps, and then bounded off the track and away into some large bushes on the banks of the river that glinted and shivered with iridescent light: a hundred spider's filaments were catching the light. I went on up. By now it was late afternoon, and the sun was forward of me, and shining uncomfortably into my eyes. Looking back, it appeared to me that I had half-covered the distance between the shore and my goal, the rockfringed plateau, but the great crack or sliding away in the body of the land where I had climbed up beside the cataracts did not show at all; it all seemed like a long steady slide to the beach, with only some plumes of grey mist to show where the water fell. The land's fall was marked more by sound, the still audible roar of the Falls. If I had not climbed up myself and experienced that rift, I would not have believed in its existence, and therefore in front of me might very well be other falls or slides that were now swallowed and smoothed over by the forest. Here the river poured past me, in a deep-green roll between high banks. It was a paradise for birds and for monkeys, and as I stood to rest and to relieve my eyes for a while of the sun's glitter here, under trees, I saw on the opposite bank, on a white stretch of sand, some little deer step down to drink. I decided to rest. I found a grassy

slope where the sunlight fell through layers of lightly moving leaves, and fell asleep in a dapple of
light. When I woke I found the golden spotted beast
stretched out beside me. It was getting dark under
the trees. I had slept longer than I had meant to. I
decided to stay where I was for the night, since I
took it that my friend the big cat would stay by me
to guard me. Having found a tree laden with a kind
of purpley-orange fruit, rather like a plum, I made
my evening meal of these, the first land food I had
eaten for so long it was like eating fruit for the first
time in my life, every mouthful a delightful experi-
ment. Then I sat down again and waited as the light
ebbed in that hour when everything in nature is sad
because of the sinking sun. The yellow beast moved
closer to me, so that it was within my outstretched
arm's length, and it lay with its great head on its
outstretched forepaws and gazed across the river
with its green eyes, and I felt that it was pleased to
have my company as the sunlight left our side of the
earth and the night came creeping up from the sea.
We sat there together as sight went: first the deeply
running river, then the trees on the far bank whose
highest boughs held light longest, then nearer
bushes, and finally individual blades of grass that I
had marked as small guideposts, trying to fix their
shapes—as if the heavy downsettling of the dark
could be withheld by such small sentinels. Sound
came in, with more weight to it in the dark. The
thunder of the beaches that were now miles away
still made an undersilence, the river's spiral rolling
in its bed was an undersound to its surface splash-
ings and runnings, and the night birds began to stir
and talk in the branches that hung very low overhead. And once the great beast lifted his head and
roared, and the sound crashed in dull echoes back
and forth off hillsides and escarpments I could not
see. I heard a movement in the bushes at my back,

and thought that perhaps my friend the beast had gone off to hunt or to travel, but when I peered through the thick but sweet-smelling dark I saw that now there were two beasts stretched out side by side, and the newcomer was delicately licking the face of the first, who purred.

The dark lay heavily, but it was not cold at all, there was a moist warmth in the air that I took into my lungs which were slowly giving up the salt that had impregnated them so much that only now breath was again becoming an earth-, rather than a sea-creature's function. Then the dark glistened with an inner light, and I turned my head to the left and saw how the glade filled with moonlight, and the river showed its running in lines of moving light. The moon was not yet visible, but soon it rose up over the trees that from where I sat on turf seemed close to the sky's centre. The stars went out, or were as if trying to show themselves from beneath a sparkling water, and the glade was filled with a calm light. The two yellow beasts, not yellow now, their patterns of dark blotched light having become like the spoor of an animal showing black on a silvery-dewed earth, were licking each other and purring and it seemed as if they were restless and wished to move about. And as I thought this I decided to continue my journey by night, for it was warm enough, and the track running up alongside the stream was of sand unlittered by rocks or ruts, and everything was light and easy. I got up, leaving my sweet-smelling glade with regret, and went on up towards the heights, and the two big cats followed me at a few paces, their green eyes glowing in the moonlight when I turned to make sure that they were still there, for they moved so quietly it was like being followed by two silvery shadows.

The night seemed very short. It seemed no time before the moon, as the sun had done earlier, was standing full before my eyes in the Western sky, and its solemn shine filled my eyes with its command until it seemed as if the inside of my skull was being washed with moonshine. Then I turned to look back and saw that the morning was colouring the sky pink and gold over the sea. But my two friendly beasts had gone. I was alone again. The river on my left, now grey with the light that comes before sunrise, was no longer a full steady glide, but was wider and more shallow and broken by rocks, little falls and islands. Ahead it was rushing from another but much wider cataract, and the path I was on mounted steeply between trees that had the twisted stubborn gallantry of those forced to live in a mountain air and on a sharp slope where the soil is continually thinned by rain. I was by now very tired, but I thought it would be better to walk on and up until the sun had again moved forward and was shining into my face and eyes. I did walk on, but now it was slow going, for the track was a path, sometimes not much more than footholds in rocks feet apart, and often slippery from the spray of the river.

I went on up and up, half stunned by the crashing of the waters, and by nasty tearing winds that seemed to blow from all sides, buffeting the breath half out of me. Yet I was exhilarated, by the liveliness of that air, and the fighting to keep my lungs filled, so that everything about me was made distinct twice over—by my clearminded condition, and by the fresh shadowless light of dawn. The edge of the plateau and its clustering rocks now seemed so close above me that the winds might roll down rocks to crush me, or as if the whole mass might slide in, as lower down the mountainside the weight of earth had already slid away. But I still went on, pulling myself by branches, and bushes, and even clumps of tall reed, which cut my hands and arms.

If the wind had not beaten all clear thought out of my head I might by then have become too discouraged to go on, but although what my eyes saw filled me with foreboding, I continued like a robot. For it was now evident that ahead of me was a narrow cleft, possibly too dangerous to use in my ascent, and that above that—should I reach that height—a perpendicular rock rose smooth as glass to the edge of the escarpment. There seemed no way around the cleft. On one side of the sharp rock which it split the waters were thundering down, more through the air than over a rocky bed. All I could see on that side of me were masses of water mostly spray. On the other side was a very steep shaley slope beneath which was a precipice. It could not be possible to make my way to the right across this slope, for even a small pebble thrown on to it started an avalanche which I could hear crashing into the forest far below. Yet the track had followed the river all the way up here, somebody or something had used that track—and its destination seemed in fact to be this cleft in the rock ahead. So I went on up into it. The morning sunlight was a glitter in the blue sky far above my head, for I was enclosed in a half dark, smelling of bats. Now I had to squirm my way up, my feet on one wall, my back and shoulders against the other. It was a slow painful process, but at last I scrambled up on to a narrow ledge against the final glassy wall. Looking down, it was a scene of magnificent forests through which the river went in a shining green streak, and beyond the forests, the circling white rim of sand, and beyond that, a horizon of sea. Up here all the air was filled with the sharp smell of river spray and the flowering scents from the forests below. The evil-smelling cleft I had come through now seemed to have had no real part in my journey, for its dark and constriction seemed foreign to the vast clear space of the way I had been—but that had not been

so, and I made myself remember it. Without the
painful climb through the cleft I would not be
standing where I was—and where I was had no way
on and up, or so it seemed. I had to go up, since
there was nothing else to do, but I could not go up.
The ledge I stood on, about a yard wide, dwindled
away into air very soon, as I saw, when I explored it
to its end on either side. In front of my face was this
smooth dark rock like glass, into which I peered as I
had into the sides of glossy waves in the sea. Only
here there were no fish staring out at me, only a
faint reflection of a face shaggy with many weeks'
growth of beard. And now I did not know what to
do. It was not possible to climb up that glassy rock.
It was twenty, thirty feet high, and it had no crack
or rough place in it. I sat down, looking East into
the morning sun, back over the way I had come,
and thought that I might as well die in this place as
in any other. Then there was a movement in the
cleft, and I saw the head of the yellow beast come
cautiously up, for it was a tricky climb even for
him—it must have been as much too narrow for him
as it had been too wide for me. After him came his
friend, or his mate. I moved well over to give the
big animals room to stand on the ledge, but they did
not remain beside me. First one and then the other
turned to give me a long steady stare from its green
eyes. Their great square tufted yellow heads were
outlined against the deep blue of the sky beyond—
and then first one and then the other went on up
the precipitous glassy rock, in a couple of big easy
bounds. I saw the two heads, still outlined against
the blue sky, peering down at me over the rocks
thirty feet above. I got up and moved to the place
on the ledge from where these two had just bounded, unable to believe what I had seen, and then I
noticed that on the smooth glassy surface was a
roughened streak, like a path, which was only visi-

ble when the light struck it at a certain angle. This
was not as rough as the trunk of a thick-barked tree,
but it was as rough as weather-worn granite. Without the example of the two beasts I would never
have even thought of attempting to climb like a fly
up this ribbon of rough across the smooth, but now I
stood as high as I could, reaching up and up with
my palms, and I found that by not thinking of how
terrible and dangerous a thing it was I was doing,
my hands and feet clung to this rough breathing rock
face, and I found I had come to the top of the
impassable mirrorlike rock, and I fell forward among
rocks on the edge of the plateau for which I had
been aiming. It was at once evident that this height,
the summit of my aims since I had landed on the
beach far below the day before, was the lowland
plain to mountains that rose far ahead, to the West,
on a distant horizon, probably fifty miles away.
Looking down over the frightful path I had ascend-
ed, it now seemed nothing very much, and the sharp
glass summit that I had thought it impossible to
surmount was no more alarming than—anything
that one has done, and apparently done easily. The
broad river was a shining silver streak. The lower
falls ten or twelve miles away where the whole land
with its burden of forest slid sharply down was no
more than a shadowy line across treetops, and a
white cloud low over the forest was the miles-long
cataract. The high falls, close under the escarpment,
whose spray reached almost to the summit, was
sound only, for that long tumbling descent was not
visible at all.

All the coast lay open to me now, and the blue
ocean beyond. And it was as if there was nobody in
the world but myself. There was not a ship on the
sea, or so much as a canoe on the river, and the long
forests lay quiet beneath, and in those miles of trees
there was not even a single column of smoke that

might show a homestead or a traveller making himself a meal.

On the plateau where I stood, the vegetation was different. Here were the lighter, gayer, layered trees of the savannah, with its long green grasses that would soon turn gold. As I looked West to the mountains that in winter must have snow massed on their peaks which were now summer-blue, the sound of water still came from my left. About half a mile South, over a fairly level ground, I found the source of this noise. The river whose course I had traced up from the sea here ran fast along a shallower rockier bed. It was a stream, a wide bird-shrill splashy stream with gentle inlets and beaches a child could play safely on. But this river did not fall with a roar over the edge of the escarpment, and down those glassy sides which indeed looked as if they had at one time been smoothed by water. No, at about half a mile from the cliff's edge there was a chasm in the riverbed a couple of hundred yards wide. The great mass of water simply slid into it, almost without noise, and vanished into the earth. But it was possible to see where the riverbed had run, thousands or millions of years ago. For on the other side of the hole where the water rushed into the earth, the river's old bed still existed, a shallow enough channel, but wide, and widening towards the cliff where it had once fallen, and overgrown with shrubs and grass, and very rocky. The channel was worn down more deeply on one side, where the water had believed that it must make a loop in the riverbed, as is the way of rivers which cannot by nature run straight, and whose bodies spiral around and around exerting a pressure on one bank and then on the other. But the water had not known about the plunge over the cliff which lay just ahead and which would make its preparations for a bend useless: the water had crashed straight over the edge, and when

I stood there to look down, I saw that the worn smoothed path of the stream when it had been a waterfall still showed among the littered rocks below the glassy coping over which I had believed it impossible to climb. The river emerged suddenly, a hundred feet below after its long dark passage through the rock. Out it came, as sparkling clear and noisy as it had been above, before it had ever tasted the air of the underearth. After its emergence it crashed and plunged and roared and dashed itself to pieces as I had seen that morning while I climbed up beside it.

I returned to look down into the hole in the plain where the river fell as neatly as bathwater into a plughole, and saw that above the great chasm the air swirled with iridescent spray. I was now again looking Westwards into the setting sun, and I had to find a place to sleep that night. I was not able, looking back along my days and nights, to remember when I had slept well and calmly. Not since I landed on this friendly shore—for by sleep I did not mean that snatched half-hour while the sun set and the yellow beast watched. Not on the dolphin's friendly back, and certainly not on the rock or on the raft. Time stretched behind me, brightly lit, glaring, dangerous, and uniform—without the sharp knife-slices of dark across it. For when we normally look back along our road, it is as if regularly sharp black shadows lie across it, with spaces of sunlight or moonlight in between. I had come to believe that I was now a creature that had outgrown the need to sleep, and this delighted me.

I decided to watch night fall beside my friends the great coloured beasts, and wandered back in a sunset-tinted world to where they had shown me how to scramble over the impassable glass. But they were not there. Again the air was filled with the loneliness of the sunset hour. I was melancholy

enough to cry, or to hide my head under a blanket—
if I had got one, and slide with my sadness into a
regression from the light. But the scene was too
magnificent not to watch as the sun fell sharply
behind the distant blue peaks, and the dark fell first
over the sea, then over the forests, and then crept
slowly up to where I sat with my back against a tree
which was still small and elastic enough for me to
feel the trunk moving as the night breeze started up.
And again I watched the moon rise, though this
evening I was so high I could see first the blaze of
clear silver in the dark of the Eastern sky, then a
crisping sparkle of silver on the far ocean, and then
the first slice of silver as the moon crept up out of
the water. And again it was a night as mild and as
light as the last. I sat watching the night pass, and
waited for my splendid beasts. But they did not
come. They did not come! And they never came. I
did not see them again, though sometimes, when I
stand on the very edge of the rock-fringed plateau
and look down over the tops of the forest trees
below I fancy I see a blaze of yellow move in the
yellow-splashed dark, or imagine that by a river
which from here is a winding blue-green streak, I
see a yellow dot: the beast crouching to drink. And
sometimes the loud coughing sound of a beast, or a
roaring louder than all the noise of the falling waters
makes me think of them—and hope for their assistance for the next traveller who makes his long
delayed landfall on this glorious coast.

Again the night was short. I may have slept a
little, but if so it was a sleep so dazzling with the
light which lay full on my lids that in the morning
what lay behind me to the time of the sunset was a
broad space of time evenly filled with a cool refresh-
ing silver. I thought that I should perhaps try to
make my way to the distant mountains when the
sunlight had fully come back, but when the light did

come—when the little bubble of earth turned itself around so that the patch I stood on stared into the sun's face, then I saw that the tree I had been leaning against all night grew out of a large flat rock, and that ...

And now I must be careful to set down my mind's movement accurately. For suddenly it had changed into that gear when time is slower—as when, falling off a ladder, one has time to think: I shall land *so*, just there, and I must turn in the air slightly so that my backbone does not strike that sharp edge. And you do turn in the air, and even have time to think: this fall may hurt me badly, is there someone in the house to help me—and so on and so forth. All this in a space of time normally too short for any thought at all. But we are wrong in dividing the mind's machinery from time: they are the same. It is only in such sharp emphatic moments that we can recognize this fact. As I was staring at the flat rock, which had unmistakably been dressed, for I could see manmarks at its edges, my mind slowed, while time went faster; or time went slower while my mind speeded—to use our ordinary way of reckoning. Whatever the process, I was suddenly quite remarkably alert and excited, and had even got to my feet without knowing I had, and I was standing upright looking around me. I was looking at the foundations of a great house, or temple, or public building of some sort, which now lay clear to see for a couple of hundred yards all around me in the fresh green grass. But I had not seen anything yesterday but a grassy savannah with some rocks scattered about among low trees. Now the ruinous foundation was unmistakable. It was as if the knowledge of what I would see caused me to see what otherwise I could not—for I already half-believed that my seeing had created what I saw. For it was so hard to believe that yesterday I had clambered up over the edge of the escarpment ready to accept anything at all, from peopled cities to men with one eye in the middle of their foreheads, and yet I had not seen what was so clearly to be seen. This city, or town, or fortress, had been of stone. Everywhere around me the floors and foundations lay clearly visible. Everywhere lay pillars, columns and lintel stones. I walked North for a while—but in this direction there seemed no end to this evidence of men having lived here once. I walked West—the city continued well beyond where I tired and turned South. The slabs and hunks and floors of dressed stone continued as far as the riverbank I had walked along yesterday—and had seen nothing of ruins. And they extended right to the edge of the cliff. Once there had stood here, on this escarpment's verge, overlooking the sea and the forests, a very large and very fine city.

Now it was not possible for me to leave the place. Before the sun had risen, I had intended to travel onwards to the mountains, but now this old place drew me. I could not leave it. And yet there seemed no place I could shelter. I walked back and forth for some time, while the sun rose up swiftly over the blue-green ocean. In my mind was a half thought that I might find a house or a room or something that might shelter me if it rained or blew too hard. And so it was. Where I had walked—or so I believed, but it was hard now to see exactly where I had moved, in so many stridings back and forth—but certainly where I had looked often enough, I saw ruins standing up from the earth, and when I walked towards them, saw that the mass of stone had once been a very large house, or a meeting- or storage-place. Dry stone walls were whole, reaching up perhaps fifty feet. The matching and working of the stone, which was of a warm earthy yellow, that stone which is time-hardened clay, was very fine and accomplished, with many patterns worked into it. The floor, only lightly covered with blown yellowy earth and rubble, was of a mosaic in blue, green and gold. I stood in a large central room, and doors led off at the corners into smaller rooms with lower walls. But there were no roofs or ceilings. I walked back and forth over the patterned floor, between the many and various walls, and the place was whole, save for the absent roof, in whose place was first a clear sparkling blue, and then the sun itself, pouring down, so that the interior became all sharp black shadows and washes of golden light. There was not so much as a stone loose or fallen from the walls, not so much as a half-inch of mosaic lost from the vast floor. And yet I had not seen this building standing quietly among the coloured grasses. I walked to where the door had been, and looked out, and was not surprised at all to see that I was surrounded by the ruins of a stone city, that stretched as far as I could see from the top of these deep stone steps. Trees grew among the buildings, and there had been gardens, for there were all kinds of flowering and scented plants everywhere, water channels ran from house to house, their cool stone beds still quite whole and as if invisible workmen maintained them. I now had a wide choice of buildings of all kinds for my home, but there was not a roof among the lot of them. Probably these buildings had once been thatched? This sharp tender young grass became, as it aged, the wiry-stemmed reed man uses for thatching? What kind of city was this which was in such good preservation that it seemed it was inhabited by friendly hardworking ghosts—and yet had no roofs? And what stone city of such size and magnificence ever has had thatched roofs?

I chose a smaller house than most, which had a rose garden, and water running everywhere, both in closed and in open channels. It was almost on the escarpment's edge, and from it I could see clear across to the sea and to the sky, so that the eye made a slow circuit, from the rocky falls beneath the glassy cope, to the falling waters, to the deep shady forests, the beaches, the ocean, the sky, and then the gaze travelled back along the path of the sun until it was staring straight upwards, and flinching because of the sun's fierce glare, and so it lowered again to my feet, which were planted on the very edge of the cliff.

What should I roof my new home with? This question answered my other: What had the original inhabitants used as roofing? Clay was the answer. Between the stones of the old foundations and the stone channels, the earth showed as clay. And when I splashed water on it, the dense heavy substance potters use formed at once in my palm. Once this city had had roofs of tiles made of this clay, and clay being more vulnerable to time than rock, these tiles had dissolved away in heavy rain or in the winds that must tear and buffet and ravage along this exposed high edge whenever it stormed. No people, where were the people? Why was this entire city abandoned and empty? Why, when it was such a perfect place for a community to make its own? It had good building material close at hand, it had houses of every kind, virtually whole and perfect save for the absent roofs, it had good pure water, and a climate which grew every sort of flowers and vegetables. Had one day the thousands of inhabitants died of an epidemic? Been scared away by threat of an earthquake? All been killed in some war?

There was no way of finding out, so I decided not to think about it. I would stay here a while. And I would not trouble to roof myself a house. The walls gave shelter enough from the sun. It was not yet the rainy season, but even if it had been, the rain would soon drain away off this height, and it was not a place to stay damp or cold.

I found a tree which had aromatic foliage, something like a blue gum, but with finer leaves. I stripped off armfuls of the leaves and carried them to the shelter of a wall. With them I made a deep warm bed I could burrow into if the night turned cold. I picked some pink sweet fruit, in appearance like peaches, that grew bending over a water channel. I drank the water—and understood that my needs as an animal were met. I need do nothing but pick fruit and gather fresh leaves when those that made my bed withered. For the rest I could sit on the cliff's edge and watch the clouds gather over the sea, watch the moon's growing and declining, and match my rhythms of sleep and waking to the darkening and lightening of the nights.

And I need not be solitary. For this city had an atmosphere as if it were inhabited, as I've said. More, as if this city was itself a person, or had a soul, or being. It seemed to know me. The walls seemed to acknowledge me as I passed. And when the moon rose for the third time since I had arrived on this coast, I was wandering among the streets and avenues of stone as if I were among friends.

Very late, when the moon was already low over the mountains, I lay down on my bed of deliciously smelling leaves, and now I did sleep for a time. It was a light, delightful sleep, from which it was no effort to wake, and I was talking to my old shipfriends, George and Charlie, James and Stephen and Miles and the rest, and into this conversation came Conchita and Nancy, who were singing their songs and laughing. When I woke, as the sun came up shining from the blue-green sea, I knew quite clearly that I had something to do. My friends were all about me, I knew that, and in some way they were of the substance of this warm earthy stone, and the air itself, but it was not enough for me just to live here and breathe its air. I sprang straight up when I woke, driven by this knowledge that I had work to do, and went to wash my face and hands in the nearest water channel. I admired my fine mariner's beard, and my hard dark-brown salt-pickled arms and face, ate more of the peachlike fruit, and walked out among the sky-roofed houses to see what I could see ... it was very strange indeed that I had not noticed this before: among the buildings, in what seemed like the centre of the old city, what might very well have been the former central square, was an expanse of smooth stone which was not interrupted by flowers or by water channels. The square was perhaps seventy or a hundred yards across, and in it was an inner circle, about fifty yards across. It was a little cracked, where earth had settled under it, and some grass grew in the cracks, but it was nearly flat, and it waited there for what I had to do. I knew now what this was. I had to prepare this circle lying in its square, by clearing away all the loose dirt and pulling out the grass. And so I began this task. It took longer than it should have done, because I had no tools at all. But I tore off a strong branch and used it as a broom. And when the dirt was all swept away and the grass pulled up, I brought water in my cupped hands from near channels, and splashed it down. But this took too long, and then I searched until I found a stone that had a hollow in it which might have been used as a mortar for crushing grain once, and I used that to carry water. To clear and prepare that circle in the midst of the city took me nearly a week, during which I worked all day, and even at night when the moon came up. Now I lay down to rest between the sun's setting and the moon's rising, and worked on under the moon, lying down again to rest between moonfall and sunrise, if there was this interval.

I was not tired. I was not tired at all with the work. I was not even particularly expectant of anything. I knew only that this was what I had to do, and could only suppose that my friends must have told me so, since it was after my dream of them that I had known it.

Now the moon was in its last quarter and making a triangle, sun, earth, moon, whereas when I had reached that coast it was full, and sitting on the plateau's edge and staring into the moon's round face I had had my back to the sun, which was through the earth, and the sun stared with me at the moon. Then the pulls and antagonisms and tensions from sun and moon had been in a straight line through the earth, which swelled, soil and seas, in large bulges of attraction as the earth rolled under the moon, the sun; but now the tension of sun and moon pulled in this triangle, and the tides of the ocean were low, and the great sky was full of a different light now, a fainter bluer moonlight, and the stars blazed out. I did not know why I thought so, but I had come to believe that it was the next full moon that I was waiting for.

I moved my pile of drying leaves to the edge of the circle in the square. Now that all expanse of stone was washed and clean, patterns glowed in it, continuous geometrical patterns that suggested flowers and gardens and their correspondence with the movements of the sky. Even in the thinning moonlight the patterns loomed up milkily, as I lay on my elbow in my pile of leaves. I lay there in the dimming moonlight, and listened to the wind in the grasses, the tinkling of the water that ran invisibly in its channels, and sometimes the hard crackle when one of the dried leaves of my bed cartwheeled and skittered across the stone floor as I watched and

watched all night, in case I might be wrong, and the
visiting Crystal descended now, in the moon's wane.
When I was ready to sleep, I lay on my back, with
one arm out over the stone which held the day's
warmth, and I closed my eyes, and let the moon and
the starlight drench my face. My sleep was ordered
by the timing of the moon. I was obsessed by it, by
its coming and going, or rather, by its erratic circling
in wild crazy loops and ellipses around the earth, so
that sometimes it lay closer to the North, sometimes
circled lower over my head, at 15 degrees South,
sometimes it looped lower still, so that with my head
to the North, and my feet pointing to the Antarctic,
the path seemed at knee level. In the dark of space
was a blazing of white gas, and in the luminous
envelope of this lamp some crumbs of substance
whizzed around, but the crumbs further out from the
central blaze were liquefied or tenuous matter, gases
or soups also spinning in their orbits, and some of
these minute crumbs or lumps of water that spun
about had other tinier crumbs or droplets swirling
about them in a dance, a dance and a dazzle, and
someone looking in, riding in, from space, would see
this great burning lamp and its orbiting companions
as one, a unit; a unit even as central blaze and
circling associates, but even more if this visiting
Explorer had eyes and senses set by a different clock,
for then this unit, Sun and associates, might seem
like a central splurge ringed by paths of fire or light,
for the path of a planet by a different scale of time
might be one with that planet, and this Celestial
Voyager with his differently tuned senses might very
well see the Earth's circling streak and its Moon as
one, a double planet, a circling streak that sometimes showed double, as when the hairs in a paint-
er's brush straggle and part, and make two streaks
of a single stroke. The Voyager, too, would see the
tensions and pulls of the lumps or drops in their

orbiting about the Sun in a constantly changing pattern of subtle thrills, and currents and measures of movement in the rolling outwards of the solar wind, and he might even see in the little crumb of matter that was the Earth, the tuggings and pullings crosswise of the Moon and the Sun, which were at right angles, this being the Moon's last quarter and the tides of water and earth and air being low.

The moon held me, the moon played with me, the moon and I seemed to breathe at one, for my waking and sleeping, or rather, being wakeful and then dreaming, not the same thing, was set by the moon's direct pressure on my eyes. And then, as it waned, by my knowledge of its presence, a dark orb with its narrowing streak of reflected sunlight, and then at last the two days of the dark of the moon, when the moon, between earth and sun, had its back to us and held its illuminated face inwards, to the sun, so that great Sun and minute Moon stared at each other direct. The sun's light, its reflected substances, were reflected back at the sun's broad face, and we received none, instead of being bathed in sun-stuff from two directions, immediately from sun, and reflected from moon. No, the moon had her back to us, like a friend who has gone away. In the few days when the moon was dark, when the earth was warmed and fed and lit only by the sun, only that part of the earth which was exposed to the sun's rays receiving its light, I fell into a misery and a dimming of purpose. In the daytime I walked among the buildings of this city which was whole except for its absent roofs, and watched the turning of the earth in the shortening and lengthening of shadows, and at night I sat by the edge of the great square of stone where the circle lay glowing—yes, even by starlight it showed a faint emanation of colour—and lived for the return of the moon, or rather, for its circling back to where it might again shed the sun's light back on us.

As my head, when climbing the last part of the ascent to the plateau, had been filled with the din of falling water and the buffeting of mountain winds, so that I could not think, could only ascend without thought, so now my head was full of light and dark, filled with the moon and its white dazzle—now alas reflected out and away back at the sun, back at space—and my thoughts and movements were set by it, not by the Sun, man's father and creator, no, by the Moon, and I could not take my thoughts from her as she dizzied around the earth in her wild patterning dance.

I was moonstruck. I was mooncrazed. To see her full face I sped off in imagination till I lay out in space as in a sea, and with my back to the sun, I gazed in on her, the Moon, but simultaneously I was on the high plateau, looking at the moon's back which was dark, its face being gazed upon by the sun and myself.

I began to fancy that the moon knew me, that subtle lines of sympathy ran back and forth between us. I began to think the moon's thoughts. A man or a woman walking along a street gives no evidence of what he is thinking, yet his thoughts are playing all about him in subtle currents of substance. But an ordinary person cannot see these subtle moving thoughts. One sees an animal with clothes on, its facial muscles slack, or in grimace. Bodily eyes see bodies, see flesh. Looking at Moon, at Sun, we see matter, earth or fire, as it were people walking in the street. We cannot see the self-consciousness of Moon, or Sun. There is nothing on Earth, or near it, that does not have its own consciousness, Stone, or Tree or Dog or Man. Looking into a mirror, or into the glossy side of a toppling wave, or a water-smoothed shining stone like glass, we see shapes of

flesh, flesh in time. But the consciousness that sees
that face, that body, those hands, feet, is not inside
the same scale of time. A creature looking at its
image, as an ape or a leopard leaning over a pool to
drink sees its face and body, sees a dance of matter
in time. But what sees this dance has memory and
expectation, and memory itself is on another plane
of time. So each one of us walking or sitting or
sleeping is at least two scales of time wrapped together like the yolk and white of an egg, and when
a child with his soul just making itself felt, or a
grownup who has never thought of anything before
but animal thoughts, or an adolescent in love, or an
old person just confronted with death, or even a
philosopher or a star measurer—when any of these,
or you or I ask ourselves, with all the weight of our
lives behind the question, What am I? What is this
Time? What is the evidence for a Time that is not
mortal as a leaf in autumn, then the answer is, That
which asks the question is out of the world's time
... and so I looked at the body of the moon, now a
dark globe with the sun-reflecting segment broaden-
ing nightly, I looked at this crumb of matter and
knew it had thoughts, if that is the word for it,
thoughts, feelings, a knowledge of its existence, just
as I had, a man lying on a rock in the dark, his back
on rock that still held the warmth from the sun.

> Misshapen Moon
> Tyrant
> Labouring in circles
> Reflecting hot
> Reflecting cold
> Why don't you fly off and find another planet?
> Venus perhaps, or even Mars?

> Lopsided Earth.
> Reeling and heaving

Wildly gyrating
Which is the whip and which the top?
We have no choice but to partner each other,
Around and around and around and around
    and around ...

The thoughts of the moon are very cold and
hungry, I know this now. But then, enamoured and
obsessed, I simply longed. I merely lay and let myself be drunk. But that cold crumb that waltzes and
swings about us so wildly is a great drinker of men's
minds. By the time of the first quarter when the
moon had again moved a fourth of its journey
around the earth, and there was a week to the full
of the moon and the expected landing of my crystal
visitor, I was lunatic indeed. I did not sleep, oh no, I
could not sleep, I walked or I lay or I knelt or I sat,
my head sunk back into the muscles of my neck,
gazing up and up and up and the cells of my
eyeballs were ringing with light like a fevered man's
ears.

This sound shrilled and grew, and late one
night, when the half-disc was right overhead, I
heard mingled with this another, an earth noise, and
I knew that whatever it was was out on the plain
beyond the ruins of the city, between it and the
distant mountains. I walked through the ruined
houses that had seemed so intimate with me, so
close, but now they had set themselves from me,
they had turned away, and when I came up to a jut
of wall, or the corner of a building, or a threat of
shadow, my hands clenched themselves, and my
eyes darted of their own accord to every place that
might shelter an enemy. Yet I had not once before,
since making my landfall, thought of enemies or of
danger.

I walked down a broad paved street that rang
out echoing answers to my footfalls, and reached the

dwindling edge of the city, and saw, under the bright stars and the brightening moon, a mass of cattle grazing out on the plain. There were thousands of them, all milk-white or gently gold in this light, all large, fed, comfortable beasts, and there was no one there to herd them. They had all the vastness of the plain for their home, and they moved together, in a single impulse, a single mind, sometimes lowering their heads to graze as they went, and sometimes lowing. It was this sound that had brought me from the centre of the city to its edge. As I stood watching, there was a sudden frightened stirring on the edge of this ghostly herd, and I saw a dark shadow move forward at a run from a ruin at the city's edge, and then crouch to the ground. Then one of the big beasts fell dead, and suddenly there was a strong sickly smell of blood on the air that I knew, though I had no proof of this, had not been made to smell of blood before.

And now I understood my fall away from what I had been when I landed, only three weeks before, into a land which had never known killing. I knew that I had arrived purged and salt-scoured and guiltless, but that between then and now I had drawn evil into my surroundings, into me, and I knew, as if it had been my own hand that had drawn that bow and loosed that arrow, that I had caused the shining milk-white beast to fall dead. And I fell on my knees as the herd, alerted, thundered past and out of sight, lowing and shrieking and stopping from time to time to throw back their heads and sniff the air which was sending them messages of murder and fright. Soon I was there alone in the dim moonlight with one other person, a young boy, or perhaps a girl in men's clothes, who had walked over to the carcass and was standing over it to pull out the arrow. And without looking to see who it was, though I knew that I could recognise this person if I did go close enough, and without caring if I was seen by him, or by her, I fell on my face on the earth and I wept. Oh, I'll never know such sorrow again, I'll never know such grief, Oh, I cannot stand it. I don't wish to live, I do not want to be made aware of what I have done and what I am and what I must be, no, no, no, no, no, no, around and around and around and around around and around . .

> *I must record my strong disagreement with this treatment. If it were the right one, patient should by now be showing signs of improvement. Nor do I agree that the fact he sleeps almost continuously is by itself proof that he is in need of sleep. I support the discontinuation of this treatment and discussion about alternatives.*
>
> DOCTOR Y.

DOCTOR Y: Well, and how are you today? You certainly do sleep a lot, don't you?

PATIENT: I've never slept less in my life.

DOCTOR Y: You ought to be well rested by now. I'd like you to try and be more awake, if you can. Sit up, talk to the other patients, that sort of thing.

PATIENT: I have to keep it clean, I have to keep it ready.

DOCTOR Y: No, no. We have people who keep everything clean. Your job is to get better.

PATIENT: I was better. I think. But now I'm worse. It's the moon, you see. That's a cold hard fact.

DOCTOR Y: Ah. Ah well. You're going back to sleep are you?

PATIENT: I'm not asleep, I keep telling you.
DOCTOR Y: Well, goodnight!
PATIENT: You're stupid. Nurse, make him go away. I don't want him here. He's stupid. He doesn't understand anything.

> *On the contrary. Patient is obviously improving. He shows much fewer signs of disturbance. His colour and general appearance much better. I have had considerable experience with this drug. It is by no means the first time a patient has responded with somnolence. It can take as long as three weeks for total effect to register. It is now one week since commencement of treatment. It is essential to continue.*
>
> DOCTOR X.

I did not wait to see the beast cut up. I ran back to the edge of the landing-ground and tried to bury my fears in sleep. I didn't know what I was afraid of, but the fact I was afraid at all marked such a difference now and then that I knew it was a new condition for me. I could feel my difference. Now, I was afraid of the moon's rising and its rapid growth towards full. I wanted to hide somewhere, or in some way, but to hide in a perpetual daylight until that night of the Full Moon when—I was certain of this—the Crystal would descend to my swept and garnished landing-ground. But daylight was not a time to take cover in, to use for concealment. I piled branches over my head and lay face down with eyes blotted out and made myself sleep, when I had no need of it, but my sleep was not the sleep of an ordinary man. It was a living in a differ-

ent place or country, I knew all the time that I was
living out another life, but on land, very far from the
life of a seaman, and it was a life so heavy and
dismal and alien to me that to go to sleep was like
entering a prison cell, but nevertheless, my new
terror of the night and its treacherous glamourous
sucking light was enough to make me prefer that
landlubber's living to the Moon Light. Yet I woke,
and although I had not wanted to, and had decided
to stay where I was, watching the skies for the
Descent, yet I could not prevent myself getting to
my feet, and walking through the now mocking and
alien city. This time I went Northwards, and beyond
the city I saw great trees, and somewhere under the
trees a gleam of red fire. I walked openly, without
disguising myself or trying to be quiet, through the
patched moon-and-shadow of the forest glades, till I
stood, on a slight rise, looking down into a hollow
that was circled by trees, yews, hollies, and elms.
There I saw them. They were about fifty yards
away, and the intervening space was all sharp black
shadows and gleams of brilliant moonlight, and the
leaping running shadows of the fire played all
around the scene, so that I could not see very clearly. It was a group of people, three adults and some
half-grown ones, and as I leaned forward to stare
and settle my eyes against the confusion of lights
and shade, I saw that they were roasting hunks of
meat on the fire, and singing and shrieking and
laughing as they did so, and a terrible nauseating
curiosity came over me—but that curiosity which is
like digging one's fingers into a stinging wound. I
knew quite well who they were—or rather, I knew
what faces I would see, though there was a gulf in
my memory, blotting out the exact knowledge of
where these people fitted into my long-past life.
They turned, as the sound of my footsteps alerted

them, and their three faces, women's faces, all the same, or rather, all variations of the same face, laughed and exulted, and blood was smeared around their stretched mouths, and ran trickling off their chins. Three women, all intimately connected with me, alike, sisters perhaps, bound to me by experience I could not remember at all. And there were three boys; yes, the boys were there too, and a baby lying to one side of the fire, apparently forgotten in the orgy, for it was crying and struggling in tight wrappings, its face scarlet, and I rushed forward to pull the child out of the way of those hostile tramping feet, and I opened my mouth to shout reproaches, bul Felicity pushed a piece of meat that had been singed a little, but was still raw and bloody, into my mouth—and I fell on the meat with the rest, pulling gobbets of it off a bloody hunk that was propped over the fire with sticks that sagged as they took fire, letting the lump of meat lower itself to the flames, so that all the forest stank of burning flesh. But I swallowed pieces whole, and at the same time laughed and sang with them, the three women:

Under my hand,
        flesh of flowers,
Under my hand,
        warm landscape
Give me back my world,
In you the earth breathes under my hand . . .
Now we reach it, now now,
Now we reach it, now now now,
Now we reach it, now,
Now now now now now now now now . . .

and the three boys my sons who were as bloody-drunk and as crazed as their mothers kept up a stamping dance of their own and sang

Now we reach it, now, now,

over and over again. They were all laughing at me, laughing with malicious pleasure because I had joined this bloody feast, and later I saw that it was over, the women were walking soberly away, leaving the fire burning, and the piles of stinking bloody meat lying to one side of it. I looked for the baby, but it was not there. Then I saw that it was dead and had been thrown on the heap of meat that was waiting here, quite openly in the glade, all purply red and bleeding, for the coming night's feast. The baby was naked now, a little reddish newborn babe, smeared with blood, its genitals, the big genitals of a newborn boy baby, exposed at the top of the bloody heap. I understood that I was naked. I could not remember when I had lost the clothes with which I had left the ship. Presumably I had landed naked on the beach off the dolphin's back, but I had not thought once about being naked, but now I needed to cover myself. The bloody hide of the dead cow lay in its rough folds to one side of the glade, where the women and the boys had thrown it. I ran to it, and was about to wrap myself in it, all wet and raw as it was, when I chanced to look up and saw that the sun stood over the trees and the treacherous moon had gone. And so was the fire, the pile of bloody meat, the dead baby—everything. There was no evidence at all of that night's murderous dance.

I walked back through the forest, which was now full of a calm morning light, and then across grasslands, and then into the suburbs of the empty ruined city until I reached the central square, and I examined it anxiously to see if the past night had affected it at all. But no, there it lay, exposed and tranquil under the clean sunlight, and there was no sound but the invisible water's running, and the song of birds.

I was terribly afraid of the coming night. I was afraid of the laughing murderesses and their songs. I knew that when the moon rose that night I would be helpless against its poisons. I tried to think of ways I could tie myself, bind myself, make myself immune from the Moon Light, but a man cannot tie himself, or not with bonds that cannot be undone— can't, that is, unless he kills himself. There is no way of making himself immune to the different person that may come to life in him at any moment—and who does not know the laws of being of his host. But I was already beginning to doubt that I knew who was stronger, which was host, what was myself and what a perverted offshoot.

Finally, I worked out that if I walked as fast as I could away from the city, and kept walking until the moon rose that night, then it would be too great a distance for me to get back to the forest before the sun rose in its turn and banished the witches and their feast. While I was myself, the sun's child, I would have the will to walk away from what the night would lure me to. And so I did walk, at a fast steady pace, away to the South, skirting the river by going between the great chasm and the cliff's edge, across the dry riverbed, and then on across the savannah, all through that long hot day, and when the moon rose I was twenty miles away in a higher, dryer air where there were few trees and those stunted and meagre. I looked back over the plain where I could see the herds of cattle grazing, but from this height and distance, they were small clusters of light moving on the moon-green of the grass. I could see, too, but far away, the tiny dark that was the edge of the forest where the women must be. The moon was three days from its full. I was in despair. I knew that I should rather go on walking all night straight on, straight on and away from the tug of that forest, but I did not. I turned around and walked straight back, down off this rare highland where the air was so pure and so fine, down, and by the time the moon lay at my left hand, low over the mountains which I would have reached by now and understood had I not been waylaid by the ruined city, I was at the city's outskirts, and I ran like a maniac through it, but skirting the centre of it, the square with its circle, because I did not want to see the reproach of that clean waiting landing-ground, and then I ran through the suburbs on the other side, and into the forest and there, exactly as I had seen them the night before, were the three women, the three half-grown boys, the baby, dead and festering on the pile of meat. But it was late, the moon was down, and the sun would soon rise. The women were about to move away. I had saved myself by walking so hard and fast in the opposite direction. They all went off into the trees without looking at me, and one of the boys leaped on a young steer he had tethered by its horns, and he went galloping on this crazed beast around the glade, kicking the embers of the fire, the piles of meat, the baby's corpse, scattering them about. And then he rode off while the beast roared and screamed. And again the glade was empty and clean in a morning sunlight.

I went back to the square, thankful that I had saved myself. But I knew that I was too tired now to walk away for the second night running from the approaching feast. And I knew that there were still two nights of a strong moon before the Full Moon. And I lay down and slept by the square—and that night joined in the bloody banquet under the trees, and this time they had killed the half-grown steer, and all the glade stank of blood and guts and murder, and now I knew that I would never do this again, for I was filled with strength from my sleep of the day and from the meat of the feast, and on that last day I walked twenty miles South as I had before, and turned around as the moon rose, as I had before—very nearly the full moon now—and I walked back through the night, not running, or wanting to go back to the forest, and I did not go back to the forest, for by the time I reached the city, it was too late. For the sun had come up out of a red sky over the ocean, and this was the day of the full moon. But I was tired. I was so very tired. I had not eaten that night, and I had walked forty miles. I washed myself carefully, using the largest of the water channels, sinking myself right down into it, so that the water came to my waist. I combed my beard and hair as well as I could with my fingers, and I watched the foulness run away from me with the water. And I drank and drank water as much as I could hold, hoping that its cleanliness would wash the insides of my body free of its loads of bloody meat that it could still feel from the night before last. And I lay down then to rest and wait. And, in the heat of that day, despite everything I could do, I fell asleep. I slept heavily and dreadfully, and my dreams were of that other life in a damp sunless country where my life was a weight of labour every hour, every minute, and when I woke it was long past moonrise, though I had meant to wake well before that Rising; and it was midnight. I had missed the descent of the Crystal, for it was here now.

But I could not see it.

A full white moonlight lay evenly over the empty city, and over the square floor of stone on whose edge I was sitting, dreadfully heavy with sleep and foreboding. The circle in the square was still clean and faintly glowing with colour, though some leaves had blown over it during the last few days' neglect. That the Crystal was present, there, quite close, a few yards from me, was evident to me because ... I knew it was. As I looked it was as if the light there lay more heavily—no, not that, it was not a heaviness, a weight, but more of an intensity. Just there, in the centre, it was hard to see quite through to the buildings on the other side—not impossible, no, but they quivered and hung in the air like stones in the quiver of air that comes off sizzling sand or rock. And more than by sight, it was through my ears that I knew, for they sang and keened so shrilly that I had to keep shaking my head to clear away the sound. It was almost too fine and high a sound to bear. If I had been a dog I would have howled and run away. And the effort of staring in was almost too much for me. My eyes tried to close, because whatever it was that I could not quite see, but was there, belonged to a level of existence that my eyes were not evolved enough to see. And more than that, my whole body, and the level of life in it, was suffering. Beating out from that central point came waves of a finer substance, from a finer level of existence, which assaulted me, because I was not tuned to them. And I remembered how as I stood on the deck of the ship and watched the shining crystal shape, the disc, that was at the same time in an unimaginably fast movement and stationary, a visible flat spiralling, and how when I saw it come in towards me and then envelop me, it was as if my whole being had suffered a wrenching away from its own proper level. I felt this again now. I was feeling sick and low and shaken, strained out of myself with the effort of seeing what I could not really see, and hearing what I could have heard with different ears, so that I had to hear it now as an intolerable shrill note. I got to my feet with difficulty and staggered in towards the centre. As I came closer the noise got shriller, my eyes pulsed and burned, and all my body felt blasted and empty. I knew that what I was doing was futile. I knew I had missed my

opportunity—for the second time, for the first had
been on the deck of the old ship when the Crystal
had taken my friends but left me behind. But although I knew this was an empty attempt, because
it had none of the quiet ease of confidence, which is
in itself a sign or condition of success, I had to make
it. Emptiness was in me and all about me. Pulling
my eyes away from that central compulsion, to rest
them, I looked about the quiet roofless houses lying
there, and saw first of all, their quality of peaceful
trust, a waiting. An emptiness very different from
my frantic hunger. But they were turned inwards, to
the centre; it was a city which had found its core, its
resting place, in that whirl of intensity which laid
claims on it and shot it through and through with its
own fine substance, as a thought can take over a
man and change everything about him. (Oh, for bad
as well as for good, as I had learned so recently.)
Looking at the houses, and then glancing in at the
whirling presence in the centre, and glancing away
again, for respite, I managed to come within fifteen
yards of the thing—and could not come closer.
Again I stood and looked from very near at a wall or
sheet of shining substance in which creatures were
imprisoned by their nature, as I was imprisoned in
the air I had to breathe. From so very close, and by
not looking direct, but out of the side of my eyes, as
star watchers observe stars in, paradoxically, a more
delicate and finer vision, I could see it pulsing there,
a shape of light; and (almost seen, more sensed,
known, recognised) the creatures that belonged to
that state in nature. Like the shadows of flames
running liquid on a wall of fire, like the reflection of
broken water on a fall of water, inside that pulsing
light I could see, from the side of my eye, the
crystallisations of the substance which were its functions, its reason for being, its creatures. There they
were, beings divided away from me as fish in a wall

of water are divided from the man six inches away in air, but they were known to me, I knew them, I felt that I ought to slide in there, somehow, in some way, by thinking differently, by breathing that fast spinning vibration—but I could not go nearer, and I knew it was because I had let myself be drawn into the forest with the blood-drinking women, and because I had slept like a dog in the hot sun. I tried to force myself in to the place, although the laws of my density held me back. I felt too ill even to stand. In a last effort of will, which I knew was wrong and useless, I collapsed, and fainted, my eyes blazing light as they were extinguished by dark. And when I woke up again it was morning, the hot sunlight lay everywhere about me, and I knew that the Crystal was gone. The square and the circle inside it were empty. I had been sick and my nose had been bleeding. I lay in blood and the smell of vomit. Where I had been lying smelled vile. And as I sat up, to stare inwards at my terrible loss, I knew again what I had known on the deck of the ship, when all my friends had vanished away with the shining visitor. I had been left behind. I had not been taken. I had failed most dreadfully and through my own fault. I had had nothing to do but wait quietly for the moment of the full moon, and keep myself light and alert and wakeful. But I had not done it.

I stood up and looked about me at a city which seemed as if it had changed, though I could not say how it had. There was a new feeling about it, its peace and silence had gone. It had a look of frivolity, a sort of drunkenness. If a town, or a building, or a shape of stone could be said to giggle, then it was that: a silly silent giggling, an infantility, a coarseness. It was like that moment when the women turned towards me in the firelight under the trees, and showed their faces smeared with blood, but they were laughing and smiling, as if nothing much was happening to them, or to me.

I dragged myself off towards the river, to bathe and become fresh again. But I stopped. For on to the square of stone stepped a—but I did not know what it was. I thought at first, that this must be a man, for he stood as tall as one, and had the shoulders and the arms and legs of one, though strained and distorted in their shape. But his head . . . was it some kind of monkey, who shambled on to the square of stone, and then in right to the very centre? Here he squatted down and looked about him. But the body was covered all over with a fine close hide, shining brown, like the hide of a dog, and the head was like a dog's, with sharp cocked ears and dog's muzzle. Yet there was a ratlike look about it. The creature had a rat's long scaly tail. I was afraid. It was bigger and much stronger than I was. I thought it might come over and attack me. But I walked towards it and it looked at me without concern. I was thinking then that I should attack and kill it, for I found it disgusting and ugly, as it squatted there, exactly where last night the Crystal had lain shining and vibrating. I thought that if I killed it then the city would have to be cleaned again. I came close to it. The creature looked idly at me and away, it moved about, scratched for fleas, sniffed the air with its sharp dog's or rat's nose. I understood that it probably did not see me, or, if it did, that I was of no interest to it whatsoever.

I stayed where I was. So did the creature. I hated everything about it, it was a creature alien to me in every way. Yet I was thinking that someone standing a hundred yards away might say, at a casual glance, that it and I were of a similar species, for I stood nearly as tall as it did, and I had a head growing where this dog-rat had one, and roughly similar arms and legs. Coming closer this observer would see that I was hairless whereas this animal had a hide ... well, not quite hairless. I now had thick curling brown hair to my shoulders, and a deep curling brown beard to my waist and thick dark hair on my chest and from my navel to my crotch. Dark brown hair on skin burned brown by wind and sun. I was covered and decent! Whereas this beast ... but I felt too disgusted with it to stay there matching myself point by point, and I walked away off the square, and as I did so the creature gave a high squeaky call, and it was answered by other calls, half bark, half rat's high shrilling, and on to the stone square came running and scampering and shambling, a dozen or so of these creatures. They were all males. They had the genitals of a big dog, large globular testicles and penises like rods, for they all seemed in a state of sexual excitement. Later I saw that this was more or less permanent with them. Then they stood upright, they looked as close-haired dogs look when made to stand on their hindlegs, the lower part of the belly all genital. They stood in a group right in the centre and faced outwards. They were on their hindlegs. They had sticks or stones in their hands, and were keeping some sort of a watch. Then I saw others moving in from the avenues in troops. I ran out, to the very edge of the escarpment, where I flung myself down and lay looking out over the land that lowered itself through the deep old forests to the blue ocean. I lay there, with the sun beating down from overhead, and knew that I had to wait another month until the moon again came to the full, and that the city, in which I had lived quite alone, was now full of these hideous dog-rats. I could hear their barking and whistling and scuffling all over the city.

I did not feel I was able to bear living there, waiting, with such companions. I made every sort of wild plan—to go back to the coast again and build myself a raft from driftwood, to make my way to the mountains and construct there a new landing-ground and hope that the Crystal might take pity on me and descend there instead, or to return to that cold damp country where from time to time I seemed to live, and labour out my time there, giving up all hope of the Crystal ... but I knew quite well that I would stay here. I had to. At last, knowing that I had no alternative but to do exactly what I was doing, I went to the river, careful to move out of sight of the Rat-dogs, and washed and bathed. I gathered some fruit. I cut fresh branches of the aromatic bush and laid them down at the edge of the escarpment, looking out and away from the city and its restless noisy inhabitants. I slept. In my sleep one or more of the Rat-dogs came to examine me, for I saw their spoor and dung when I woke. But they did not harm me. I dreamed of them though, and cried and struggled in my sleep, imagining myself their prisoner.

It was now a question of arranging matters so that I could last out a month without becoming a slave to the moon and being forced back into the bloody ritual in the forest, or falling a victim to the curiosity of these invaders in this city which I had been thinking of as mine.

During the three or four days of the moon's wane from the full, more and more of these ratlike dogs came in to the city. Since they did not harm me, I decided to move among them and observe them. They did not seem to have any particular pattern to their lives. Some moved about in mixed groups or packs, males and females together, with or without young. These tended to have one animal dominant, either male or female, but not always. They bickered and quarrelled incessantly, and individuals went to other groups, so it was the groups that were continuous, not the individuals in them.

Some separated into smaller groups based on a mating couple, and these appropriated separate rooms
in the houses. Some were solitary, a great many, and
they did not seem to have any particular function in
any group, large or small, but they tried to attach
themselves to groups and couples, and while occa-
sionally they were tolerated for a short while, more
often they were driven away or ignored. These solitary ones sometimes met together in what looked
like efforts to relieve loneliness, and sat about in
twos and threes, watching the larger groups. But
mostly they moved around, watching, and this was
an unpleasant mirror to what I was doing, and I
imagined that I saw in their sharp forlorn postures,
and sharply critical but avid eyes, what I might
appear like to them—if they looked at me at all. But
these were a species which seemed extremely busy
all day, or rather, occupied, and self-absorbed. They
were always moving about, never still, gathering
fruit and eating it, moving from room to room and
from building to building, settling in one for a day
or an hour and then moving on, talking in their gruff
squeak in a way that suggested that most of the talk
was for the sake of relieving a pressure of energy,
scuffling and fighting—and sexual activity. These
animals seemed extraordinarily highly sexed, but
perhaps it was because of their always displayed
genitals. The males I have described. The females
had scarlet-edged slits from anus to their lower belly. The males were roused to sexual excitement any
time a female of any age approached, and the females were nearly as sensitized. And a greater part
of their time was spent in sexual display, in attract-
ing each other's attention, appropriating each other's sexual partners and in watching other animals'
sexual behaviour. When a pair had actually come
together and had agreed to mate, they went off
behind a wall or a bush, for a part-private mating,

and these had the variety of human matings. Others came to watch the sexual act, and let out high excited yappings and squeakings and, stimulated past bearing, fell on each other and went off to nearby bushes or sheltered places. So that one mating might start off a frenzy that could last half a day. It was noticeable that this sexuality was strongest while the moon was nearer the full, and lessened as the nights grew darker. Yet the matings were as common in the day as at night. It seemed that these animals were afraid of the dark, congregating together more as night fell, and this fear was the first time I was able to achieve some pity or affection for them, for they really did seem so very forlorn, and bravely so, rounding up the younger animals as the sun went down, posting lookouts on the high walls, moving about with fearful looks over their shoulders. Yet there was no enemy that I could see. And now I had experienced an impulse of fellow-feeling for them, I began to see them more sympathetically and I disliked them less. For instance, it became evident to me that these animals had only recently begun to walk on their hind legs, which accounted for their way of staggering, or jerking from a precarious balance to another, at each step, as a big dog does, when made to stand on its hind legs. And this accounted for more: their most pitiable and characteristic gesture. As their eyes, like a rat's or a dog's were made to be used as they moved forward on all fours, their sharp pointed noses tended, now they were upright, to point upwards to the sky, while their eyes squinted to either side downwards, in their effort for a clear view. And they kept bending their heads down and sideways, first on one side and then on the other as they walked or staggered about, all the time trying to force down their neck muscles. Putting myself in their position I saw that they must have a view of

the world as two different semicircles, one on either
side. And unlike men, who are blind at their backs,
so that they continually have to turn their heads to
one side and then the other, for the most part on a
horizontal axis, and are nevertheless blind around
two thirds of a possible sweep of vision, these animals were always squinting up, skywards, and their
head and neck movements were very rapid, to correct this, and this continuous jerking about of the
head contributed to their look of general restlessness. It was the younger and more flexibly-muscled
of them that seemed able to keep open a fairly-wide
scope of vision by the fast jerkings-about of their
sky-pointing muzzles, each sideways jerk an inter-
ruption in a cross-sweep usually diagonal. These
head movements gave the effect of the stills of an
old film or cartoon running together not quite fast
enough.

I noticed too that when they were tired, or
believed themselves to be alone, they would let themselves down on all fours and run about for a time like
this. And they ran very fast and ably indeed, for this
was how their bodies had been designed to move. But
when an individual or a group behaved like this for too
long, the others would begin to make irritable movements, and then would set up a chiding critical chattering, while the culprits looked defiant, then guilty,
and sooner or later staggered back to the upright
position.

When they were huddled together in their
roofless rooms or on the stone of the square, at night
when there was no moon, they sat like dogs or
monkeys, squatting, their front limbs straight down
in front of them for support, and they moved about
on all fours much more in the dark. They seemed so
very different in these two different conditions, their
clumsy half-staggering on their hind legs, with their
awkward jerky vision that gave them such a look of

pomposity and self-importance, and the rapid running and scampering when on all fours, that they really seemed like two different species, and I suppose I was unconsciously thinking of them as such, for I do remember very clearly that at the first appearance of the apes, I did not at once react with alarm at a new invasion, but thought vaguely that perhaps the Rat-dogs were moving in yet a third way.

These apes were of a kind familiar to us humans. They were a variety of chimpanzee, but larger than the ones we keep to show off in zoos. They came swinging into the city through trees and along the walls, and when they saw the Rat-dogs their reaction was not one I could at once interpret. Although they stopped still and massed together, they did not seem particularly afraid, nor did they seem pleased. They conferred among themselves, on the North side of the city, till there were a couple of hundred or so massed there. Meanwhile, the Rat-dogs, turning their squinting eyes this way and that towards the newcomers, also massed together, and did not make any aggressive action as the monkeys came in further, and then scampered and swung all over the city finding out corners and rooms that were not inhabited. There was a great deal of sharp scolding and complaint as the newcomers tried to take places that were occupied, but it seemed as if both species recognised the right of the other to live in this place. More and more of the apes came trooping in. The city was crammed with animals. It seemed that the first kind, the Rat-dogs, saw the monkeys as inferior, and the monkeys agreed, or were prepared to appear to agree. They would do small services for the big staggering beasts, and tended to move out of their way. Yet to me, a man, the monkeys were altogether more likable and sympathetic, perhaps because I was familiar with them. I felt no strong antipathy, as I still did for the Rat-dogs, in spite of my growing compassion for them. And it seemed to me that the eyes of the monkeys showed sympathy for me, a comprehension, although they neither made attempts to approach me, nor molested me, ignoring me for the most part, as the others did. A monkey's eyes, so sad, so knowledgeable, they are eyes that speak to the eyes of a human. We feel them to be human eyes. And what sort of self-flattery is that? For the eyes of most human beings are sharp, knowing, clever and vain, like the eyes of the Rat-dogs. The depth that lies in a monkey's eyes by no means lies behind the eyes of all men. I found now that I moved around that populated, noisy, scuffling, dirtied city, avoiding the big Rat-dogs when I could, meeting with relief the monkeys who seemed so very much more *human*. But there were more and more of both species, the city was crammed, and the days were passing, so that only half the moon's lit face showed on our earth, and then more of a dark back than her lit face, and it was dark, all dark, and I knew that soon, not much more than two weeks away, I must be ready for the Crystal's descent. Yet all of the central square was always full of animals, as once long ago it must have been full of people meeting to talk or exchange or barter, and every inch of it was littered with fruit rinds, dung, stones, bits of stick or branch or blown leaves. I might never have cleaned the place.

The dark of the new moon held the city in a warm bad-smelling airlessness, and all the animals were massed together, watching the tiny sickle of light in the sky, and with sentinels posted on trees and walls everywhere. They were quieter than usual. It was not a good quiet. On the big square were mostly Rat-dogs, except for the monkeys who had chosen to groom them, or play the fool to amuse them. I went boldly into the square late one evening, as the sun went, thinking that perhaps in that sad hour when every creature seems to be thoughtful that these creatures would be ready to listen and to understand. I stood there like a fool and said to them in human speech: "My friends, we have only fourteen days. Two weeks is all we have. For they are coming, and they will land here, on this circle in the centre of the square. But they will not land on a place which is foul and littered, so please, for your sake as well as for my sake, for the sake of all the creatures that live on this poor sick earth, let us clean this place, let us sweep it with branches, and then bring water and wash away the stains of the filth that is here." I kept my voice steady and I smiled, and I tried to show by gestures what we should do, but they moved about as I spoke, or turned their pointed noses down sideways so that one of their two planes of vision could include me, and the servantlike monkeys hopped closer and looked at me with their sad eyes, trying to understand—but of course they could not understand, how could they? Perhaps I was half-hoping that the meaning of my words would communicate itself to these so differently planned brains, because of the desperation of my need that it should.

The dark came up in a rush from the ocean and the forest, enveloping the plateau and the teeming city, and I went away to the edge of the escarpment and sat there, watching the stars and listening to the multifarious but subdued din from the animals behind me, who were also watching the skies, where the moon's back was a dark circle with a hairline of light at one side.

Perhaps it was their fear of the dark; perhaps that fear stopped a normal exuberance of movement and of voice and left them banked with unexpended energy; or perhaps it was simply that the city had grown too full for their civility to continue—

however it was, that night the fighting started. I
knew it first by the smell—the smell of blood, which
by now I did know so very well. And there were
sudden scuffles much louder than usual, and cries
and shrieks. These last sounded like the blood-
crazed women around their fire in the forest, and in
the morning, after a long dark stuffy night, I walked
into the city and saw corpses lying on the central
square and also here and there among the houses.
Most of these dead were the monkeys, though there
were one or two of Rat-dogs. And now the two races
had separated off, except that a few of the monkeys
had chosen to stay as servants or jesters with the big
beasts who tolerated them. The city was roughly
divided, and now the sentinels on the trees and the
walltops watched each other, were turned inwards
instead of outwards.

The morning slowly passed in this new hot suspicious tension. There was no new outbreak of
fighting, and when the sun stood overhead, it
seemed as if a truce had been declared in the bark-
ings and squeakings and chatterings I had heard but
not understood. Each army sent out representatives
and the corpses were dragged away. These were not
buried, but pulled through the city and then its
suburbs, and thrown into the great hole where the
river plunged down into the earth. I cried out to
them No, No, No, not to foul the clean river and
then the sea, but remembered how men had poisoned all the oceans and rivers so that beasts and
fish were dying there, and so, feeling sick and
hopeless, I went away, thinking that what corpses
succeeded in making their way from out the dark
riverine channels through the earth, and out to the
waterfalls and cataracts, and from there to the wide
level river, and at last to the sea—these corpses
would at least be cleaner offal than the lethal filth
men feed to the sea currents.

Towards night, and the light's draining away in sadness in a red-stained sky, the fighting broke out again, and they fought all night, and I sat on my cliff's edge and tried not to hear it or to follow the carnage too closely in my imagination. There were thirteen days to go to the moon's full, and I knew I had no hope of cleaning the city, no hope of the Crystal's coming, unless by some fortune I had no reason to expect, the animals went away from the city again, as apparently casually as they had come.

Next morning the dead lay in heaps, and the whole city smelled of blood. And now these animals, whose food was fruit and water, were gathered around piles of corpses and were tearing off lumps of hairy flesh and eating it. As I came in close to look, I felt afraid for the first time of these beasts, apes and Rat-dogs. I was now, as they were to each other, potential meat. They ignored me, though I was standing not twenty yards away, until I saw three of them become conscious of my being there, and they turned their pointed muzzles to me, with their sharp teeth white and smeared red, and I saw the blood dripping down as I had off the faces of my women. I went back to the edge of the sea and fell into a despair. I gave up hope then. I knew that the fighting would go on. It would get worse. They would now kill for food. I knew that I was in danger and I did not care. In such moods there are many arguments you can find to support the wisdom of despair. The advocates humanity has found to argue on the side of despair have always been more powerful than those other small voices. I lay myself down on the escarpment's edge and looked down into the deep forests which had taken so many centuries to grow, where my beautiful yellow beasts must be and where birds as brightly coloured as sunset or dawn skies followed the curve of lives as brief as mine. And then I slept. I wanted to sleep away time so that the end would come more quickly.

When I woke it was late afternoon and while the sunlight still lay sparkling over the distant ocean, beneath me, over the forest, it was almost night. The fighting still went on. I could hear animals chasing each other not more than a few yards away in the buildings that reached almost to the escarpment. I did not want to turn my head to look, for out of the corner of my eye I could see a dying rat-beast rolling and squeaking and kicking up puffs of dust in its death struggle. I looked forward and out again over the forest where Jaguar, Parrot and Lizard blazed and burned, older than man, and then I saw lying on the air in front of me a great white bird who, instead of sailing right past my eyes on its current of air, at the last moment turned and landed beside me on the cliff's edge, its great wings balancing it to a safe perch. It was not a species of bird I knew. It was about four feet tall as it sat, white plumaged, and it had a straight streak of a yellow beak that gave it a severe appearance. I thought enviously of how in a moment it would let itself slide off on a warm wave of evening air, as a swimmer slides off a warm rock into a swirling sea. As I thought this it turned and looked steadily at me with very round golden eyes. I went to it and it squatted low, like a hen settling in a smother of outstretched sheltering wings over its eggs, and I slid on to its back, and no sooner than I was safely there than it glided off into the air, and we were dropping down lightly over the rocky sliding hill, and the waterfalls and then over a deep forest now silent with the approach of night. The bird's back, its wing span was ten or twelve feet. I sat up, with a fistful of feathers to keep me steady, but a wind that came sweeping up from the sea nearly sent me toppling off and down over and over to the treetops, so I lay face down, with my arms on either side of the bird just above where the wings joined. The slopes of white feathers were sun-warmed still, and slippery, and smelled clean and wholesome like a hen's egg when it is fresh. The light shone off the white feathers immediately below my eyes like sun off a snowfield, and I turned away my face and laid it to one side, and looked down past the bird's neck and shoulders and we swooped out over the sea and sped along the waves' crests that still, even though all the land between shore and the plateau's edge was plunged in dark, sparked off light from the setting sun. It was a red sun in a ruddy sky, to match the carnage that went on in the city beneath it—which I could just see, white walls and columns in miniature, miles away, high through darkening air. And on we went over the waves and I breathed in great gulps of cold salty air that swept my lungs free of dirt and blood. And on we went until the shore and continent beyond had dwindled to a narrow edge of dark against a sky that was piled high and thick with glowing clouds, and then as my bird dipped one wing to swerve around and back I cried No, not yet, go on, and the bird sped on, while the air whistled past my cold-burning ears and I could taste the salt spray on my lips and beard. And on and on we went, and then I turned over carefully on my back, with my arms bent back and clutching at the finer feathers in the warm caverns under the bird's beating or balancing wings, and I looked up into a star-sprinkled sky where the moon was with her back to the earth, and showing a slice of its edge one finger wider than yesterday's to remind me of my sorrow and my failure. And now in front of us was the coast of Portugal and there was Conchita on her headland looking out to sea. Behind her the red blotch of new suburbs spread out like measles, and below the sea pranced and tossed. She was singing

or half-chanting, or even speaking—for it was halt-
ing, worrying, blocked song—which showed poor
Conchita was as little fitted for her nunhood as she
had been happy in my arms,

> "Come on, shout!" the brass sun said,
> The peacock sea screamed blue, the turkey
>   houses red,
> Sun and sea, they challenged "Come!"
> The earth sang out, but I was dumb.

> Slow, slow, my feet down thick sand dunes,
> Curled shells recalling old sea tunes
> Cut my slow feet until they bled.
> "Who cannot dance must bleed," they said.

> Not ape, nor God, to swing from tree to tree,
> Or bid the sea be still from fear of me,
> Divided, dwarfed, a botched thing in between,
> I watched the sky burn on, the grass glow deeper
>   green.

> To sing! To sing! To squeeze the flaring after-
>   noon
> Like warm fruit in my hand! Then fling it out
>   in tune!
> To take the waves, the freedom of their beat,
> And dance that out on sea-taught feet.

> But blood and nerves are crucified too long
> That I should find a sweet release in song.
> Not I to sing as free as birds
> Whose throat forms only human words.

> Renounce the sea, the crooning sands,
> My ease, bought not by loosed feet, hands,
> Or love which breaks the mind in pain
> To make the flesh shine whole again.

These are mine still, but only in the long
Cold reaches where the mind coils strong
To re-create in patience what the slow
Limbs, bound, knew simply as a song, but long
   ago.

I called to her, Conchita, Conchita, but she did
not hear me, she was looking out over her sea, and
now my bird had swept around and was heading
back and soon we were over the sea's edge where I
had landed, and then over the forests, and then we
were on the cliff's edge again. The alighting of this
great white bird frightened a number of monkeys
that had been hiding where some bushes grew
thickly. They went chattering off, and I sat myself in
my usual place, and the bird sat with me a little in
silence, and then sailed off again on its white wings
into the dark of that night.

And so that night passed, with the screams and
the sound of the fighting going on behind me, but
now I felt less oppressed by it, for I kept my mind
on the long cool flight I had had on the great bird's
sunwarmed back, and on my old love Conchita
stammering her separate failure on her separate coast.

I did not go into the city's centre again for three
days, but sat on the cliff hoping to see the bird, but
he did not come, and at last I ventured in, and the
fighting still went on, and so many had been killed
that they could not either eat or dispose of the
corpses, which lay in heaps everywhere. All the
animals were exhausted from the long fighting.
Their fighting had become more frightful and desperate and mechanical. They were very crazy now,
and their eyes were reddened, and their fur and
hide roughened and dirty. The Rat-dogs no longer
attempted to stand upright, they ran about on all
fours, killing the monkeys by random snapping bites
with their sharp fangs. Again they took very little

notice of me as I went across the square to see how I could prepare it for the full moon not much more than a week away now. I saw nothing hopeful, and so went back to my cliff again. Now I abandoned my dream of preparing the landing-ground, and I dreamed instead of returning to the sea, of letting myself slide into the fresh salt like a bird into the air. I sat there as the days and nights came and went, my eyes fixed on the distant ocean, wishing I had slid off the bird's back into the healthful sea, and there found some plank or spar or fish or floating thing I could have clung to like a barnacle until perhaps the Crystal took pity on me and swept me up at last. And as I sat there on the morning three days before Full Moon, wondering if I should slide back down the glassy wall, and run down, down to the sea, the white bird came back and sat by me, greeting me with its friendly yellow eyes. Again it squatted as I climbed up on to it, and again sped down over the forests to the sea and again circled there just above the breaking waves. But now I understood why the bird had come to fetch me, for the sea was no longer the fresh cold salty well of sanity it had been. There was a sluggishness in its moving, as if it had thickened. There was a taint of decay. Bobbing on the waves I saw hundreds of corpses from the war on the plateau, which had been flung into the great chasm and had been carried by the stream over falls and cataracts to the sea's edge. And everywhere I saw fishes and sea creatures floating bellies up, and on the sea were patches of oil, dark and mineral-smelling. And over the sea, in patches, was a pale phosphorescence like an insidious decay made visible, and these were poisonous gases that had released themselves from the containers man had sunk them in to the sea's bottom, and elsewhere were sheets of light like a subtle electric fire which was radioactivity from the factories and plants on shores oceans or continents away. The bird swept me back and forth across miles of ocean in the frying sun, making me look at the sea's death, and even as we flew there, all the surface of the sea became choked with death, dead fishes and seaweeds and clams and porpoises and dolphins and whales, fish big and small, and all the plants of the sea, sea birds and sea snakes and seals—then my beautiful white bird lifted me up and up and up into the sky and sped back over the trees to the plateau, but now it circled down over the city with its roofless buildings and made me see how underneath me all the city, every building in it, was fouled by war, how everwhere lay the loads of corpses, how in every street groups of beasts fought each other, and now so crazed and weary were they that they fought within the species, without even the excuse of a difference in fur or hide or shape of muzzle or eye. They fought monkey with monkey, rat-beast with rat-beast. Fighting had become its own justification and they could not stop. And under every bush and in the corner of every house lay the wounded moaning and licking their wounds. Just as we came sweeping low in a final circuit, not twenty paces from my cliff's edge, I saw a female Rat-dog, with its sleek brown hide all bloodied and gashed, sitting up with its back to a wall, snapping at a couple of male Rat-dogs, and at the same time she was giving birth. Puppies tumbled out of her scarlet slit in a spout of blood and tissue, while she fought for her life. The two round mounds on her chest which were her breasts, were swollen and had been torn, so that blood and milk poured out together. Her sharp muzzle had hairy flesh hanging from her teeth, and as she snapped and bit at the two tall staggering males who menaced her, she became so crazed with fear and the need to help her puppies' birth, that even as she fought, she would give a deadly snap in front, at an antagonist, and then snap downwards at her young, and perhaps wound or kill one, and then another random desperate bite at an antagonist, and then snap downwards again, and then back at the pressing enemies, so that it looked as if she were fighting her puppies as much as the two males who were as mad with long fighting as she was, for notwithstanding they were trying to kill her (or at least acting in such a way that she had to defend herself) and indeed succeeding, for she sank down in her own blood as we swept past the group, their sexual organs were swollen with excitement, and one of them attempted to mate with her even as she died. She died in a spasm that was as much a birth- as a death-spasm.

On the cliff's edge I tumbled off the bird's warm strong back, and lay face down, weeping. Now I believed that everything was ended, and there was no hope anywhere for man or for the animals of the earth.

But at last, when I lifted myself up, the white bird was still there, and it was looking at me with its golden eyes, its straight yellow beak bent towards me, in its severe but kindly way. It seemed to want me to attend to it, and when I was properly recovered and standing up, it began walking in through the houses of the city to the centre. Now I looked up and saw that the moon must be near full, and I could see the sheet of silver stretching up into the sky over the sea where the moon would rise. I wanted the bird to stop, for I was afraid this marvellous creature might be killed by the warring beasts. But it seemed as if they were quieter. The war had worked itself to its end. Scuffling and sparring went on; couples or small groups fought. But packs of both Rat-dogs and monkeys sat licking themselves and whining and moaning. And although they had all been fighting each other to the death for days, now they seemed almost indifferent to each other's presence, and monkeys licked the sores of Rat-dogs, and Rat-dogs accepted it as homage or submission.

The bird took to its wings and swooped low over the earth along the streets, inwards to the square. I followed. There the bird settled, folding its wings, and standing erect, its narrow yellow beak held stiffly down, with its usual effect of propriety. And just as my heart beat with terror that it would be killed, I saw that all the beasts were afraid of it. Everywhere over the great stone square, animals backed away, the monkeys gibbering and grimacing, and the Rat-dogs back on their feet again, retreating, squinting down one side of their faces and then the other—until they felt themselves safe, when they let themselves drop back on all fours and slunk away.

The bird stood quietly in the centre of the circle. And now I understood it was there to protect me. I began on the work of dragging away the dead animals as far as I could. As I did this, both races of animals came to these piles, and carried their dead right away, probably to the chasm where the river plunged in, or perhaps for a final cannibal feast—though it seemed as if they had lost their taste for flesh again and were tasting and trying the fruits as if these were a new sensation and not their proper food. But I had too much to do, and could not watch them any longer. When the square was clear of the dead animals, I again tore off branches and swept it. Then I had to clear water channels that were choked up with leaves and dirt and dung. And finally I again carried water in the hollow stone that once had been a mortar and I poured water everywhere, and swept that away with sweet-smelling branches. All that night I worked under the blazing white moon, and all the following day under a hot dry sun. There sat the companionable bird, white and glossy, its golden eyes watchful, its severe yellow beak kept in my direction. At the start, some animals came near in a decision to reclaim the square, but when they saw the bird they went away again. At last I realized that they were not in sight at all. Then, that I could not hear them. They had gone from the city's centre altogether. Perhaps they had even left the city. By the end of that day the square and the beautifully patterned and coloured circle it enclosed were clean and fresh, the air smelled of aromatic leaves and water, and as I stood quietly in the dusk I could hear the water running beneath my feet in its stonelined channels. The air was full of the scent of flowers. A last bird sang from a tree near the square.

Full Moon came straight up from the sea and laid silver light over Earth from the sea's edge to the towering mountains. The moon rose up through the stars and the white bird lifted its wings and soared up and up and up and away, back into the moon.

I walked in now from the edge of the square, and took up a waiting position at the outer edge of the circle, looking in towards the centre.

> *I hope it may now be conceded that this drug is contraindicated in this case. After an absence of five days I was shocked at the deterioration in the patient. When I saw him this morning it was clear that he has less grasp of reality than when he was admitted. From what nurse says I should diagnose that he is in coma a good part of the time.*
>
> DOCTOR Y.

> *This case was thoroughly discussed at the conference Thursday at*

92

which you were not present. This drug's effects are often not fully developed for three weeks, as I have already tried to explain. Patient has been on it for twelve days.

DOCTOR X.

There was a pressure of silence, which swirled me into a singing calm. I was inside the Crystal, whose vortex had gathered in all sensation as a dust devil gathers in dust and leaves from yards around, or as bath water spiralling its way down a hole exerts its pull on every part of the water in the bath. Looking outwards from it nothing that had been there re-mained—or so it seemed at first, for the beginning of my being absorbed into the Crystal was a darkness of mind coupled with a vividness of sense that only slowly I was able to balance. It seemed that the Crystal was having difficulty in absorbing my com-parative crudeness. This fighting went on in me as well as in it, during the few moments of the begin-ning. I say "a few moments." But the very thing I became aware of first was that time had shifted gear and was vibrating differently, and it was this that was the first assault on my own habitual pattern of substance. To my eyes it seemed as if I was in a world of lucid glass, or perhaps better, of crystalline mist. My body felt a nausea which I became proper-ly aware of as it began to abate, for it had been gripping me in a totality that was a basic—of which one is unaware. For instance, as we breathe ordinary air, our lungs are adapted to absorb a poisonous gas (poisonous to other visiting creatures, or to ourselves perhaps, once) called air. The nausea had been a tight vice, locking me in tension against it. It went at last and a delightful lightness took me over. The dragging pain of gravity had gone: this dimension was as free and delicious as a skater, or flight lying between the wings of a guardian bird. Yet I had a body. But it was of a different substance, lighter, finer, tenuous, though I recognised its likeness to my usual shape of matter. Slowly my senses, my new senses, steadied. I was inside a tinted luminosity, my new body, and this luminousness was part, like a flame in fire, of the swirl of the Crystal, and this burned whitely, an invisible dance, where the centre of the circle in the square had been—and still was, for I could see its outline, but it was the ghost of its outline. And, holding fast to the start or centre of my vision, or, rather, feeling, I let that vision—or perhaps the word was understanding, move out and around. Or perhaps it would be more accurate to say, allowed it to enlarge, as light spreads, and I saw that this city on this plateau did indeed exist in the new dimension, or level, of vibration. But, as my own body was now a shape in light, though not as fine and high a light as the substance of the Crystal itself, so too was the city: it was as if the city of stone and clay had dissolved, leaving a ghostly city, made in light, like an illuminated mist that has shadows or echoes held in it. Yet the city that rose everywhere about me in the same shape of the city I knew so well was thinner, more sparse. It was a more delicately framed and upheld place. This is not to say that the houses or public buildings, delicately outlined, like a tracery in frost on a window-pane, all a patterning of stars or hexagons, were less firm and distinct than the shapes of the solid city built in stone, but that there were fewer houses and buildings in this shadow city than in the earthy one. As if this tenuous city, which was a pattern and a key and a blueprint for the outer city, only fitted certain parts or areas or individual buildings in the outer city. It seemed as if the delicately fine city "fitted" best over some public buildings and some houses. In between were areas where the mist lay blank, without shapes built into it. And yet I knew very well—since by now I did know so very well the real city where I had walked and watched and waited for weeks—that this "real" stone-built city had houses and buildings here and here and here and there—where there were none in the inner pattern, or template. I seemed to understand as I stood here in my new spritely shape that the areas of the city where the inner pattern was not strong enough to impose itself were where there was an extra heaviness and imperviousness in their substance. Whereas the parts of the city that were mirrored in the inner blueprint had as it were built into the stones a sample or portion of that fine inner light or substance.

And now it was plain to me that when walking in my normal shape through the stone city, and becoming conscious, as most people are at times, of a finer air in this or that house or hall or public place, what I was registering was the places or areas where the inner pattern lay vibrating on its self-spun thought.

Thought ... I was thinking ... the Crystal was a thought that pulsed and spiralled. My sympathies enlarged again, my mind washed out, and now I saw on the outskirts of this city moving spots or blobs of light. These were in groups or patches, and were moving away from the city. I saw that they were the troops of the Rat-dogs, and apes, but again they were fewer than I remembered, just as this new delicate city was thinner and sparser than the outer one. In this inner atmosphere only some of the beasts were mirrored. My mind moved among them like a bird on wings, and I understood that among these poor beasts trapped in their frightful necessities, some sometimes snuffed this finer air, but that most did not. Most of them were as thick, heavy and unredeemed as the bulk of the stone and earth that

had no crystalline air kneaded into it. Yet some did
have a light in them. And this did not seem to
match with any quality of group or pack morality.
For instance, one sad little blob of faintly pulsing
light which nevertheless was brighter than most in
its constellation, belonged to a beast I was able to
recognise—and he was one of the most violent, energetic and busy of them all; and another brave little
pulse belonged to a clowning, jesting ape. And yet
another marked an ape quite different from either,
one much obsessed with her twin apelets, a fussy
nagging nattering little animal, yet her star shone as
bright as the two assertive male animals. These
flocks of moving lights, or lit drops, like globules of
gleaming wet in the swirl of a luminous mist, moved
out and away. I understood that if I were to move
out there now on my ordinary gravity-subjugated
legs, the city would be clear and clean again. The
warring and killing beasts had moved away beyond
the suburbs of the city and beyond even the forest
where I had seen the orgiastic women. This forest I
now explored with the tentacles of my new senses
and found a paradise of plant, leaf and pattern of
branch all structured in light. A scene in the ordinary world nearest to it would be that in a forest
after a light snowfall when it is the essential shape
of branch and tree that is presented in white shimmering outline to eyes used to a confusion of green,
lush, loving, lively detail. In this paradisical forest
Felicity and Constance and Vera were not represented at all, yet as my thoughts hung over the
memory of what had been there, a compulsion or
pressure or need grew into them: a demand from
the excluded, a claim. The memory of the nights I
had drunk blood and eaten flesh with the women
under the full moon struck my new mind, and there
was a reeling and then a rallying of its structure,
while I accepted and held the memory, and then I

had moved out and beyond, but now the women were lodged in my mind, my new mind. I knew, though dimly enough at that time—for so many "knowings" began then, that those frightful nights when I had been compelled away from the city's centre to the murdering women had become a page in my passport for this stage of the journey. As this thought came in, so did another—or, as I've said already, the beginnings of one, these were all beginnings, that the women were now faceted in my new mind like cells in a honeycomb, gleams of coloured light, and that my comrades, whom I had seen flickering, flaming and flowing inside the greater white blaze of the Crystal were also faceted with me, as I with them, in this inner structure, and that I had understood this from the moment the Crystal had swept me up into itself, which was why I had forgotten my search for them. In that dimension, minds lay side by side, fishes in a school, cells in honeycomb, flames in fire, and together we made a whole in such a way that it was not possible to say, Here Charles begins, here John or Miles or Felicity or Constance ends. And so with us all. But while their new swelling into understanding was taking place in my mind, a move outwards into comprehension, only possible at all because of my fusion with the people who were friends, companions, lovers and associates, a wholeness because I was stuck like a bit of coloured glass in a mosaic—there was somewhere close all this time a great weight of cold. I realised that all the time there had been this weight, this pressure of freezing cold, but that I had not been aware of it as I had not been aware to begin with of my griping nausea. That had been total, and not to be isolated away from my overall condition. This terror of cold was like that. That was when I first became aware of it, or I think it was, for as I've said, in those early explorations of my new mode of feeling, it was only afterwards that I was able to trace strands back to a particular bud or start in my thought. But there was no doubt that about that time this knowledge became firmly lodged in me: the cold weight, a compulsion, a necessity, as it were, a menace only just held at bay by humanity, and always waiting there, the crocodile's jaws always there, just under the water. It was a grief and a fear too ancient for me, it was a sorrow bred into the essence of the race. I saluted it, and passed on, for like the early all-pervading nausea, this was part of my living, kneaded into my fibres, a necessity like breathing and associated with it: this cold, this weight, this pulling and dragging and compelling. It was too old a lodestone for any individual to fight away from, or even accurately to know and place. It was there.

The world was spinning like the most delicately tinted of bubbles, all light. It was the mind of humanity that I saw, but this was not at all to be separated from the animal mind which married and fused with it everywhere. Nor was it a question of higher or lower, for just as my having drunk blood and eaten flesh with the poor women had been a door, a key, and an opening, because all sympathetic knowledge must be that, in this spin of fusion like a web whose every strand is linked and vibrates with every other, the swoop of an eagle on a mouse, the eagle's cold exultation and the mouse's terror make a match in nature, and this harmony runs in a strengthened pulse in the inner chord of which it is a part. I watched a pulsing swirl of all being, continually changing, moving, dancing, a controlled impelled dance, held within its limits by its nature, and part of this necessity was the locking together of the inner pattern in light with the other world of stone, leaf, flesh and ordinary light.

In this great enclosing web of always changing

light, moved flames and tones and thrills of light that sang and sounded, on deeper and higher notes, so what I saw, or rather was part of, was neither light nor sound, but the place or area where these two identities become one. The pulsing ball of light or sound was fitted to the earthy world it enclosed, and as I had seen before with the buildings of the city and with the troops of animals, those poor ravaging beasts, everywhere in the earthy world lay the cracks and seams of higher substance, a finer beat in time or light or sound, which formed channels for the higher enclosing sphere to feed its self into the lower. Lying there out in space, as it might be within the great wings of a white bird, I could see through the coloured spinning membrane, as one can see through the spinning walls of a soap bubble as it hangs growing from a fine tube held in lips that blow air into it, and I saw how the coloured world we know, seas and soil, mountains and desert, was all in a spin of pressure of matter, and this creature hanging there in space surrounded by its delicate outer envelope, was at a first and a very long look, empty, for mankind was not visible until one swooped in close, where his evidence, cities and conglomeration and workings, showed as lice show in seams and crevices. Mankind was a minute grey crust here and there on the earth. Within patches that seemed stationary, motionless, minute particles moved, but in set patterns, so that looking down at one fragment of this crust of matter, smaller than the tiniest of grains of sand or dust or pollen, it seemed that even the curve made by a journey of a group of such items from one continent to another was flicker of an oscillation in a great web of patterning oscillations and quiverings.

The earth hung in its weight, coloured and tinted here and there, for the most part with the blueish tint of water ... the great oceans had become not more than a film of slippery substance covering part of the globe's surface. Yes, all that drama of deep blue oceans that held their still unknown and secret life, and roaring storms and crashing restless waves, and tides dragged about by the moon had become a thin smear of slippery substance on a toughly textured globe of matter, and humanity and animal life and bird life and reptile life and insect life—all these were variations in a little crust on this globe. Motes, microbes. And yet—it was mostly here that the enclosing web of subtle light touched the earth globe. It was for the most part through the motes or mites of humanity. Which, viewed from the vantage point of the enclosing web of light (inner or outer as one chose to view it) was not at all a question of individual entities, as those entities saw themselves, but a question of Wholes, large and small, for groups and packs and troops and crowds made entities, made Wholes, functioning as Wholes. Bending closer in the web of understanding which was the nature of this enclosing bell of light I could see how the patterns of light, the colours, textures, pulses of faint or strong light, were not only similarity, but identity. All over the globe ran these pulses or lines, linking groups of individuals, which groups were not necessarily nations or countries—I saw at moments how a patch of mould or lichen glowed up in a burst of colour (or sound) and this was a civil war or a burst of national emotion, but more often, when an area of colour moved and concentrated, singing on its own note, it was composed of sections of nations or countries that had left or detached themselves from their parent groups and were at war with each other, and it was noticeable how a flare-up of a tiny area was so often the coming together of two fragments or pulses, which then became the same colour, the same sound. But the lines or pulses running and darting everywhere over this globe that were most consistent were not the flareups of war but those that were the different professions, so that legislators over the earth were not merely "on the same wavelength" they were the *same*, part of the same organ, or function, even if in warring or opposing countries, and so with judges and farmers and civil servants and soldiers and talkers and moneymen and writers—each of these categories were one, and from this vantage point it was amusing to see how passionate hatred, rivalries and competitions disappeared altogether, for the atoms of each of these categories were one, and the minute fragments that composed each separate pulse or beat of light (colour, sound) were one, so there was no such thing as judges, but only Judge, not soldiers, but Soldier, not artists, but Artist, no matter if they imagined themselves to be in violent disagreement. And on this map or plan that showed how myriads of ridiculously self-important identities were reduced to a few, was another, different, but, in some places, matching pattern, of a stronger, rarer light (or sound) that varied and pulsed and changed like the rest but connected direct, made a link and a bridge, a feeding channel, between the outer (or inner, according to how one looked at it) web of thought or feeling, the pulsating bubble of subtle surrounding colour, and the solid earthy watery globe of Man. Not only a link or a bridge merely, since this strand of humanity was open like so many vessels open to the rain, but part of the shimmering web of fluid joyful being, which was why the scurrying, hurrying, scrabbling, fighting, restless, hating, wanting little patches of humanity, the crusts of lichen or fungi growing here and there on the globe, the sea's children, were, in spite of their distance from the outer shimmering web, nevertheless linked

with it always, since at every moment the glittering
tension of singing light flooded into them, into the
earthy globe, beating on its own delicious pulse of
joy and creation. The outer web of musical light
created the inner earthy one and held it there in its
dance of tension. And a scattering of people, a
strand of them, a light webby tension of them everywhere over the globe, were the channels where the
finer air went into the earth and fed it and kept it
alive. And this delicate mesh imposed on (or stronger
than) the other pulsing patterns had nothing to
do with humanity's ethics or codes, the pack's morality, so that sometimes this higher, faster beat sang in
the life of a soldier, sometimes a poet, sometimes a
politician, and sometimes in a man who watched
and mapped the stars, or another who watched and
mapped the infinitesimal fluid pulses that make up
the atom, which atom was as far from the larger
atoms that make up that mould or growth, humanity, as humanity is from the stars. And the items of
this connecting feeding mesh (like an electric grid
of humanity) were one; just as there is no such
thing as "soldiers" but only Soldier, and not "clerks"
but Clerk, and Gardener, and Teacher. For since
any category anywhere always beat on its own wave-
length of sound/light, there could not be individuals in this nourishing web. Together they formed
one beat in the great dance, one note in the song.
Everywhere and on every level the little individuals
made up wholes, struck little notes, made tones of
colour. On every level: even myself and my friends
whom the Crystal had absorbed into a whole, unimportant gnats, and my women and my children and
everyone I had known in my life—even someone
passed on a street corner and smiled at once—these
struck a note, made a whole. And this was the truth
that gave the utter insignificance of these motes
their significance: in the great singing dance, every-

thing linked and moved together. My mind was the facet of a mind, like cells in a honeycomb. Letting my mind lie dark there, quiescent, a mirror for light, I could feel or sense or recognise a pulse of individuality that I had known once as poor Charlie or Felicity or James or Thomas. Pulses of mind lay beating and absorbing beside my own little pulse, and together we were a whole, connecting within this wholeness with the myriad differing wholes that each of these people had formed in their lives, were continuously forming in every breath they took, and through this web, these webs, ran a finer beat, as water ran everywhere in the stone city through channels cut or built in rock by men who were able to grade the lift or the fall of the earth.

But yet, while I observed this, felt this, understood at last, I was conscious always of that old, that very ancient weight, the cold of grief I had become aware of so early on after my absorption into this new area of being. There it lay, just out of sight, deadly and punishing, for its pulse was that of a cold heaviness, it had to be a counterweight to joy. There it was, close, always—I acknowledged it and in doing so moved out and on, since now everything was open to me, and I floated deliciously, like a bubble in foam or as if lying at ease between a bird's stretched wings.

The corporal earth, like a round boulder, lay revolving erratically at about the distance it would take a shout or a hail to carry. It spun slowly about, wobbling badly. This spinning made a system of streaks, brown, blue and white, show on the surface of the globe, but I knew that these streaks were the seas and continents and icecaps in motion. The globe lay surrounded by its envelope of pulsing light, through which, however, I could see, as if I were peering through a thin opalescent cloud. I was seeing this earth spinning in a time that was not humanity's time. Somewhere behind me, or to one side, was the vast white blaze of the sun, and in this steady blaze the earth spun. I lay steady, a minuscule planet of the sun, watching the earth in its spin. Day and night were not visible except as a soft flicker, and the violent rocking back and forth that makes our seasons, seemed like a green flush that passed in a wink, and a momentary thickening of the white streaks at North and South poles. At this speed all I could see was a whizzing around on its axis and a whirling around the sun—and there was the weight of cold grief present here too, the compulsion, but I did not now attend to this, for as I thought of the speed of the planet, it began to slow, and now it was turning no faster than needed for me to take in a pattern of earth and water before the pattern turned out of sight. Since I was now further away than before, when the chart of darting impulses had shown itself to me, I could examine in less detail but in more perspective how the illuminated envelope about the earth thrilled and glowed and changed and shivered in its dance, and I could see very clearly how this envelope which clung to the earth's surface like a white summer fog on a warm morning matched and spoke to the areas beneath. A continent, I saw, gave off the same subtlety of shade—not absolutely uniform all over, of course not, but enough to be a recognisable basis to whatever other currents then ran and danced over it in their netting of sympathetic movement. It seemed as if there was something, but I could not see what, which made, let's say, that mass of land which we call Russia, European Russia, give off a glow which did not change, and this shade was different from that shade which pervaded the mass we call Asia, and these were different, but steadily different, from other areas of the world. Each part of the globe's surface of course had its own distinctive physical shade, that was its vegetation (or its lack of it), its plant setting for its animal life, but as distinctive, as clearly differentiated as jungle and desert and swamp and highland was the light that lay above in the aerial map that was its mirror and its sister—its governor. In this map of the currents of the mind and sympathies and feelings, countries—that is, nations—were marked out, and held what was necessary and appropriate to them, and it mattered very much whether a concept "nation" matched with the physical area beneath it, and where these were in discord then there was a discord of light and sound. I had an old thought, or rather, an old thought was transplanted upwards into the keener swifter air of this realm, that no matter what changes of government or what names were given to a nation's system of organisation, there was always the same flavour or reality that remained in that place, that country, or area—and seen from where I was, where time was speeding so that one revolution of the globe was like a slow human breath, so that I was watching great movements of human events, but as I might, as a human, watch for an hour the change, growth, and sudden destruction of an anthill. I looked close in at little England, catching a quick glimpse as it turned past, and saw how it kept its own pulse, which was a colour, a condition, a note of sound—for all countries, every one, every crust of mould, or part of humanity, were held in laws that they could not change or upset. They were manipulated from above (or below) by physical forces that they did not even as yet suspect—or that they did not suspect at this moment of time because it was part of this little organism's condition to discover and forget and discover and forget—and this was a time when they had forgotten and were about again to discover. But their terrible bondage, the chains of necessity that grasped them—it was this thought that came in again, bringing the dreadful breath of cold, of grief.

As I thought that I would like to see the earth speed up a little, but not as fast as before, when a year's turn around the sun seemed like the spin of a coin, it did speed up—and now I saw other patterns of light, or colour, deepen and fade and marry and merge and move, and as I thought that all these patterns were no more than a composite of the slower individual pulses and currents I had seen earlier, and that they were making up the glowing coloured mist that was the envelope of the globe, it came into my mind that the glowing envelope of the globe seemed to be set, or held, by something else, just as it, in its place, held the rhythms of the earth, our earth. My mind made another outwards-going, outswelling, towards comprehension, and now I saw how lines and currents of force and sympathy and antagonism danced in a web that was the system of planets around the sun, so much a part of the sun that its glow of substance, lying all about it in space, held the planets as intimately as if these planets were merely crystallizations or hardening of its va-porous stuff, moments of density in the solar wind. And this web was an iron, a frightful necessity, imposing its design.

Now I watched, as the earth turned fast, but still so that I could see the change and growth and dying away of patterns, how as the planets moved and meshed and altered and came closer to each other and went away again, exerting a pressure of forces on each other that bound them all, on the earth the little crusts of matter that were men, that were hu-manity, changed and moved. Just as the waters, the oceans (a little film of fluid matter on the big globe's surface) moved and swung under the compulsion of the sun and the moon, so did the life of man, oscillat-ing in its web of necessity, in its place in the life of the planets, a minute crust on the surface of a thickening and becoming visible of the Sun's breath that was called Earth. Humanity was a pulse in the life of the Sun, which lay burning there in a vast white explosion of varying kinds of light, or sound, some stronger and thicker, some tenuous, but at all forces and strengths, which fluid lapped out into space holding all these crumbs and drops and little flames in a dance—and the force that held them there, circling and whirling in their dance, was the Sun, the energy of the Sun, and that was the controlling governor of them all, beside whose strength, all the subsidiary laws and necessities were nothing. The ground and soul and heart and centre of this little solar system was the light and pulse and song of the Sun, the Sun was King. But although this central strength, this majestic core of our web, was an essence to the whole system, further out and away from the centre, where poor dark Pluto moved, perhaps it might be that the tug and pull and pressure of the planets seemed more immediate; perhaps out there, or further, the knowledge that the Sun is still the deep low organ note that underlies all being is forgotten—forgotten more even than on earth, spinning there so crooked and sorrowful and calamitous with its weight of cold necessity so close. And perhaps, or so I thought as I saw the dance of the sun and its attendants, Mercury the Sun's closest associate was the only one which could maintain steadily and always the consciousness of the sun's underlying song, its need, its intention, Mercury whose name was, also, Thoth, and Enoch, Buddha, Idris, and Hermes, and many other styles or titles in the earth's histories, Mercury the Messenger, the carrier of news, or information from the Sun, the disseminator of laws from God's singing centre.

Yes, but farther out, on the third crookedly spinning planet, it is harder to keep that knowledge,

the sanity and simplicity of the great Sun, and indeed poor Earth is far from grace, and so it was
easy to see, for at that tempo of spin that enabled
me to watch clearly the marrying of events on earth
and in the rest of its fellow planets, I watched how
wars and famines, and earthquakes and disasters,
floods and terrors, epidemics and plagues of insects
and rats and flying things came and went according
to the pressures from the combinations of the planets and the sun—and the moon. For a swarm of
locusts, a spreading of viruses, like the life of humanity, is governed elsewhere. The life of man,
that little crust of matter, which was not even visible
until one swooped down close as a bird might sweep
in and out for a quick survey of a glittering shoal of
fish that puckered a wave's broad flank, that pulse's
intensity and size and health was set by Mercury
and Venus, Mars and Jupiter, Saturn, Neptune,
Uranus, and Pluto, and their movements, and the
Centre of light that fed them all. Man, that flicker of
life, diminished in numbers and multiplied, was
peace-loving or murderous—in bondage. For when a
war flared up involving half the earth masses of the
globe, or when the earth's population doubled in a
handful of years and for the first time in known
history, or when in every place that men lived they
rioted and fought and scuffled and screamed and
killed and wept against their fate, it was because
the balance of the planets had shifted, or a comet
came too close—or the moon spoke, voicing the
cold, the compulsion; and now, bending in as close
as I dared to watch, I saw how the earth and its
moon cycled and circled and how both earth and
water pulsed and swelled and vibrated on Earth, as
matter swelled and moved and vibrated on the
Moon, on the cold moon, on the cold dead moon,
the warm Earth's cold sister, the stepchild, the terrible moon who sucks and leeches and clutches on to

the warm earth that was alive, for the moon wanted to live, the moon *would* live, the moon was like a poor sad still-born babe, but the baby would live, it fought to live, as eggs drag lime from hen's bones, and foetuses pull life from their mothers, the moon sucked and leeched and was like a dragging magnet of need that was the earth's first metronome in the dance of the planets, for it was nearest, it was the deprived and half-starved twin, the earth's other self, the Necessity.

Here was the frightful cold weight of sorrow that had lain on the edge of my mind since I had first been absorbed into the Crystal—the knowledge of the moon and its need. So close was the moon, so much part of earth, that it *was* earth—for seen even from that short distance they looked like a pair of brothers always in movement about each other. The moon was so very close, the always present force that is easiest overlooked when the tiny human mind looks for reasons and answers. Much easier to look out—right out, beyond even the furthest orbits of Uranus and Pluto, out to Riga, even to that other mirror, far Andromeda and beyond that to . . .

Oh yes, that's what our mind does most easily, but right here, in close, so close it is locked with us in a dance that moves waters and earth in tides twice a day, and swings in our veins and arteries and the tides of thought in our minds—close, flesh of our flesh, thought of our thought, Moon, Earth's stepchild, setting our stature, setting our growth, feeding appetites and making them. Moon spinning closer in to Earth makes animals and plants such and such a size and Moon lost or disintegrated or wandering further away changes animals, plants, the height of tides and probably the movement of land masses and ice masses, changes life as draconically as a sudden shower in a desert will change everything overnight. On the surface of the little Earth, a little green film, and part and parcel with this film, being fed by it, the crust of microbes, mankind, mad, moonmad, lunatic. To celestial eyes, seen like a broth of microbes under a microscope, always at war and destruction, this scum of microbes thinks, it can see itself, it begins slowly to sense itself as one, a function, a note in the harmony, and this *is* its point and function, and where the scummy film transcends itself, here and here only, and never where these mad microbes say I, I, I, I, I, for saying I, I, I, I, is their madness, this is where they have been struck lunactic, made moon-mad, round the bend, crazy, for these microbes are a whole, they form a unity, they have a single mind, a single being, and never can they say I, I, without making the celestial watchers roll with laughter or weep with pity—since I suppose we are free to presume compassion and derisiveness in the guardians of the microbes; or at least we are free to imagine nothing else— compassion and amusement being our qualities, but who knows what sort of a colour or a sound laughter, tears, make there in that finer kind of air?

Some sort of a divorce there has been some- where along the path of this race of man between the "I" and the "We," some sort of a terrible falling- away, and I (who am not I, but part of a whole composed of other human beings as they are of me) hovering here as if between the wings of a great white bird, feel as if I am spinning back (though it may be forwards, who knows?) yes, spinning back into a vortex of terror, like a birth in reverse, and it is towards a catastrophe, yes, that was when the microbes, the little broth that is humanity, was knocked senseless, hit for six, knocked out of their true understanding, so that ever since most have said, I, I, I, I, I, I, I, I, and cannot, save for a few, say, We.

Yes, but what awful blow or knock? What sent us off centre, and away from the sweet sanity of

We? In a moment I'll know, I'm being sucked back like a mite revolving in the vortex of the bathwater, eddying into the millrace, back, back, and then, Crash! the Comet; it comes hurtling out of the dark space, gives Earth a blow to midriff, and, deflected in its course, rushes off into the dark again, taking some of the atmosphere with it, and, leaving Earth no longer circling sane and steady, but wobbling back and forth, gyrating like a top, and all askew, which is when the seasons were born, beloved of poets, but worse, the air changed, the air that they breathed which kept them sane and healthy, saying We in love and understanding for the developing organ in a celestial body which they were. The air that had been the food of sane and loving understanding became a deadly poison, the lungs of these poor little animals laboured and changed and adapted, and their poor brains, all muddled and befuddled laboured to work at all, and worked badly, a machine all awry, but always teased and tormented by a queer half memory of the time before they became poisoned and spoiled and could not think and hated each other instead of loving. And there hung Earth, a casualty, all amiss, but soon they forgot, their newly-poisoned air became their normality, a forgetting by vanity, and . . . but Crash, look, I'm on the other side of Catastrophe, I'm before it. Though I'm free, too, to say "after," since like "up and down" it is interchangeable and entirely how you look at it, how you are situated, as is backwards and forwards. But man-wise, microbe-wise, I am before the Crash and in a cool, sweet, loving air that rings with harmony, is harmony, Is, yes, and here am I, voyager, Odysseus bound for home at last, the Seeker in home waters, spiteful Neptune outwitted and Jupiter's daughter my friend and guide.

All men make caves of shadow for their eyes
With hats and hands, sockets, lashes, brows,
So tender pupils dare look at the light.

In Northlands too where light lies shadowless
A man will lift his hand to guard his eyes;
It's a thing that I've seen done in strong moon-
light.

At any blaze too fierce, that warden hand
Goes to its post, keeping a dark:
Like cats', men's eyes grow large and soft with
    night.

New eyes they are, and still not used to see,
Taking in facets, individual,
With no skill yet to use them round and right.

Think: beasts on all fours we were, low,
With horizontal gaze kept safely from
That pulsing flaming all eye-searing bright.

Yet had to come that inevitable day
A small brave beast raised up his paw to
    branch,
Pulled himself high—and staggered on his
    height.

Our human babes have shown us how it was.
They clamber up; we, vigilant,
Let them learn the folly of their fright.

At that first venture, light stooped in salute,
Like to like, a shimmer in the mind,
And the beast thought it "angel"—as indeed we
    might.

One paw, earth-freed, held fast the slippery
    branch;
The other, freed, waited, while the eyes
Lifted at last to birds and clouds in flight.

And so he balanced there, a beast upright,
And the angel, saving what he'd hardly won
Jerked up that idle hand to guard his sight,
In that most common gesture that is done.
Man may not look directly at his sun.

I gotta use words when I talk to you. Probably
that sequence of words, I've got to use words, is a
definition of all literature, seen from a different perspective.

Enmeshed like a chord in Bach, part of a disc
as exquisitely coloured as a jellyfish, all pulsing harmonies, the disc being a swirl or spiral, made up of
sun and planets and baby planets and all their ac-
cretions, enmeshed, too, in Andromeda time, galaxy
time, moon time (oh woe and alas) looking at the
thing from any point of view but Earth Time, it is
possible a change of emphasis from Saturn to Jupiter
involving a change in all conditions on Earth and
taking centuries (our time) may perhaps have had
to find its message thus: That Jupiter fought Saturn
(or Zeus, Chronos) fair and square in mortal (or
immortal) combat and—not killed—but defeated
him, and thereafter Jupiter was God to Earth. But
here is a thought and not for the first time—of
course not, there is no thought for the first time—
why God? The vastest, most kingly and, so they say,
most benign of planets whose rays envelop Earth in
justice and equanimity (so they say) and touching
certain sections of humanity, that grey mould struggling for survival in its struggling green scum, with
more particularity than other sections. And on

Mount Olympus bearded Jove, or Jupiter, lorded it over the subsidiary Gods—not without a certain magnificent tetchiness. But why Father? Why Father of Gods and Men? For who is our Father? Who? None other than the Sun, whose name is the deep chord underlying all others, Father Sun, Amen, Amen, as the Christians still pray. Why not Father Sun, as Lord on Olympus, why Jove, or Jupiter, Zeus? For on that mountain Phoebus Apollo was a god like others, among others—very odd, that! Of course, man cannot look directly at his Sun. Gods go in disguise, even now, as then they were, or might be, Pillars of Fire—Forcefields, Wavelengths, Presences. It is possible that the Sun, like other monarchs, needs deputies, and who more suitable than Jupiter, who is like a modest little mirror to the Sun, being, like the Sun, a swirl of coloured gas, and having, like the Sun, its parcel of little planets. After all, Sun is an item in the celestial swarm on an equal basis with the other stars, chiming in key with them, and having its chief business with them—for this is nothing if not a hierarchical universe, like it or not, fellow democrats. Sun can probably be viewed, though for any mortal to think such a thought comes hard, a lèse-majesté indeed, as an atom on a different time-and-motion scale, having comradeship with other, equal atoms, all being units of the galaxy, while galaxies are units and equals on another level, where suns are as tinily swarming as men (that broth of microbes) are to planets. Russian dolls, Chinese boxes!—and this is why it is not unreasonable to imagine the Great Sun, giving Jupiter a careless nod: "Be my deputy my son! I have other more important business to attend in my peer group!"

Why Jupiter at all, if Saturn once held that place?—or at least, so the old myths do suggest. But why is it unreasonable to suppose that planets, as indeed, stars—like people—change character; for a weighty, responsible old planet in its maturity may give a very different report of itself than the same creature in its skittish youth. Perhaps Jupiter grew into the post, Lord of the Gods (as butlers are lord in the servants' hall, the Master and Mistress being too far out of sight to count), a deputy God, while Saturn got too bad-tempered for the position. After all Saturn ate his children. They do say that Saturn's rings are the smashed remnants of former planets.

Who knows but that our little system is an unfortunate one, and peculiarly vulnerable to visiting comets and intermittent visitors of various kinds? Or perhaps all stars, planets, planet's planets, are as subject to sudden calamity as men are, and the correct government and management of a star and its planets, or indeed, a galaxy and its suns, is a prudent balancing and husbanding of probabilities and substances? Who knows but that beings are not moved about among the planets, in one shape or another, as plants are moved about in a garden, or even taken indoors when frost is expected? When that comet came winging in from the dark beyond Pluto and went Bang! into poor Earth, perhaps there were warnings sent then from Jupiter (or Saturn, if it was his regency)—Take Care, Earth! the message might have gone. Or even: "Poor Earth, would you like to send us some of your inhabitants to live out a hundred or so generations as Our guests, until the unfortunate results of that Collision subside. Not on Us, of course: pure flame we are, burning Gas, like our Father, the Sun—but one of our planets would do nicely, with a little adaptation on your part." For we may suppose, I am sure, that Planets are altogether gentler and more humane than poor beast Man, lifting his bloody muzzle to his lurid sky, to howl out his misery and his exhaustion in between battles with his kind.

And who would convey these messages? (They

have to use words when they talk to us.) For one may imagine that Hermes or Mercury (or Thoth or Buddha), the planet nearest to the Sun our Father, may transmit messages from the Gods by the fact of his condition, the shifting and meshing of the planets causing him (at certain times) to shed substances on Earth as invisible to Earth's senses (though not to her new and her soon-to-be-invented or re-invented instruments) as the solar wind. But why Mercury—why Mercury messenger to Jupiter . . . there is an idea of doubleness here, of substitution, like Jupiter with the Sun. For consider how Athene, Minerva, is as much a messenger as is Mercury, the Sun's nearest child. We may play with the idea—why not? Gnats may sing to kings, and their songs have to be guessing games. Gnats are sure they have a few ideas of their own, for the seconds their lives last. But perhaps Minerva, Jupiter's daughter, has the same position vis-à-vis Jupiter as Mercury with the Sun. Our great lump of cold glassily ringing Moon, planet to our planethood, is in intimate enough relation with us, what of Jupiter with his—is it now twelve, subsidiaries? Perhaps the largest of them, a healthy, bouncing, rather managing girl, but handsome enough with her flashing blue eyes, runs errands for her father. A pulse darts earthwards from Jupiter's child, a synchronising in the machinery of Jupiter, the other planets, his planets, makes an impulse that becomes thoughts in the minds of men.

Or, words having to make do for pulses, impulses, dartings, influences, star-stuff, star-winds, up she gets, that responsible elder Daughter, and says to Jupiter: "Father, isn't it about time you gave a thought to poor humanity in its plight, poor Odysseus pining there in the arms of the enchantress and wishing only to go home. Haven't you punished him enough?"

"I?" says her Father. "You are always so personal, my dear, so emotional. In the first place, I'm as bound by the cosmic harmonies as everyone else. And in the second place, it wasn't me at all—surely you remember it was Neptune who hated him? He fell foul of the sea, that favourite of yours."

Who was Neptune, when Homer lived and sung. Oh, the sea, of course . . . but then, as now, seas like all the other forces and elements had their sympathetic planets. Neptune the planet is a new discovery, or so we think. However that may be, Odysseus the brave wanderer was hated by some force to do with the sea, the ocean in its drugged condition, its moon-madness, always tagging along after the moon. It was the ocean Odysseus displeased, could not remain in harmony with, the ocean, our moon's creature and slave.

Neptune had not been discovered, was discovered by us, modern man. So we know, quite definitely.

A hundred years or so ago (earth time), divines and historians and antiquarians of all kinds stated categorically that the world was created 4000 odd years ago, and anyone who did not go along with this thesis had a hard time of it, as the memoirs, biographies and histories of that period make so sadly clear. What a great step forward into sanity and true thinking has taken place in such a very short time: they'll concede now that the age of the physical world is longer than that—oh, quite considerably, by many millions. A hundred years of scholarly thinking has stretched back a millionfold the age of the earth. But these same divines, antiquarians and scholars are thinking now as they did a hundred years ago, when it comes to the age of civilisations; they can't even begin to concede that civilisations might have very old histories. The earth is allowed to be millions of millions of years old, but

the birth of civilisation is still set somewhere between two thousand and four thousand B.C., depend-
ing on the bias of the archeological school and the
definition of civilisation. We, now, are civilisation,
we are the crown of humanity, the pinnacle to
which all earlier evolution aimed, computer man is
the thing, and possessed of wisdom those earlier
barbarians did not have: from our heights man
dwindles back to barbarism and beyond that to
apehood. They say (or sing) that writing was first
invented in the third millennium B.C.; agriculture is
so old; mathematics so old; and astronomy is dated
exactly like the rest, having become scientific at that
moment it divorced itself from astrology and super-
stition. And everything is dated and known by
things, fragments of things: the children of a society
that is obsessed with possessions, objects, have to
think of previous civilisations in this way: slaves of
their own artifacts, they know that the old barbarians were too.

Every time a new city is dug up, the boundaries
(in time) are grudgingly shifted back—a couple of
hundred years perhaps, half a millennium. On a
plateau in Turkey part of a top layer of a city has
been laid bare, which takes a high form of human
living (one dare not say civilisation) back ten thousand years, and underneath that layer are many
other layers, still unexcavated . . . but do the special-
ists say: We cannot make any pronouncements at all
about human history, because our knowledge (or
our guesses) is limited to the last site we have
(partly) dug? No, no, not at all, what their
present knowledge is—is knowledge, for this is how
they always go on, it seems they have to, it is how
their unfortunate brains are formed.

Well, it is at least possible that astonomers of
ten thousand, or even twenty thousand, or even
thirty thousand years ago were as clever as ours are;

it is at least possible that the evidence for this lies easily available in easily excavated cities—available to people whose minds are less bound by the prejudices of our time.

We may suppose that ancient astronomers did not necessarily believe that the world was created on a certain day four thousand odd years before their own time, and by God in person. That they understood that words *had* to be used for their benefit—and understood what the words were symbols for.

That long before the Roman Gods and the Greek Gods and the Egyptian Gods and the Peruvian Gods and the Babylonian Gods, astronomers listened to Jupiter and his family, or to Saturn, and knew that Thoth (however he was called then) served Amen the Father, (and here again comes in the idea of deputy, of substitution, for Thoth created the world with a word); and that there were names for planets, suns, stars, and crumbs, blobs, and droplets of earth and fire and water; and that their patterns and sounds and colours were understood, and tales were told of them, instructive of Times and Events—why not? For no one knows what lies under the sands of the world's great deserts. No one knows how many times poor Earth has reeled under blows from comets, has lost or captured moons, has changed its air, its very nature. No one knows what has existed and has vanished beyond recovery, evidence for the number of times Man has understood and has forgotten again that his mind and flesh and life and movements are made of star stuff, sun stuff, planet stuff; that the Sun's being is his, and what sort of events may be expected, because of the meshings of the planets—and how an intelligent husbanding of humanity's resources may be effected based on the most skilled and sensitive of forecasting, by those whose minds are instruments to record the celestial dance.

"Father," says Jupiter's efficient and bossy daughter, "why don't you send down Mercury to do something about that poor voyager, stranded there on his drugged island? He could ask Neptune to let up a bit. It's not *fair*, you know. It's not *just*."

"Well you see to it then, daughter," says Jupiter, a busy man, Sun's deputy, and with all those bounding children, tugged this way and that like a busy housewife and mother with her large brood. "You just see what you can do, but mind you, don't forget that We, Jupiter, are not the only influence on the traveller's journey. No, it's a harmony, it's a pattern, bad and good, everything in turn, everything spiralling up—but yes, it's the right moment for a visit to Mercury. It is the exact time—thanks for reminding me."

"Timing is everything," murmurs Minerva the Flashing-Eyed, bustling off to find Thoth, or Hermes, and finding him speeding around the sun in an orbit so dazzling and so lively and so gay and above all so many-sided and accomplished that it was hard to keep up with him.

"Ah," says he, "it's time again, isn't it? I was thinking it must be."

"You sound reluctant," said Minerva.

"I've just been visiting Venus."

"Everyone always likes her best," says Minerva, drily. "As everyone knows, she and I don't get on. She's so *silly*—that's what I can't stand. People say I'm jealous—not at all. It's that damned stealthy dishonesty I can't tolerate—that appalling hypocrisy. I've never been able to understand how it is that intelligent men can put up with it—but there you are. And I didn't come to talk about Aphrodite. I'm here about poor Earth, poor traveller!"

"Your kind heart does you credit. But don't forget, it was partly their fault."

"Stealing the fire?"

"Of course. If that fellow hadn't stolen the fire, then they would never have known what a terrible state they are in."

"You, Mercury, God of letters and of music and of—in a word, *progress*, complaining about that! You wouldn't want them still in that dark and primitive state, would you?"

"They don't know how to use it."

"That remains to be seen."

"All I'm saying is that knowledge brings a penalty with it—of course, it *was* enterprising of him—what's his name, Jason, Prometheus, that fellow—in his place I might have done the same. Eating the fruit when I was told not to . . ."

"Stealing the fire," says Minerva, always with a tendency towards pedantry.

"Come now, don't be so literal-minded, that's to be like them," says Mercury.

"And there's the other thing," says Minerva, rather stern—at her tone Mercury began to look irritated. For Minerva was also a bit of blue-stocking; her feeling of justice and fair play (regarded as childish by some of the Gods who regarded themselves as more advanced, philosophically) usually led her to the question of women's rights, and men's vanity.

"All *right*," says Mercury, "understood."

"But is it?" says she, severe. "His mother was an earth-woman, certainly, but who was his father? Well?"

"Oh don't start, please," says Mercury. "You really are a bore, you know, when you get on to that."

"Justice," she says. "Fair play. I'm my father's daughter. And who was *his* father? With such blood, or rather, fire, in his veins, he was not to be expected to live like a mole in earth knowing that Light existed, and yet never reaching out after it."

"There was reason to believe," says Mercury, "that he was in it all the time. He walked in the Garden with God."

"And then he ate what he should not have done. He stole the Apple, dear God of Thieves. And paid for it."

"And in short everything is going as was expected, and according to plan, and with Our assistance."

"Progress has to be seen to be made."

"All right, I'm ready to leave when the Time is Ripe."

"Are you quite sure of your mandate?"

"Dear Minerva! Is it any different this time?"

"It is always the same Message, of course . . ."

"Yes. That there is a Harmony and that if they wish to prosper they must keep in step and obey its Laws. Quite so."

"But things are really very much worse this time. The stars in their courses, you know . . ."

"Fight on the side of Justice."

"In the long run, yes. But what a very long run it must seem to them, poor things."

"Partly through their own fault."

"You sound very severe today. Sometimes we even seem to change roles a little? You must remember that you are God of Thieves because you inspire, if not provoke, curiosity and a desire for growth, in such actions as stealing fire or eating forbidden fruit or building towers that are intended to reach Heaven and the Gods. Punishable acts. Acts that have, in fact, been punished already."

"Perhaps it isn't always easy to take responsibility for our progeny? Is it, dear Minerva? For acts can be our children . . . tell me, is it easy for your Father, or for you, to recognise as kith and kin acts of justice that are in fact the results of your influence—can in a sense be regarded as you, though in extension of course? Justice is Justice still, in the sentencing of a thief to prison—and the thief has stolen books because he has no money to buy them. In such a drama both you and I are represented— and there's little doubt which of us appears more attractively? Are you sure you aren't finding my celestial role rather more attractive than yours, and it is that which accounts for your concern—which I very much value, of course."

"I should have known better," says Minerva. "Only an idiot gets into an argument with the Master of Words. Well, I can't really wish you an enjoyable visit, when things have never been so bad."

"But one hopes, and indeed expects, that they have a potentiality for good in proportion to the bad—for that is how things tend to balance out."

"The sort of remark that I usually make, if I may say so—and which tends to irritate you, dear Messenger. But you are right. This particular combination of planets will be really so very powerful—the equivalent of several centuries of evolution all in a decade or so. I don't think I *am* exceeding my mandate if I say there *is* anxiety. After all, no one could say they have ever been distinguished by consistency or even ordinary common sense."

"I am sure the anxiety is justified. But I expect there'll be the usual few who will listen. It's enough."

"So we must hope, for everyone's sake."

"And if the worst comes to the worst, we can do without them. The Celestial Gardener will simply have to lop off that branch, and graft another."

"Charmingly put! Almost, indeed, reassuring, put in such a way! But so much trouble and effort have already been put into that planet. Messengers have been sent again and again. The regard of Our Father (as of course it comes down to us through his Regent, my own Father) is surely expressed by the long history of Our concern? And there was the Covenant—the fact they continuously disregard it, is not enough reason to abandon them altogether. *After all, when all is said and done . . .*"

"You are tactfully referring to that ancestry business again? Well, whatever the stark and dire nature of the shortly-to-be-expected celestial configurations, and whatever man's backslidings, the fact that I am about to descend *again* (yes, I grant that I say that with a bit of a sigh) shows that our respective fathers are well aware of our situation. And more—that there is confidence in the outcome."

"I'm glad I find you in such good heart."

"Dear Minerva, do come out with it. You want to give me some good advice, is that it?"

"It's just that—well, after all, there *are* a dozen or so of us, Jupiter's children, and it *is* an enlarging family, and some of us are not unlike Earth, and as the oldest sister you must see that I have had so much experience and . . ."

"Dear, dear Minerva."

"Oh well, I really didn't mean to irritate you. I'll leave you, then."

"Yes, do, goodbye."

And Minerva flies off.

As for Mercury the Messenger, he divides himself effortlessly into a dozen or so fragments, which fall gently through the air on to Earth, and the Battalions of Progress are strengthened for the Fight.

Ah yes, all very whimsical. Yes, indeed, the contemporary mode is much to be preferred, thus: that Earth is due to receive a pattern of impulses from the planet nearest the Sun, that planet nearest on the arm of the spiral out from Sun. As a result, the Permanent Staff on Earth are reinforced and

THE CONFERENCE

was convened on Venus, and had delegates from as far away as Pluto and Neptune, both of whom normally asked for transcripts to be sent. But this time, everyone in the solar system would be affected. The Sun Himself was represented. But his Presence was general and pervasive: the light glowed more strongly after a certain point in the proceedings, and a silence fell for a moment—that was all. But everyone knew how rare an event this was, and the sense of urgency deepened.

Minna Erve was in the Chair. A forceful and animated woman, with particularly arresting eyes, she was the obvious choice, because of her position as Chief Deputy's oldest daughter.

The conference was already nearly over, with not much more than the Briefing to come. Already those who were not in on the Descent were getting up and collecting their gear.

Minna Erve was still speaking. "In short, this is the worst yet. The computers have checked and doublechecked—and checked again. This was on advice from on High—" here the Light pulsed in acknowledgement—"but there is no doubt. The balance of planetary forces already exercises strong adverse pressures, which will reach a peak in about ten to fifteen years from now. Their years, of course. Before you leave, I'd like you to watch this second film, *Forecast (Detail)*."

Delegates glanced at each other, but sat down again. Minna might be overconscientious, but it was true enough that until most of them had reached here and had been hit by the atmosphere of this particular conference, they had not really appreciated the urgency.

They had already seen the *Forecast* film, showing Earth as an item in its place in the solar system. Earth had showed it was under pressure, as it and the other planets moved into the expected positions, first of all by the increased activity on the surface. This was slight to begin with, but earth-quakes, tidal waves, excessive movements of all kinds become increasingly noticeable. The weather, always inhospitable to life on that planet, became more extreme. The icecaps melted slightly, causing havoc along the seaboards. The Comet added its quota of disturbance to the already delicate-enough balances between Earth and its neighbours. The representatives of Mars and Venus had sat with particularly long faces. What happened anywhere in the System (and of course, beyond) affected every-one, but near neighbours were bound to feel it first: the last time Earth was in a crisis, both Mars and Venus had suffered, and the memory of that time was still strong. But it had not been possible for any delegates, not even those from Pluto and Neptune, to whom the Earth's inhabitants were alien indeed, to watch the end of the *Forecast* film without awe.

But this was *Forecast (Detail)*; Earth in closeup, by herself, and without even the Moon. The previous film showing Earth and Moon as—as it were—an atom of the molecule, had brought home first the change in the seasons, weather, crustal activity, vegetation. This film, on a smaller and slower scale, showed the drastic increase of population as Forests and Plant Life and Animal Life diminished, and deserts spread. For as animal and bird life dwindled, human beings multiplied, to preserve the balance. Organic life, necessary in the cosmic balance, had to be maintained on Earth, and as humans killed and destroyed the organic life of which they were a part, their own increase kept the balance. But their aggressiveness and irrationality increased steadily. As usual it was a total process—one strand or factor not to be separated from another. It was not that human aggression and irresponsibility increased because of the population explosion, and that this explosion was because of the planetary movements—all these were strands in a single process.

The delegrates watched with steadily deepening grimness as wars, previously kept local, got worse and enlarged. Towards the end the destruction ceased to have even a pretence of consistency. Nations became allies in one decade who had been enemies the last; enemies who had been devoting every technical resource to mutual slaughter suddenly became allies. But the technical devices were out of control; the instruments of mass slaughter and destruction took over. As that planetary position was reached that was by now designated everywhere in the System as FIRST CLASS EMERGENCY, the increasingly poisoned atmosphere on Earth, the emanations of mass Death and Fear, reflected back and affected—first of all, Mars and Venus; and their imbalance in its turn spread out to the other planets—and, as was signalled by the presence of the Sun Himself, to the Sun Himself.

By the time the planets had moved out of the Danger position, changes must occur in every part of the System which even now, at this moment, the computers in a million laboratories were busy forecasting.

The penultimate stage showed by *Forecast* (*Detail*) was more violent than the last stage. Earth rocked and hissed, and heaved, showered locally by falling rock, flame, boiling liquids, and convulsed by quakes. Men fought and struggled. There were mass movements of lower forms of animal and insect, locusts, rats, mice. There were sudden epidemics. Whole nations of people died in these epidemics, and as poisoned air and water reached their patches of the planet. So much of animal and human life died it was as if the globe quietened, stilled. An awful emptiness distinguished the final stage. It seemed as if no life remained. But even while this cauldron of poison bubbled, it was possible to see the beginnings of another pattern—some of the humans busied themselves in a different way. Even as the Earth's convulsions began to subside, the planetary Emergency over, they were again rebuilding, re-creating—and, as was obvious from their increasingly meaningful activity, the crisis on the planet had bred a new race. It was a mutation. While not much different in appearance from the previous human, the new human being had increased powers of perception, a different mental structure. This remnant of an old, or the beginnings of a new race, had as heritage all the accumulated experience of the human race, plus, this time, the mental equipment to use it.

Forecast (*Detail*) ended, and the delegates left. When no one remained but the Descent Team and Minna Erve, the hundred or so of them waited politely for the Sun to leave, if He so wished, but the pervasive golden glow remained steady. Some thought It even brightened a little, and they took courage from this, thinking it to be a message of hope, and of belief in their powers to accomplish what they had all volunteered to do.

Now Minna Erve was joined on the platform by Merk Ury.

Minna said: "Merk will brief you. But I must remind you all that Time is running out."

Merk said: "Thanks, Minna. I had in fact already decided to limit this to the main points, particularly of course as you have already so ably done the groundwork.

"The first point is this—and the second and the third—you should not underrate the difficulties. Every one of you in this room has of course travelled extensively inside the System—some of you perhaps outside of it—and you won't need to be told that to hear a place described is not the same as experiencing it. Which is another reason to keep these few remarks short.

"Now, you will probably all know that at first there was a doubt whether life could exist on Earth at all, after the previous Crisis which altered the atmosphere. But Nature is infinitely resourceful, making virtues from deficiencies. We had thought that nothing could live in that tempestuous, erupting, unstable, accident-prone planet, but in fact the life forms did adapt, but most are only able to live in certain dry areas of the Earth and where the temperature is more or less equable. Most parts of the planet are too cold, too hot, wet, frozen, mountainous or dry. But you are all familiar with the dominant creature that has evolved, its most striking physical feature being its pumping system for air and liquid. In other words, it is distinguished by the organs it has evolved for living in a particularly difficult and poisonous air. But it is as yet an inefficient adaptation and the creature's mental processes are defective.

"Now, the Permanent Staff on Earth has always had one main task, which is to keep alive, in any way possible, the knowledge that humanity, with its fellow creatures, the animals and plants, make up a whole, are a unity, have a function in the whole system as an organ or organism. Our Permanent Staff's task is always extremely difficult, the main feature of these human beings as at present constituted being their inability to feel, or understand themselves, in any other way except through their own drives or functions. They have not yet evolved into an understanding of their individual selves as merely parts of a whole, first of all humanity, their own species, let alone achieving a conscious knowledge of humanity as part of Nature; plants, animals, birds, insects, reptiles, all these together making a small chord in the Cosmic Harmony."

Here there was a discreet, slight, and not uniformly approving applause. For Merk had a literary turn. Merk smiled slightly on hearing it. He knew quite well that some of them there believed that as he was a technician he should not be indulging himself with the inexact arts. It was an affectation among some of them to use jargon, despise literature and to arm themselves with a jaunty facetiousness when approaching the serious.

"Each individual of this species is locked up inside his own skull, his own personal experience— or believes that he is, and while a great part of their ethical systems, religious systems, etc., state the Unity of Life, even the most recent religion, which, being the most recent is the most powerful, called Science, has only very fitful and inadequate gleams of insight into the fact that life is One. In fact, the distinguishing feature of this new religion, and why it has proved so inadequate, is its insistence on dividing off, compartmenting, pigeon-holing, and one of the most lamentable of these symptoms is its suspicion of, and clumsiness with, words." Here he smiled again, winningly enough. A few laughed.

"To sum up these few remarks: our task, that of the Permanent Staff, is always to inculcate and maintain a truth to which these creatures are so far able only to pay lip service, a phrase of theirs which is their way of summing up their most powerful defect, the inability to see things except as facets and one at a time. The truth is that We—speaking of course in our roles as delegates and deputies—" and here the all-pervading Light brightened for a moment, as it were in acknowledgement of their stewardship—"We can only tolerate them insofar as they obey instructions, manage their affairs, their communal life, in such a way as to adjust to the Systems' needs. But they seem unable to retain this very simple truth for long, although they have been told again and again, and this is because of another and most powerful feature of their thinking, which is that anything they are told is distorted to fit their own particular personal or group bias and then added, like another pebble to the pile of the half-truths they already cherish. So that we confidently expect—or could have expected in the past, before this present great (forgive me for another lapse into the literary) leap forward, under the influence of the Solar Wind of Change—" and here the Light brightened and, as it were, smiled—"that anything we have to say will be retained in its pure form for only a short time and by a few people, because in the nature of things, or rather, it is in *their* nature, this simple fact—human duty as part of the Harmony—will be off running like a mad dog, will be twisted out of itself, will have become the property of a hundred warring sects, each claiming that their version, which they have concocted, is correct. But that time is past, or nearly so. An ability to see things as they are, in their multifarious relations—in other words, Truth—will be part of humanity's new, soon-to-be-developed equipment. Thanks of course, not to Us, but to . . ."

The Light deepened a chord, and held it. Everyone showed that he or she was conscious, with Merk Ury, that the main point, the central issue, had been reached. There was a general brightening and steadying of their individual atmospheres, force-fields or auras.

"As everyone here knows, has had drummed into him or her from the moment he or she volunteered—it is not at all a question of descending into that Poisonous Hell and remaining unaffected. Every one of us takes his life in his hands. For these

creatures are for the most part malevolent and murderous by nature, able to tolerate others only insofar
as they resemble themselves, capable of slaughtering
each other because of a slight difference in skin
colour or appearance. Also they cannot tolerate
those who do not think as they do. Although they
know perfectly well, theoretically, that the surface
of the inhabited globe is divided into thousands of
areas, each with its system of religious or scientific
belief, and although they know that it is entirely by
chance that any individual among them was born
into this or that area, this or that area of belief, this
theoretical knowledge does not prevent them from
hating foreigners in their own particular small area,
and if not harming them, isolating them in every
way possible. This means, that unless we can perfect
our own adaptation to them, they will attack us,
the Team's members. This we must expect. Further,
we must expect that the colonies on Earth that are
the result of previous Descents will have acquired—or
many of them will—these same qualities of separative-
ness, and unharmony and hostility to others. Or,
retaining in that poisonous brew they call air only
the memory that they should *not* allow themselves to
be affected, they devote all their energies to elaborate
systems whose function was once to keep them sane,
but which now have become their own justification.

"Now, as you know, this will not be my first
Descent."

Here, again, many glances were exchanged. This
time for mutual comfort and support. For not one of
those present were unaware of the dramatic histories of some of the previous Descents. Or rather of
those which were documented—for most were not,
since they had been designed to remain unknown to
the inhabitants of Earth. But throughout the Solar
System, tales of the various Descents were told and
retold—as fables, as far as most people were con-

cerned. But to the few who knew they were literally true, they were grim enough hearing. For the first Law enjoined on them all, the children of the System, by their Father, was to love one another—that is, to respect the laws of Harmony. And yet so very close to them, their neighbour, strand of their strand, pulse of their pulse, energy of their energy, was Earth, whose inhabitants not only did not respect the Law, but who tended to persecute or kill, if they did not ignore, Those who came to remind them of it. And such a backsliding and a falling-away on the part of close neighbours tended to make them uncertain of their own continuing safety and health of mind—for after all, every one knew perfectly well that accidents could happen anywhere, that the planetary housekeeping and estate managing was, and had to be, subsidiary to a structure of Law much greater than that of the Solar System. In short—they, too, could become victims; there but for the grace of Light, went they.

Merk continued: "When the time comes, it will be our task to wake up those of us who have forgotten what they went for; as well as to recruit suitable inhabitants of Earth—those, that is, who have kept a potential for evolving into rational beings; and to generally strengthen and defend our colonies on Earth for their task. That has always been so, of course. But this time it will be all that and more—it will be an assisting of the Earth's people through the coming Planetary Emergency in which all life may be lost. But we have already dealt with that earlier in the Conference.

"At the risk of boring you, I must repeat, I am afraid—repeat, reiterate, re-emphasise—it is not at all a question of your arriving on Planet Earth as you leave here. You will lose nearly all memory of your past existence. You will each of you come to yourselves, perhaps alone, perhaps in the company of each other, but with only a vague feeling of recognition, and probably disassociated, disorientated, ill, discouraged, and unable to believe, when you are told what your task really is. You will wake up, as it were, but there will be a period while you are waking which will be like the recovery from an illness, or like the emergence into good air from a poisoned one. Some of you may choose not to wake, for the waking will be so painful, and the knowledge of your condition and Earth's condition so agonising, you will be like drug addicts: you may prefer to continue to breathe in oblivion. And when you have understood that you are in the process of awakening, that you have something to get done, you will have absorbed enough of the characteristics of Earthmen to be distrustful, surly, grudging, suspicious. You will be like a drowning person who drowns his rescuer, so violently will you struggle in your panic terror.

"And, when you have become aroused to your real condition, and have recovered from the shame or embarrassment of seeing to what depths you have sunk, you will then begin the task of arousing others, and you will find that you are in the position of rescuer of a drowning person, or a doctor in a city that has an epidemic of madness. The drowning person wants to be rescued, but can't prevent himself struggling. The mad person has intermittent fits of sanity, but in between behaves as if his doctor were his enemy.

"And so, my friends—that's it. That's my message to you. It's going to be tough. Every bit as tough as you expect.

"Which brings me to the final point. Which is that there is to be no Briefing. How could there be? You'd be bound to forget every word you hear now. No, you will carry Sealed Orders."

Here, as some of them unconsciously glanced

around for evidences of these, Merk joked: "Come, come, what do you expect? A roll of microfilm? Perhaps a manuscript of some kind, that you'd have to chew up and swallow in moments of danger? No, of course not, give me some credit—brainprints, of course."

At this, they were obviously much relieved and reassured, brain-printing being, after all, as brain-printing does.

"And in fact you have already been printed, thanks to . . ."

The Light glowed up for a moment—glowed up and held the increase.

"Yes. We have the Absolute assurance that our brain-printing was the best possible quality. You'll find it is all there, when you need it . . ." The glow was deepening, and there was a steady vibrating hum, which was having the effect of encouraging and steadying them all—was even, as some of them believed, the final pressure of the Printing. But they all knew now that this was the Time. Minna Erve, her eyes flashing tears, although tempted to remain with them, slipped away, without formal goodbyes, as Merk Ury stepped down off the platform and sat in the body of the hall with the rest. They all sat quiet, adjusting their breathing apparatus. There was a deep mellow silence, the underside of the powerful humming sound. Each held his or her mind steady in the thought: Don't forget, keep the memory of this moment, keep it steady . . . but the golden spin of the moment swept the whole space they occupied into a vortex of ringing Light in which they were spinning atoms. The pressure increased. The Sound became higher. It was like a flute. The Light was now an explosion of orange, which deepened into red. This pulsed and beat. The high dizzy whine of the Sound had become absorbed into the steady pulse of the dark red glow.

Each was alone now, all his knowledge of himself, his understanding, absorbed into his ears where beat, steadily on and on and on and on, the dark red pulse.

Sucked into sound, sucked into sea, a swinging sea, *boom*, shhh, *boooom*, shhhh, *boooom* . . . thud thud, thud thud, thud thud, thud thud, thud thud, in and out, in and out, yes, no, yes, no, yes, no. Black and white, coming and going, out and in, up and down, *no*, yes, *no*, yes, *no*, yes, one, two, one, two, one two, and in the three is me, the three is me, THE THREE IS ME. I in dark, I in pulsing dark, crouched, I holding on, clutching tight, booom, shhh, boooom, shhh, rocked, rocking, somewhere behind the gate, somewhere in front the door, and a dark red clotting light and pressure and pain and then OUT into a flat white light where shapes move and things flash and glitter.

He is a *good* baby, it was a good quiet birth and he went straight off to sleep.

Oh sick and queasy, all mouth and the smell of sick, a stomach rocking as baby rocks, oh so sick, and too full and too empty, and hungry and wet and smells and oh smells and dark and light, dark and light, one and two, the three is *me*. And

He is a *good* baby, he sleeps all the time.

I struggle up clutching and fighting away from the sick rocking stomach, the smell of sick, I fight and clutch and roll and roar immersed in a hell of want, I must have, I must have, I must have, oh rise on your two legs then, I must rise and walk, walk anyhow and any way and any way up and away from this I must, I want, but they rock me, hushhhhh, they crooooon me, shush, they knock me over the head with sleepers, soothers, syrups, drugs and medicines.

Be a *good* boy, baby, and go to sleep.

Oh I sleep, down among the dead men, wrapped in cocoons of warmth, all belly and wet stinking bum, I must wake, I must wake, I *know* there is something more awake than this, I *know* I have to be awake and be, but

Be a *good* baby, I'll rock you to sleep,
He is a *good* baby, he has always slept a lot,
He is a *good* baby, he doesn't give any trouble,
He is a *good* baby, and he has always slept the
night right through.

I run and crawl and all the world's my oyster, I touch and finger and sniff and taste and a streak of dust on the floor is a wonder, and sunlight on my skin is a continent and light is and dark is, and dark is for remembrance, behind there is a door, I came in at there, pulsing, pulsing, one and two and I makes three, and now is a million-textured light changing as the day changes, light the wonder, light out of dark, and oh let me smell and grow and find and fight but

Be a *good* baby and do keep still
He's such an energetic baby, he wears me out,
Sleep, baby, for good Lord's sake!
Can't you ever keep still,
You used to be such a *good* baby.

Pushed back into sleep as I fight to emerge, pushed back as they drown a kitten, or a child fighting to wake up, pushed back by voices and lullabies and bribes and bullies, punished by tones

of voices and by silences, gripped into sleep by
medicines and syrups and dummies and dope.

Nevertheless I fight, desperate, like a kitten
trying to climb out of the slippysided zinc pail it has
been flung in, an unwanted, unneeded cat to drown,
better dead than alive, better asleep than awake,
but I fight, up and up into the light, greeting dark
now as a different land, a different texture, a different state of the Light, I lie in dark and recognise
Night but

    Sleep, child, why aren't you asleep?
    He gives me trouble, he never wants to sleep.

But I'm up and on my feet and running and a
discovery of the tones and sounds of Light is my day
with sleep and bed waiting to catch me by my heel
and drag me down down down, and in the day,
they say, when I rage peevish and restless, with
tiredness the enemy overcoming the discovery, the
wonder and the delight

    Lie down and *sleep*, lie down and *rest*
    Be a *good* boy now and *sleep* awhile.

And when night comes and I'm struck with
anger again that tiredness undoes me, again and
again, or struck with rage because I'm still awake
and still got far to go, the gleam of light on a leaf a
signal and the drip of rain a most potent drum

    Oh do go to *sleep* now baby, it is time for *sleep*,
    For God's sake give me some peace and quiet,
    For Christsake *sleep*.

And alone in the dark and out of the way I
shout and shake my bars and at last so that they
love me, I sleep, I learn to sleep.

He is such a good boy, he's sleeping well.
He doesn't give me nearly so much trouble now,
he's stopped being so wakeful.
Thank God, he's asleep.

I'm off to their school now and I'm learning to
be good.
I'm a good boy now, I am quiet and good.
One and one are two
And the third is Me.

Me half beaten back into dark, me quietened,
regulated, time-tabled, a nuisance tamed, me the
obediently sleeping.

But back in the dark in the deep of my mind is
where I know quite well the door is, back or forward, up or down, beyond the Boooom, shush, the
eternally boooooming, the pulse, the beat, the one
and two, the one and two, through there, who
knows which or where—I do. I know. I remember.
Do I remember? Yes, I remember. I must remember.
There. Where?

The little white days flicker faster faster, flick
flick flick, on and off, white with the slices of dark
between, the days for living, and the nights for

Sleep.

He doesn't sleep well doctor, he needs a pill.

The small days flicker and the nights are killed
dead with Pills. But he sleeps well, he is healthy and
regulated and *good*.

And now the greatest drug of them all, the
sweet dream, sweet night dreams and sweeter day
dreams, I dream of Jeannie with the light brown
hair and wide-apart legs like loving arms.

And now I'm grown and gone, and I work and
play all regulated ordered and social and correct,

and I sleep now less than I ever did in my life for this short brief blissful time, just away from that bed the family, before I become that feather bed the family, and I'm young and my dreams and living are all one, white arms around my neck and I drown, I drown, she and I, he and I, down among the dead men. Down.

Oh doctor can you give me a pill to make me sleep. Oh, I'm working too hard and Oh, I'm worried about my marriage, and oh I'm worried about my job, and oh I can't stand what I think. Oh give me a pill and give me a drink and give me a smoke and give me dope, give me enough food to knock me silly, give me now everything I had when I was baby, give me what you trained me to need before I even talked or walked, give me anything you like, but let me SLEEP for in the dark where the door once was (but is it still?) is the place I can tolerate being alive at all. I never learned to live awake. I was trained for sleep. Oh let me sleep and sleep my life away. And if the pressure of true memory wakes me before I need, if the urgency of what I should be doing stabs into my sleep, then for God's sake doctor, for *goodness* sake, give me drugs and put me back to dreaming again.

And now life is wearing thin and as it reaches the end the drugs are wearing thinner, less life for loving, less room for food, less stomach for drink, and sleep is harder to reach and thinner, and sleeping is no longer the Drop into the black pit all oblivion until the alarm clock, no, sleep is thin and fitful and full of memories and reminders and the dark is never dark enough and

Give me pills, give me more pills. I MUST SLEEP.

No, I don't enjoy my nights reading thinking talking and simply being alive, no, I want to sleep, I have to sleep.

In a long narrow ward where sixty old men in

charity pyjamas are put to bed like infants for the
night at nine o'clock by institution nurses, the nurse
goes around, with sixty doses of SLEEP.

SLEEP WELL.

In the outpatients of a million hospitals, in the
consulting rooms of a million million medicoes, a
million million million hands are stretched out,

Doctor give me pills to make me sleep.
SLEEP WELL.

As the earth revolves, one half always in the
dark, from the dark half rises up a wail, oh I can't
sleep, I want to sleep, I don't sleep enough, but give
me pills to make me sleep, give me alcohol to make
me sleep, give me sex to make me sleep.

SLEEP WELL.

In mental hospitals where the millions who
have cracked, making cracks where the light could
shine through at last, the pills are like food pellets
dropped into battery chickens' food hoppers, SLEEP,
the needles slide into the outstretched arms, SLEEP,
the rubber tubes strapped to arms drip, SLEEP.

SLEEP, for you are not yet dead.
I must wake up.
I have to wake up.

I can feel myself struggling and fighting as if I
were sunk a mile deep in thick dragging water but
far above my head in the surface shallows I can see
sunlanced waves where the glittering fishes dance
and swim, oh let me rise, let me come up to the

surface like a cork or a leaping porpoise into the light. Let me fly like a flying fish, a fish of light.

They hold me down, they cradle me down, they hush and they croon, SLEEP and you'll soon be well.

I fight to rise, I struggle as if I were a mile under heavy sour black earth and above the earth slabs of stone, I fight so hard and I shout, No, no, no, no, don't, I won't, I don't want, let me wake, I must wake *up*, but

Shhhhhh, hush, SLEEP and in slides the needle deep and down I go into the cold black dark depth where the sea floor is an earth of minute skeletons, detritus from eroding continents, fishes' scales and dead plants, new earth for growing. But not me, I don't grow, I don't sprout, I loll like a corpse or a drowned kitten, my head lolling as I float and black washes over me, dark and heavy.

He is sleeping well, doctor, yes, he is resting well, yes, he is very quiet, yes, he is no trouble at all.
But I must wake up.

But I am tied hands and feet, I am wrapped about and around with strands of seaweed from the Sargasso Sea, and I roll helpless on the ocean floor, down among the dead men, and my eyes are blacked out, sleep is heavier in me than the need is to wake and fight.

I must wake up.

Doctor he is very weak now. Yes he is restless between shots. Yes, he seems confused, bewildered, unable to feed himself, seems to want to go back to sleep, does not want to wake up, was angry when I said to him, We think you should wake up now.

Nurse how can I wake when you hush me, hush

me, hush me, Hushhhhhh, shhhhh, I'm down among the dead men, and sweet sleep has dreams that daylight never knew, better to sleep where the dreams may come and visit, sweet promising dreams, marvelling visitors from *there* who know and tell that behind (or before) and down (or up) is the door up and out into the sweet light of day.

Well now, and how are you feeling?

Feeling?

We'd like to know how you are?

Are?

You've had a good sleep and we think that now you are rested you ought to be able to remember who you are.

Who are you?

I'm Doctor Y.

I've never known anyone of that name.

Don't you remember me?

That's not what I have to remember.

No. Not if you don't want. But who are you?

Why, can't you see me?

I can see you very well indeed.

Then there you are.

Can you remember your name now perhaps?

My *name!* But I've had so many names.

You see, we have found out a little about you, but it would be better if you remembered it for yourself. Can you try?

I can.

Well then?

There's something I ought to be doing, I know that. Yes, I know *that*.

What?

Not this, not here. There.

There? Where? Can you remember at all?

Yes, remembering.

What?

No, who.

Yes, that's what I mean.

It was there, I know it was. We have to. We have to remember.

We?

It's the law of God.

Ah. I see. Well, well. Well, rest a bit now. You've not done badly for your first time really awake.

Oh but I've been much more awake than this. This isn't awake at all.

Oh good, good.

It's knowing, Harmony. God's law. That's what it is. Let me . . . let me . . . I must . . . *let me get up*.

Now now shhhhhh, don't get so excited, there's a good chap. Nurse, will you come here a minute? Good. I'll see you tomorrow then, Professor.

Tomorrow? *No*, that's too late. I must get up.

Sleep dear. That's it, sleep. There's a good boy.

He is Professor Charles Watkins, Classics, Cambridge. Married, two sons. Aged 50. A wallet found in the street in Parliament Square with family photograph, the rest of contents missing. Police matched photograph with the photograph taken by them at station the night he was picked up. Wife has been told her husband is here. Spoke to her on telephone. Suggested she should wait until he remembers who he is. Took this sensibly. But, find out why wife did not report him missing? I probed, but I caught something evasive here. Saw patient this morning. He is obviously rested, no longer talking to himself; in short, better. He did not respond to his name. Suggest trial of half a dozen E.C.T.

DOCTOR X.

In view of strong doubt whether treatment has in fact benefitted patient, suggest advisable postpone electric shocks for some days. Have written to Mrs. Watkins. Surely she ought to be told more than can have been possible in a telephone call.

DOCTOR Y.

Well, how are you today?

Is it today?

It is Monday the 15th September.

I should be doing something. I should be.

A lecture? A class? An address?

Yes yes yes. That's it. They told me. They said it would be. But I ought—I must get up.

You aren't very strong yet.

Am I ill then?

Not physically.

Then why am I not strong? Am I weak?

Professor Watkins, you lost your memory.

Who is Professor Watkins. Is that the name of the other one?

No, it's your name.

Mine? Oh no!

Yes it is.

What do I profess?

Greek. Latin. That field.

I profess *not*. Field? That's no word for it! I should be . . . I ought to be . . . tell me, were you there too?

Where, Professor?

At the lecture? At the briefing?

Ah, you were briefed then?

Yes, yes. I *do* remember.

Who was there?

I. And *He*, of course and . . . and—who? A lot of us, yes . . .

Go on.

The Emanence. Yes. The light. That's it, yes, of course. God the Father, Amen. Amen, Amen. And we were, yes, that's who we were and that's why I am here, but I lost my way in those fields.

You lost your memory, Professor, and you were found wandering on the edge of the river.

Oh my God, I hope it has cleansed itself by now, I do hope it is running clean again.

Wasn't it clean?

Full of corpses, you know.

Oh I'm sure it was not. The Thames may not be the cleanest of streams, but it doesn't collect many corpses.

The Thames? The Thames?

Yes, you were on the Embankment. The police found you.

I don't remember anything of that.

Well, I'll help you. You seemed as if you hadn't been in bed for a while—

Well, naturally not!

You had eaten, they thought, but you were very tired . . .

Eaten, oh my God yes, oh, oh, *no*—

And the moon is new. . . .

On the contrary, it was full.

Well, well.

The Thames you say. That's a tidal river. Not like that other. The river comes in and out, in and out, a tide, one and two and me makes three. Three. A tidal

river is like a breath, breathing, feeding the land
with fish and . . . Who? Who?

Professor, please. Do think about it. Don't start
rambling again. Please try and remember.

God I think. I gotta use words when I talk to
you, Eliot. I gotta use words. But if not God, what?

So you are God, too, are you?

You as well.

I don't aim so high, I assure you.

Stupid. You don't have a choice.

Well, well, Have a nice rest. I'll tell Doctor X
that I think you are getting on nicely. I'll see you
tomorrow. I'll be in charge of you for a few days.
Doctor X is going away for a holiday.

Doctor X?

He saw you yesterday. You said you saw him.

You can't *see* him. I told you. He's not there.

You can see me, can you?

Oh yes, very clear indeed.

But not Doctor X?

No, he's solid all through. He's all animal without light. No light. No God. No sun.

I wouldn't say that, you know.

Do you know? Can you see? From there, where
light is? From there Doctor X would not be at all.
Only those with light can be seen from the country
of light. You would be seen there, yes. Your light
burns, it is a small steady light.

What light?

Star light.

Well, thanks. But I do think you are being hard on poor Doctor X. He tries to help you. According to his lights.

There you are, that's what I said. It doesn't matter what he says or does. He's not in existence. I can't see him if I don't try to very hard.

Ah well, see you tomorrow then.

> *Patient has religious delusions. Para-*
> *noic. Disassociated. I think he is*
> *more coherent however. Have not*
> *yet heard from Mrs. Watkins.*
>
> DOCTOR Y.

DEAR DOCTOR Y.,

Thank you for so very kindly writing and explaining to me about my husband. I was rather upset after Doctor X's telephone call because I am rather ignorant about mental health and he didn't tell me very much. But I do understand that if my husband lost his memory there isn't much to tell. I don't know any particular reason why my husband should be "under stress" as you put it. Not any more than usual. But I wouldn't necessarily be the one to know. I don't pry into my husband's affairs. So I wouldn't know if something has upset him very much or anything like that. The reason why I didn't tell the police when I didn't hear from him is that he sometimes does things on his own and he would resent it if I interfered. I think it would be better if you asked Jeremy Thorne of 122 Rose Road, Little Minchener, nr. Cambridge, as he knows much more about my husband's plans than I do. I don't think Mr. Thorne will be back yet, as he has been in Italy for a summer holiday. But they will be back soon.

Yours sincerely,

FELICITY WATKINS

P.S. You asked about my husband and the children. When he is here it is a very happy family. You asked about letters that might have upset my husband. There are letters that came just before he went off to London but unless it is necessary I would rather not read them. I will send them to you if you think they would help.

Well Professor, you are looking very much better. How do you feel?

Why don't you let me go back to sleep. You keep waking me up.

Yesterday you were angry with us for making you sleep.

Was I?

Yes, you called us every kind of name and said we were trying to keep you fuddled.

Fuddled. Fuddddlled. Fudddled. Fudd . . . that word sounds like what it says. That's strange. Words . . . sounds. A dull heavy word. Fudd. Thud. Thud thud, thud thud, thud thud. Fudd, fudd, fudd, fudd. Its colour is. What? I knew. But not now. Sound— that's important . . . yes . . .

I think you are much better. Your colour is clear, you are obviously much stronger and your eyes are clear.

The azure-eyed. The flashing-eyed. Oh *no*, I must sleep again, where *They* are. Awake is asleep.

No, Professor. Sit up. I'm afraid we can't have you going back to sleep again. You've slept enough.

Why do you keep calling me Professor?

Professor Charles Watkins. 15 Acacia Road, Brink. Near Cambridge.

But I don't want that. I won't accept that.

I'm afraid you have no choice Professor. We know that's who you are.

But I know I am not.

Or is it that you are beginning to remember though you don't want to admit it?

Why do you say *Or?* *And* is more like it. It's funny, I've just noticed. People say, Either, Or, this or that, because of the thud thud, fudd fudd, in or out, black and white, yes and no, one and two, the either-or comes from that, the beat, the fudd fudd in the blood, but it isn't either or at all, it's and, and, and, and, and, and.

However that may be Professor, you must accept who you are. I am telling you the truth. Accept that—and try to go on from there.

But if I went on, that would mean I had begun. All that means nothing to me. It isn't mine at all. It is a dream.

My dear Professor, it is your life.

A dream of life. A life that is a dream. A dream ...

No, I am afraid I am not letting you go back to sleep yet.

Oh I must sleep. I *do* want to. Not here. There. What I said before isn't what I would have said if I

knew what I know now, I can sleep my life away.
Yes. We sleep our lives away. Yes. And you.

Professor Watkins, do you realise you have been
here a month now? In this hospital? It is the Central
Intake Hospital. You were in a state of shock when
you came in. You had been wandering about, and
the police found you on the Embankment. You were
rambling and confused and talking to yourself. We
sedated you. Then when you seemed much better,
we tried out a drug to help you remember who you
are—it often makes prople drowsy, but in your case
it made you very sleepy indeed. Whether or not that
is a good thing, is a matter of opinion. But the fact
is, and I am telling you again so that you don't forget
it, is that you have been in the hospital for a month.
We have just found out your name, your profession,
your address and your circumstances. We know a
little more, if you want to hear it. . . . Well? Come
on, do try.

What you say is only what you know. You tell
me it is so. But if I tell you what I know, you
disagree.

Then tell me what you know. Now then, why
are you laughing? Do you realise you haven't
laughed before? This is the first time I have seen
you laugh.

Doctor, I can't talk to you. Do you understand
that? All these words you say, they fall into a gulf,
they're not me or you. Not you at all. I can see you.
You are a small light. But a good one. God is in you
doctor. You aren't these words.

Well, well. Rest then. Lie down and rest. But
before you go off to sleep try and remember: You
are Charles Watkins. You have been living and
working in Cambridge for years now. You teach the

Classics. You give lectures. And you don't live alone—not by any means. I'll see you tomorrow.

_____

And how are you today? Oh—steady now, you've been dreaming, have you?

I am dreaming now.

No, you are awake now. You are talking to me, Doctor Y.

This is no different. A dream, like that.

Oh yes it is different. This is reality. The other is a dream.

How do you know?

You'll have to take my word for it, I'm afraid.

If I did have to, I'd be afraid. I can't take words for anything. Words come out of your mouth and fall on the floor. Words in exchange for? Is that it? Your dreams or your life. But it is not *or*, that is the point. It is an *and*. Everything is. Your dreams *and* your life. You can talk there, talk. I dream whatever I do, lying or waking.

Well, well, Professor. I'll see you tomorrow. Perhaps we may have to try a new treatment.

> *This patient is no better than when I left last week. I do not see what alternate we have to E.C.T.*
>
> DOCTOR X.

> *I suggest confronting him with his wife, or if we can locate some, friends.*
>
> DOCTOR Y.

*If no change in the next two or
three days, we must transfer him to
Higginhill. Would remind you this
is for Intake.*

DOCTOR X.

*It is not unusual to extend the rou-
tine six weeks, for another three
weeks. I suggest we do so.*

DOCTOR Y.

*Only if we can agree on E.C.T.
Which would be a reason for extension.*

DOCTOR X.

*I am not against E.C.T. But as an
interim proposal: withdraw all
drugs, including sleepers, and see
what happens.*

DOCTOR Y.

Very well.

DOCTOR X.

How are you today Professor?

As you see.

You are looking much brighter.

I haven't been given any drugs for twenty-four
hours.

We thought it might help you to remember.

Nurse told me I have been drugged ever since I
came in.

I told you, we sedated you in various ways.
Then we tried a treatment which you reacted to in a

very personal way—you slept almost continually, so we stopped the treatment before we normally would have done with that particular drug.

I am thinking more clearly. Doctor Y?

Professor!

I have to ask you a serious question.

Please do.

Your attitude to me is this. I've got to make him remember what I know to be true about him.

Yes it is. Of course.

But that means that you don't take *me* seriously. You haven't once taken me seriously.

In reply to that I can only say that you have had more of my personal time and care than any patient I've had in months.

No, I don't mean that. I say to you, I'm not what you say I am. I *know* that. I'm not Professor Charles What's-his-name. Or if I am nominally that, it isn't the point. But you just go on and on and on, sticking to that one point.

Go on, explain. I am listening.

I might be anything else. I could be. . . .

What? God perhaps?

Who said that?

You did.

I might have died in the war.

Oh, you were in the war then.

So was everyone.

Some more than others.

We were all there.

What were you doing in the war?

If you know what it is I profess, don't you know who it was I fought?

No, your wife didn't mention it. I must ask her.

I have a wife?

Yes. Her name is Felicity . . . is that funny?

Ha, ha, ha, I have absented myself from Felicity. Ha, ha, ha.

I'm a married man, myself.

Felicity.

And you have two boys.

If I am a professor I can have a wife, but my knowledge is, I am just as well a sailor with a wife in the West Indies. *Her* name is Nancy.

Ah, so you are a sailor again, are you? Were you a sailor in the war?

No, I was an onlooker and then the Crystal came. *They* fought. They ate each other.

Ah. Now I want you to help me with this. If you aren't Charles Watkins, who are you?

I think I am my friends. And they are—in the name of the Crystal. Yes. A unit. Unity.

Your name is Crystal?

That's crystal clear. Ha, ha, ha, ha.

You're very jolly this morning.

Words are so *funny*. Felicitously funny.

I see. Well, I'll drop in for a chat tomorrow. We aren't going to give you any more sedatives or drugs. Not for a time anyway. You'll probably find it harder to sleep. But try and stick it out. And perhaps you could try and see if you remember anything about your family. Two sons. Two boys.

My son is dead.

I can assure you that none of them are dead. Very much alive. I've seen their photograph. Would you like to see? I'll bring it tomorrow.

DEAR DOCTOR Y,
Thank you for your letter.
I have decided to send you two letters I found in the jacket my husband was wearing just before he lost his memory. I don't know if they will be of any help. One is by him, but he didn't post it for some reason. I don't think my husband ever had a breakdown. But I don't really know what a breakdown is. I think he is the opposite of the kind of person who has a breakdown. He has always been very energetic and gets a lot of things done. He always sleeps much less than most people. When we were first married I used to worry but I got used to it. He sometimes sleeps four or five hours a night for weeks at a time, sometimes only two or three. But that is in summer. In winter he sleeps a bit more. He says it is because animals need to hibernate. I don't think he has been working harder than usual this year. He always works hard. It is his nature. He was rather bad-tempered and crotchetty earlier this year but at the beginning of summer he always gets difficult, but it is because it is examination time. He was stammering quite badly in the spring, a

new thing for him, but our family doctor gave
him some sedatives and the stammering
stopped, but it was bad enough for a time to
make him cancel some lectures he was going to
give.

Yours sincerely,
FELICITY WATKINS

DEAR PROFESSOR WATKINS,
　　It has been agreed that I should write to you.
You won't know me—or rather, you won't know
my name. Yet, we did meet briefly after your
lecture. I hope you will remember because it
was what you said that started it off. Was a
catalyst, touched a spring, something like that.
What? Well, nothing common or obvious and
that is my trouble in writing to you. It is all
intangibles. If you don't remember, then it will
still be true that your saying what you did that
night began a remarkable process in me and
this coincided with a similar process in a close
friend of mine—and as we are beginning to see,
in more than one of the people closest to us. Yet
it is hard indeed to define it. For me, it was
definitely listening to you talk. We have wondered if it is possible for you not to remember?
Can a yeast not know it is a yeast? I suppose so.
Or perhaps it is not like that at all—it might be
that a man talking on a platform in a particularly inspired frame of mind may match up to, or
coincide with someone listening, and who has
gone to listen with no particular expectation, in
ways we know very little about. But in writing
to you, this act of sitting down to put words
together, in the hope that the words will be as
strong as those used by you that night, it is like
the spreading of a yeast or some sort of chemical that has started working in one place, and

then moved out, feeding and inciting, then curved back again to where it began. This letter is like a snake swallowing its tail. By now you will see that it does not matter that you do not know me, because I am not important individually. Nor of course are you. I am writing because I have more time than my friends. I am retired. My children are grown up and I am a widow. Perhaps it had to be me because of my having been there that evening and coming back as if I'd been slapped out of a daydream. We have been wondering too, about the others who were there that night. Did some of them go away feeling as if they had been infused with a new sort of intelligence? Or was I the only one. You probably don't know. But I find it hard to believe. I have heard very many lectures in my time—alas. And even given them. It is not a new thought for me that the quality of a lecture or lecturer need not have much to do with the actual words used. No, I do not mean that I admire the demagogue and the inspirational speaker, not at all. But there is another quality. It is one you had that night. It is possible to imagine what you said that night being heard quite dully. The words were interesting, yes. But that is not the point. The essence of what happened in the room that night, and of what I've been learning since is that words spoken casually in the next room, familiar music heard with a particularly close attention, a passage in a book one would normally class as commonplace—even the sound of rain on branches, or lightning cracking across a night sky, sounds and sights as ordinary as an every day may hold that very quality I now understand to be that most valuable to me. And to others.

And if you do not know what it is I am

talking about—then we must accept as true that the unbelievable suggestion that not only bird, lightning, music, rain, the words of a nursery rhyme

How many miles to Babylon?
Four score miles and ten.

Can we get there by candlelight?
Yes, and back again!

but a man talking in a rather ugly lecture room can be charged with this quality and not be aware of it. As a bird can sing all summer and never know that the sounds it makes will remain for a lifetime in the ears of a child in stained streets as the crystallisation of a promise of a recurring spring.

If you do not know what I am saying, do not recognise anything, then . . .

It was early this year, at the beginning of spring. I was spending the weekend with friends near Cambridge, ex-pupils of mine. They have small children. They were very excited, because full of plans for a new kind of school—no, not to supplant ordinary education, what the State provides, but to supplement it. Some kind of a weekend school with emphasis on unorthodox individual teaching. As I write I am conscious of a feeling of staleness and boredom—yet now as then I am attracted to such ideas. It is that I have been attracted by them so often!

You were to address a couple of dozen parents, because you had been involved for some time in similar schemes. The idea of sitting through an evening in a lecture room nearly kept me at home, yet I believe that such individual efforts to educate, enliven, and provoke are vital—that any country goes as sleepy as a pear, without such efforts. More, that any democracy depends on them. I went, and found myself as I expected, in a rectangular space, coated over with plaster painted grey that was still damp—it was a new hall. It was inadequately heated. There was a wooden platform at one end on which stood the speaker—you. Rows of individuals sat to attention in front of you. The chairs were hard uprights. This is the uninspiring setting that we allow ourselves for the working-out and discussion of the dreams we dream for a better world! The village hall. The local hall. The church hall. We take it for granted of course. A man or woman stands on a low platform with a table by him that has a glass of water on it and perhaps a microphone and in front of him a collection of people who sit facing him, looking up to listen to what he, or she is saying. Out of this process come better schools, hospitals, a new society. We may take it for granted but what could it look like from outside? Very odd, I am sure. Anyway, you were the one that night, a middle-aged man, used to standing on platforms, accomplished and easy in manner, so as not to upset or offend your audience. This is not a criticism, though perhaps it sounds like it. I remember sitting there as you began speaking and thinking you had a perfect platform manner the way doctors have bedside manners.

I was restless and irritable—extraordinarily and unreasonably so, about the whole thing. And I was angry with myself for being like this. I liked what was being said. I liked the fact that all these young parents were proposing to put themselves out in time and expense to educate their children in ways the ordinary school

system could not or would not do. I approved of
you, the speaker, insofar as it was possible to
see what you were like, behind the professional-
ism of your delivery. Yet I was seething with
rebelliousness, with emotion—why *should* one always have to sit on hard chairs in a character-
less hall to hear ideas discussed, why, when one
wants to be a citizen and act with others, does it
always have to be like this—and why should
there always be this phenomenon, people weary
and angry with what is provided by society,
why did we take that for granted—that it was
so *always*, always had been so, must be so. Why
is what happens, what is provided, always so
dull and flat and negligible compared with
what any ordinary person in the street can
imagine as possible and desirable—let alone
these young professional parents, all rather
highly educated, in the hall. Twenty years ago I
had been part of such a group of young parents, on behalf of my own children. Recently
again, on behalf of friends' children. But what
we had dreamed of, and then discussed, and
then planned, and then tried to put into action,
had not taken the shape we had originally
dreamed of. Not anywhere near it . . . There
had been results, but nothing that even approached what we *knew* was possible. Why?
What went wrong? What always went wrong?

I was sitting very still between my host and
hostess, sizzling with exasperation and rebellion
and impatience, emotions all quite unsuitable for
a retired head-mistress, when you said what
struck me so deeply. I remember exactly what
you said, because I was in a state of concentrated attention on what you are saying, in spite of
my physical restlessness.

"Everybody in this room believes, without

knowing it, or perhaps without having formulated it, or at least behaves as if he believes— that children up to the age of seven or eight are of a different species from ourselves. We see children as creatures about to be trapped and corrupted by what trapped and corrupted ourselves. We speak of them, treat them, as if it were possible to make happen events which are almost unimaginable. We speak of them as beings who could grow up into a race altogether superior to ourselves. And this feeling is in everyone. It is why the field of education is always so bitter and embattled, and why no one ever, in any country, is satisfied with what is offered to children—except in dictatorships where the future of children is scaled to the needs of the State. Yet we have become used to this and don't realise how extraordinary it is, and what the fact of it is saying. For it should be enough to teach the young of a species to survive, to approximate the skills of its elders, to acquire current technical skills. Yet every generation seems to give out a bellow of anguish at some point, as if it had been betrayed, sold out, sold short. Every generation dreams of something better for its young, every generation greets the emergence of its young into adulthood with a profound and secret disappointment, even if these children are in every way paragons from society's point of view. This is due to the strong but unacknowledged belief that something better than oneself is possible. It is as if the young creatures of humanity grow towards adulthood in a kind of obstacle race, beset by hazards, with the adults trying futilely but gallantly to provide something better. Once adulthood is reached the newly grown ones join with the older ones, their parents, as they turn about and look back into their own infancy. They watch the infancy of their own children with the same futile anguish. Can we prevent these children from being trapped, and spoiled *as we have been*, what can we do . . . ? Who has not at least once looked into a young child's eyes and seen the criticism there, a hostility, the sullen knowledgeable look of a prisoner? This happens very young, before the young child is forced to become like the parents, before its own individuality is covered over by what the parents say he is. Their 'this is right, that is wrong, see things my way.' This meeting tonight, of young parents joining together to try and provide something better, a better 'education,' was nothing more nor less than this phenomenon that repeats itself in every generation. Every person sitting there on hard chairs in front of you felt as if his or her potential had been left unfulfilled. Something had gone wrong. Some painful and wrong process had been completed and had left them, and even after an expensive schooling—most of those present were middle-class people—defective, unfulfilled, if not warped. And so we were doing only what every generation had done; we were looking at our children, as if they had in them to be—that is, if we could think of the right 'education' to give them—beings quite different from ourselves. They could be better, braver, gayer. Oh, and more, much more—we thought of them almost as if they were the young of another species, a free, fearless species, full of potentiality, full of that quality which everyone recognises, yet is never defined, the quality which all adults lose, and know that they lose."

These were the things you said—and more.

It is odd that I can hardly remember what

you looked like as you spoke. I know I was awake enough—but even so I didn't have enough energy to take in what you said, and to calm my own restlessness, and to watch you closely. Yet it was a night when I was prickling with energy, vitality, interest—just because I was angry (if that is the right word) at being there *again*. What you said explained the feeling of sameness, the *againness*. Yet the words you used, the energy you put into them, what you were feeling about it all—and it was what we felt too, for the young parents were stirring and awake and while they leaned forward on their chairs to look and listen, kept glancing at each other, even at people they hardly knew, to nod and smile as if to say: Yes, yes, that's it, it is desperately true and we must not fail, we have to succeed this time . . . all this; the emotion or recognition in the hall was suddenly making us all alive. The sameness was gone. Our day-by-day selves were held at bay for a moment even while you said: Education means only this— that the lively alert fearless curiosity of children must be fed, must be kept alive. That *is* education. And, listening, we were lively and alert and fearless. Every one of us was soaked for that time with those qualities. Still stimulated, my friends and I drove back to their house. As we entered the living room, still warm and smoky from the early evening before we had left for the lecture, we began yawning. The stimulation was already gone. One of the children cried out in his sleep, and the father went up, while the mother said that she should take the child to a doctor, he was sleeping badly, was restless and had bad dreams. I understood that there was no connection at all between what was happening now—father going to soothe child, mother talking about doctor and medicines, and what these same parents had been feeling and aiming for even half an hour before, or even a few minutes before, in the car. It was all over. The time of being awake, of being receptive, of *being energetic*—had consumed itself. We don't have much energy. Your words—or rather, what you had put into the words—had fed us, woken us, made us recognise parts of ourselves normally well hidden and covered over—and that was that. The evening ended as it had begun, some adults in the livingroom, talking, drinking, smoking, discussing the projected weekend school for children, but as if it were just another of their far-too-many chores and burdens.

But I was awake. I was as if stung awake. I did not sleep. And I sat by the window that night and I thought: Don't let it go, don't forget it. Something extraordinary did happen. Perhaps during that night while I sat looking into a suburban garden, I was like a child of three, four, five, a creature quite different from the person she was doomed to grow into. I was certainly remembering what I had been as a small child. I remembered things I had forgotten for years. Before those "prison shades" had come down. Before the trap had shut.

And when I returned home to my flat in London it stayed with me. What stayed? Not the words that you used. It was the feeling of the quality of what you said. It went with recognition, as if I had been reminded of something I knew very well. I was possessed with a low simmering fear that I would forget again, let go—what I had been as a child. It was the same feeling one has after waking from a strong dream which one knows has importance for oneself, or for a friend. You wake fighting to keep the dream, its flavour, its texture. Yet within a few minutes of waking, that country of dream has gone, its taste and reality has drained away into ordinary life. All you have left is an intellectual conviction held in a set of words. You want to remember. You try to remember. You have a set of words to offer your friend, or repeat to yourself. But the reality has gone, evaporated.

But I *was* remembering. It was as if, in any moment of the day that I chose to revive it, there was a bridge across from that heightened moment when you were saying things about the children, about all of us, and the pulse of the time I was in. I began consciously looking about me for that quality in other moments of life. Like testing one metal with another, ringing one substance on another apparently dissimilar. I had been stung awake by that night, and now I was restless and searching, and I was in a fever in case this restlessness might drain away like the afterglow of a useful dream and leave me tranquilly dead again.

Then, after weeks, something else happened. I'll write it, but I can't do more than put the words down. But it was another flash of recognition, of joy, of "yes, that's it," and again, this quality of matching, of ringing together, of substances being in tune, was here in this incident, exactly as it had been in those five or ten or thirty minutes when you were speaking of keeping aliveness and awakeness in children and at the same time you were feeding a whole room full of people with liveliness and wakefulness. If only for a few minutes.

I had been, as I've said, half unconsciously, looking, watching, trying to find that "quality" again. The quality to which I'd given the tag, "the wave-length." For it was like suddenly touching a high tension wire. Of being, briefly, on a different, high, vibrating current, of the familiar becoming transparent. Well, and when it happened, I did not immediately recognise it, for perhaps I had already made too much of a fetish of what you had made of that moment in the lecture room—I wanted the same thing to happen. When it did happen, it was ordinary, just as it had been with you, talking about education in a routine lecture. And of course, I did not expect it just there, was halfway through the moment before I recognised it, and might even, if I had not been suddenly stung into attention, have missed it altogether.

And again, I suppose it won't seem much when I write it. Sometimes when you read a book or story, the words are dead, you struggle to end it or put it down, your attention is distracted. Another time, with exactly the same book or story, it is full of meaning, every sentence or phrase or even word seems to vibrate with messages and ideas, reading is like being pumped full of adrenalin.

Ordinary everyday experiences can be like that.

I was walking down the street outside London University. It was a late afternoon. May I think it was; at any rate, it was not yet summer. It had been raining. Things were glistening in the street lights. Do you find too that about the time the sun goes down the world gets brighter, and more intense. And sometimes very sad. Particularly when it has been raining. Well, I'll get on—I know that atmospheres or sights that move one person leave another cold. I had been walking briskly to keep warm; it was a typical English spring day, as cold as winter! Outside the University entrance, which I pass often enough, since I live near there, I slowed and began glancing in at the great porticoes and pillars, the formal pompousness of the place, and I was thinking that such impersonality, formality, is how one can most easily identify a place of learning—school, university, college, and that this atmosphere in itself must set a condition of thinking for a young person being educated in it. I saw a man come down those steps, but this was a time for people to be going home, and there was a steady stream of them coming across to the gates. I was looking at them idly and thinking how tinily unimportant these human beings looked beside the great cold buildings that were supposed to be their servants, and that no young thing learning there could ever believe that human beings are more important than their institutions. Words, teachers, textbooks could say one thing: the building itself shouted the opposite.

I was watching this man for some reason, and thinking that as I stood still I was getting cold. This was my strongest thought—that I was cold. At the same time I thought that I knew this man. All at once there welled up in me a strong feeling of knowledge of him—no, not just friendship, and remember that I am sixty years old, and not a romantic girl. I can't say more than this: I can't remember a time when I've felt so powerful a kinship with someone, as if I really knew something through and through, and was linked deeply with him. As this feeling faded, leaving me rather astonished and even amused at it, I realised that of course I knew him: it was Frederick Larson. Perhaps you know the name? No, he is not a well-known

person, but I do not think it is really a foolish
question. For one thing, how often does one say
to a friend or acquaintance about another, Do
you know so and so, and he does—improbably.
But in this case there is more. It turns out that as
we—I'll explain the "we" in a moment, meet
each other, and attract others, in fact we are
already in the same orbit, if I can put it like
that. We know each other, or have friends in
common. The actual meeting is only a confirma-
tion of an existing link. Anyway—Frederick
knows your name, and your work, and he says
that in fact he met you once, but there were
people there—another lecture, it is doubtful you
will remember, if you ever heard, his name.

When he came up to the gate and saw me
standing there he said smiling: "And now tell
me about yourself."

I'll explain. It is an old joke. It was twenty-
five years ago that I first heard of him through
my sister Marjorie. She was with her first husband in Greece. He was an archeologist. He got
some form of blood disease, and was a long time
ill before he died. During this time, Frederick
Larson, who was an old friend of his, befriend-
ed him and Marjorie. He was an archeologist, too.
He got long leave to be with his friend, my
sister's husband, while he died. My sister was
lonely and miserable and wrote long letters to
me, two or three times a week. She told me all
about this marvellous friend of her dying husband's, of this friend's kindness and patience
and lovingkindness, and so on. She told me all
about him, his early life, his struggles, his education—everything. In short, I knew everything
about him and he knew everything about me,
because there seemed no particular reason why
we should ever meet. We were to each other

more like characters in a long-running serial story, but the story is being written as one reads. We knew the most intimate things about each other. It was not the first time—nor the last—that I had had this relationship with people I haven't met. But now of course I wonder if this extraordinary intimacy at second hand means that one day we are bound to meet. Well, one day at a party I was next to an American I had never met, and yet who seemed familiar. I had not caught his name when introduced. And he felt the same about me. We started telling each other things we knew about each other, as a joke, withholding our names. We knew each other extremely well— we knew more about each other than many who meet every day of their lives. Well, at last we came out with our names, and all was explained. The beginning of a beautiful friendship? Not then, at any rate. He was just off to a dig in Turkey, I was to take one of my children for a holiday, our lives were in very different grooves. We joked that there was no point in our being friends, because we already knew everything there was to know, and there could be no surprises. After that we kept running into each other, in the street, at friends' houses. Of course, he was often abroad, and when my children were half grown, we would take them travelling. Before we left on a trip I would jokingly make a bet with my husband that we would run into Frederick somewhere. We did, more than once. When we met, one or other would say: "And now tell me about yourself." More often than not, we already knew—mutual friends had kept the serial story running.

This time, when he reached where I stood, he turned and looked in at the court—but it is too big to be called a court—where tiny people hurried away from the great building. He must have seen what I was seeing, because he said: "There are buildings as large as that one which have flights of steps to them in scale with their size."

I didn't understand.

"There's a building in Peru for instance. It has stairways which could not be used by our size of human being. Imagine that building there with steps up to it in scale—steps the height of a man. The reason why that building dwarfs us so, is because of the proportions of the steps and the building itself. It is in the proportions."

"But it would be a building for giants," I said.

He quoted, laughing: "But there were giants in those days."

I was getting very cold by now, and I was late for a visit I was making. As I thought this, he said, "Well, I expect we'll run into each other again."

I had already said good-bye and turned away when I had to return. It was like a panic, a warning, a sense of possibilities being lost, of vanishing opportunities. Into my mind had come the memory of your talking on that dreary platform. Frederick had also turned back after having walked away a few steps.

He said: "I spent last summer working on a site in Turkey. About half an acre of a city has been exposed. It must have been some miles across. It looks as if under the top level are many other levels. Human beings have lived on that site for many thousands of years. Probably the climate has changed in that time, changing everything, vegetation, animals, people. Based on a summer's work and that exposed half acre we know everything about that civilisation—its beliefs, its rituals, its habits, its agriculture. Learned papers are being written by the dozen. I've writen three myself. Yesterday I did not feel very well and I stayed at home and watched television between the hours of four and seven. Based on that experience I am prepared to conclude the following about civilisation in Britain in 1969. First of all, the most outstanding characteristic of an extraordinary civilisation: all events are equally important, whether war, a game, the weather, the craft of plant-growing, a fashion show, a police hunt.

"Another, to us incredible trait, is their ability to accommodate such a wide variety of incompatible beliefs. They are a highly developed technical society, but they also believe in witches, fairies, supermen, magic of all kinds, and they take pains to inculcate these beliefs in their children side by side with scientific techniques.

"At the same time they have a deity, superior to the subsidiary gods, but this deity is more backward than they, and less powerful—for the second-rate gods, like Superman, in fact use modern techniques like levitation and space travel. The superior deity is placated or invoked by being sung to, or at, in front of priests who wear highly decorated garments, as part of an elaborate ceremonial that takes place in elaborately decorated but backward and archaic buildings. These priests, probably as part of magical ritual, use sound in all kinds of ways, chanting, intoning, droning, and so on.

"Their use of sound is altogether challenging and enigmatic. While they communicate with each other entirely verbally, usually by means of lectures—a man or woman talking at length on some isolated subject—they have little belief in the effectiveness of words by themselves, because these talks, or lectures, are introduced by, accompanied by, interrupted by, concluded by, a variety of sounds, usually musical. It is my belief that their use of music in this way, if we could understand it, would be the key to that civilisation. It is probably to do with indoctrination or brain-printing. To my mind there is no explanation for the entirely arbitrary, casual, fragmentary nature of this heightening or accompanying music except that it must be part of the technique used by a hidden priestly or technically superior caste to control the plebs. If this is the correct explanation, then this culture is remarkably advanced in some ways, even if so backward in others. Have I mentioned that they are a deeply animistic culture, believing that animals and plants have human and sometimes magical characteristics? . . . Yes," he said, "I can assure you that this is quite analogous to our methods in Turkey or in Africa or anywhere else. Now, if I had watched the television between eight o'clock and twelve, my conclusions would have been quite different, but of course, equally emphatic . . ."

We went to a pub nearby, where I telephoned the person who was expecting me, to apologise for not coming. I could not leave Frederick then. He was, in fact, in a very disturbed state. It turned out that during the last few weeks we had had the same experience. In his case he could not remember a definite beginning to it all. He could not say: It all started because one evening I sat in a cold lecture hall listening to an enthusiast about education. No, but one day he realised that he was in a different state or mood. But he couldn't define that mood. His work which he loves and usually puts before everything—even before his wife and family, as he readily admits—this work had become a routine, something to be done. He thought he might be ill. He even went to the doctor and was given a tonic. He found he was sleeping badly. He described it as the kind of sleep one has before a journey when you have to start very early, and you keep waking yourself up to make sure you don't over sleep. He was offered a chance to do some work on a site in the Sudan, and though he had been wanting to work in Africa again, he said no. Yet he knew this was foolish, and might be a decision he would later regret.

Finally he said to himself that he was slightly mad, and perhaps this was due to discovering he was indubitably middle-aged! But he stopped caring about the whys and wherefores. He said everything had become heightened and alive, and it was like being in love, that condition when for hours, days, weeks, everything is soaked with the personality of the other person. Yet he was not in love.

And there was no other person. He said it was as if everything—person, place, tree, plant, building—was full of riches, promise, yet each turned away from him as he approached. "It was as if I approached a mirror and found it blank." I know this feeling well. Do you? I told him of my experiences on "the night of the children" (which is now my label or catchphrase for it). We stayed talking until the pub closed, and then went to my flat because we both had the same feeling—each to the other was a jar full of possibility, but a closed jar, sealed. But if we talked long enough, some revelation would emerge, some clue.

One trouble was that our lives have been so different, he always travelling, always finding new places and cities, and I have been a teach-

er and a housewife and mother seldom leaving
England. Yet we did have this thing in common, the having been struck by a condition like
extra wakefulness. Other people's responses seemed
slow. They seemed half asleep. Yet this condition
was also an affliction, for it was a strain and a
difficulty—a challenge it was hard to rise to.

I've written about that meeting with Frederick in detail, because it was like "the night of
the children." Now I'll abridge things, and try
and make some order.

Frederick and I met nearly every day—we
have now reached early summer, end of May,
beginning of June. As I said, I've retired, and he
had left himself at a loose end. He is an energetic man and dislikes idleness. He set himself up
for a couple of lectures about the site in Turkey. He has done a lot of lecturing. One evening
he came to see me, about ten at night, saying
that when he had stood up to start speaking, a
couple of hours before, it being the first lecture,
he started stammering so badly he could not go
on. He literally could not bring the words out.
Excuses were made, that he had been overworking and so on. Apologies, much embarrassment. He came to see me, astonished, shocked,
and not a little afraid. He had returned to his
belief that he might be ill. Yet although he had
not been able to bring out two consecutive sen-
tences—had not brought out one word without
stammering it—with me he did not stammer at
all. He was as usual. Suddenly he remembered
that it had happened to him before, about ten
years before. But the thing had been so unpleasant he had pushed it out of his mind. He
said: "It was such a bizarre thing, when I'm so
fluent and talkative that I could not associate it
with myself. It really did seem to be happening

to someone else." He had finished a year's work on a site on a Greek island. He was lecturing on the Iliad and the Odyssey, in connection with certain discoveries he and colleagues had made. He began stammering. He battled on, because it was not something that had ever happened to him, yet after a few minutes a fit of stammering so bad he could not go on attacked him, and he had to end the lecture. It was as if, he said, his tongue had been numbed or frozen.

He went home and there finished aloud the lecture he had intended to give to the audience. He did this perfectly easily, in his normal fluent way. But he noted that as he talked, another stream of words paralleled the stream of words that he was actually using, and this parallel stream expressed opinions not precisely opposite to those he was using, like an echo or mirror image—which, said Frederick, would have made some sort of psychological sense—but opinions rather off at a tangent, and, he said, he could swear they were not opinions he had read, or heard spoken of. They were crazy, dotty, batty, cranky. But he could not prevent that silent stream going on, quite distinctly, while he came out with his ordered and sensible lecture. He said that he felt that if he relaxed a vigilance or censor for one moment, his tongue would begin voicing this other crazy stream, he would be as helpless as a ventriloquist's dummy.

Well—he cancelled the course of lectures, and went on a holiday with his family. He took sedatives prescribed by his doctor, and when the holiday was over he went off on another dig, and soon he had forgotten completely that he had stammered at all.

I am going into more detail about the stammering than I otherwise would, because on "the

night of the children" you said in passing that
you had had trouble with stammering.

Frederick cancelled his series of lectures on
Turkey. He went to a psychiatrist, who was not
able to unearth any private trouble, Frederick
insisting that he is happy in his work, his life,
his habits, his wife and his children—now
grown up. He then told the doctor about his
state of mind in the last few weeks, and discovered that he is suffering from the male meno-
pause and manic depression. This he found interesting in an academic way, but unhelpful. It
occurred to him that going to the doctor had
added another parallel track, "like a railway
line" to his life. Discussions with the doctor
about his condition went on alongside the condition, without affecting it in any way, or affecting what really interested him—which was,
and is, the discussions with me, and with one
or two other people. I'll simply say at this point
that shortly after my meeting with Frederick,
both of us made other encounters, of the same
quality. These meetings were separate, and for-
tuitous, yet Frederick's friend and mine knew
each other, and had, in fact, the sort of relationship I and Frederick had had for years—the
long-running serial story. If you come to meet
us, which I do hope this letter will have the
effect of achieving, then you will meet me,
Frederick, and two others, all of whom had
their lives changed in the last few months, yet
in ways which are very hard to describe, so
slight and imperceptible are these changes to
an outer view. Back to Frederick. After half a
dozen appointments with the psychiatrist, Frederick was still stammering whenever he approached any aspect of his professional work,

and was quite fluent and easy-tongued on any other subject.

The psychiatrist offered Frederick various treatments, all chemical, but Frederick left him and found himself a specialist in stammers, not a doctor, but someone outside the medical profession. This man uses a method which cures stammerers by making them speak very slowly, sounding every letter, with measured pauses between the words. The sounds that come out are emotionless, without the usual flow and movement of speech. It is a machine speech. But the method does cure some people. Frederick did go to half a dozen classes, and then it occurred to him that the method was a way of putting a lock on one's spontaneity, creativity. The method *was* a censorship. Watching every syllable as it comes to one's tongue means more than focussing a total attention on one's speech—it means putting the censor further back, into one's mind. Sorting out, or choosing, words when they have already arrived at one's tongue's end, that is too late. No, the choice must have been made earlier, in the mind. Frederick found that he was getting very good at it. In class he was sounding like someone who had just learned English and had to work over every sentence before using it. Or like someone living in a dictatorship, who has to keep a guarded tongue. But when he broke into uncontrollable stammering, it was as bad as ever, though less frequent. He left the classes, and decided not to return to the psychiatrist. He had understood that—there must be something that he should be understanding.

Together we went over and over the period immediately preceding the first stammering fit of over ten years ago. It was the work in

Greece, which resulted in a book called, I believe, *New Light on Homer*—or something like that. But it turned out that was not the beginning. Before Greece, he had been travelling in Africa. He had visited a tribe whose life is based on the movements of a river. The river floods every year, and a large plain disappears under water. In the plain are mounds where villages are built. When the flood rises to a certain height, the people of the villages get on to boats and go to live on the shores, until the waters subside again. Now—and this is the point—Frederick had this thought: Suppose the flood rose twenty feet higher than usual one year and inundated the villages, and the people then decided not to return to the villages, but to live somewhere else, then in a very short time indeed, probably no more than two or three years, it would be impossible to know that human beings had lived there. The huts were of wood and earth. The roofs of thatch. Most of the vessels were of wood. The earthenware was not fired, but sun-dried and made to be used and thrown away easily. The tribe had been peaceable for some time—the weapons, spears, were of iron and ritualistic. Water and ants could destroy all these things in months. The only objects in these villages that would survive were modern tinware and plastic things. But this society could have existed a thousand times over, on these mounds, with floods between, and nothing, but nothing would have remained.

Yes, Frederick said, if you judge a society by harmony, responsibility towards its members, and lack of aggression towards neighbours it was a society on a high level indeed. And—and this was the place where Frederick was hit—it was a society more integrated with Nature than any he could remember, and for Africa that is saying a great deal. Not only did this tribe's life centre on the flooding and subsidence of the river, but it was very highly ritualised around the seasons, the winds, the sun, the moon, the earth. But in conventional anthropology it is tantamount to saying that a society is barbaric, backward, to say that it is animistic, or bound with nature.

Frederick left this place deeply perturbed. Visiting this tribe, and the thoughts he had had as a result, struck at his confidence as an archeologist—that was how he experienced it. That he had the equivalent of a religious person's "doubts," and it was necessary to dismiss them before going on. The chief thought was that our society was dominated by things, artefacts, possessions, machines, objects, and that we judged previous societies by artefacts—things. There was no way of knowing an ancient society's ideas except through the barrier of our own.

This experience's effect on him he decided was "unhealthy" and "morbid."

I am sure you will have gathered by now that Frederick is and always was a man of great vitality, assurance, and has never been one to be afraid to voice opinions, take sides—assert himself.

If he had been less self-confident, probably the effect of that visit in Africa would have been much less.

However, he overcame his temporary loss of spirits, and started his lectures on Greece, which he had to abandon because of his first attack of stammering.

To come to the period just before he and I met outside the gates of the London University. There was a small, apparently minor incident

. . . he was visiting an old colleague, who was engaged in an excavation in Wiltshire. He had stayed the night in a local inn, and had walked over next morning to visit his old friend. It was mid-morning and the work was in full swing. The professor himself, half a dozen amateurs there for the love of it, and two archeological students. A trench loosely filled with rubble had been exposed. The professor was unaware that Frederick was there. He was saying that the type of trench indicated that the foundations were for a stone building—the stones that had been keyed in to the stony rubble having been taken away for other later building. At which one of the students timidly piped up that he had recently been in Africa and had observed that in a village he was visiting, the people were making a hut of poles, mud plaster and thatch. The first stage of this was to dig a trench, the second being to stand the poles of the future walls in the trench, the third being to pack stony rubble around the poles. The professor did not comment on this. He walked away and Frederick followed him and announced himself. The professor took Frederick around the site and when he came to the trench filled with the rubble he said: "In my opinion this is the foundation of a wood and not a stone building, after all, certain primitive people did start wood huts by . . ." and etc. and so on. But if there had been no student back from a jaunt to Africa, the professorial voice would have announced with total authority that this building must have been of stone. And this was how the emphatic pronouncements of archeology are arrived at. It was this minor incident that made Frederick remember certain disquiets he had suffered last summer in Turkey. If "disquiet" is the right word for it.

All through the summer in Turkey he was thinking of his visit to the river-dominated society in Africa more than ten years before. He could not shake off the memory of it, although the two places had so little in common, one being under water for months of the year, the other being so high, dry and exposed. He could not shake off thoughts about the bases of modern archeology, which usually he just accepts as not more than nuisances no one can do anything about. Particularly about finance—that the financing of an excavation was always the key to it, and particularly whether it took place at all. Certain people got money easier than others. Some people couldn't get money at all, or only with great difficulty. Some countries were easy money-extractors, others not. Countries had runs of popularity, were in vogue for a while, then went "out," like styles in dress. He, Frederick, had been working on that particular site and not one he wanted to work on, because he had been able to get money for that site from an American source—a museum short of a certain kind of artefact which was known to be freely available on that site.

Certain ideas were accepted, sometimes for decades or centuries, dominating archeology; suddenly they were doubted. That "Greece was the mother of Western civilization and Rome its daddy" directed archeology and excavation for a long time—yet he, Frederick, would be able to make out a case that the Arabs, Moors and Saracens were parents to "Western" civilisation, sources of its ideas, its literature, its science, a case based on the same kind of evidence that made us legitimate heirs to Greece and Rome . . . this case wouldn't necessarily be more true, but its bases would be as powerful.

Throughout the summer he amused himself by concocting, one after another, papers describing the civilisation he was unearthing from the point of view of civilisations not ours—Roman, Greek, Aztec, etc., and so on. With his tongue in his cheek he framed various versions of the paper that he would probably publish about his work of the summer.

This paper would begin, or end, with the ritual sentence that of course the conclusions drawn were tentative due to lack of knowledge, lack of money, lack of time, and because only a fraction of this level of the site had been excavated, let alone all the levels beneath. But this bone having been tossed to the dogs of doubt, all else would be assertion and statement. The paper would draw the fire of opposing professors, schools and theories. Textbooks for universities and schools would result. These would contain statements like: Writing was not discovered in the Middle East until 2,000 B.C. The Sumerians believed so and so. The astronomers of the Akkadians believed such and such. The Egyptians mummified their priest-kings because they wanted the corpses to last a long time. The world was created by God 4000 years ago. That African civilisations prior to the coming of the white man were nonexistent/barbaric/plentiful/backward/sparse/ or whatever was the current notion. And so on. Frederick left Turkey in a disturbed frame of mind which he associated with his previous state of mind after his African visit. It so happened that he chanced on a book describing a Victorian clergyman's crisis of Doubt over the existence of God. The clergyman's character struck Frederick as being similar to his own: energetic, and confident. The man had been upset by Doubts about the exact date of the creation of the world by God. His state of mind was very like Frederick's as he read. He was on the point of deciding that it was his moral duty to leave the Church, as he could not with honesty remain in it, when his tenth child, a girl, became engaged to a clergyman. This was a very good and by then despaired-of match, as the girl was an old maid, being nearly thirty. The father knew the girl would not keep this man, if he, the father, aired his Doubts and left the Church. For if he left the Church there would be a family-engulfing scandal and the daughter's fiancé was a conventional man with a future to guard. The father's crisis now became a nice exercise in balancing responsibilities: his conscience, or his daughter's future. With much anguish, he put off his leaving the Church until his daughter was wed. This meant he had to go through marrying (personally officiating) his daughter to the clergyman son-in-law with his mind full of Doubts. But when he examined his conscience after the ceremony he found his Doubts much less. As if the act of going through the ceremony had relieved them. "It was my love for my poor Daughter; my fears for her comfortless future; my anguish of mind that my own misery and confusion should poison Others —it was these that had caused me to act, as I then believed, Dishonestly. Thanks be to God in His Great Mercy that he led me, through my Valley of the Shadow, back to Himself . . ."

In short, that Victorian crisis was over. Frederick was left with two thoughts. One, that this frightful, painful, and very real conflict had taken place about a hundred years ago, which was nothing at all, even in human time. It had been

a very common conflict indeed. Some of the
best Victorian minds had suffered torment, even
collapse. Careers had been ruined, families destroyed, lives laid waste. But by even a few
decades later these Doubts looked ludicrous.
(In religious terms, Doubts looked ludicrous, for
in our time Crises of Doubt are experienced
most noticeably in the political context.) The
second thought was—that his state of mind after the African visit, his state of mind due to
visiting the Turkey site, were identical with
that of the Victorian clergyman in his religious
conflict. But the Victorian had not had the benefit of modern psychology. (Though he could
have remembered that the hand of the dyer is
subdued to his craft.) There was, however, no
excuse at all for him, Frederick, not to take a
cool look at what was bothering him, which was
nothing less, unfortunately, than Profound Doubts
about what was going on in Archeology, Doubts
about its bases, premises, methods and above
all, its unconscious biases.

If he were to do what that poor Victorian had
done, he should accept the job in the Sudan, on
the grounds that if he did not, his wife would
have to go without a pleasure cruise to Madeira, on which she had set her heart, and it was
not fair to make her suffer for his crisis of
confidence. But if he did this, since the Mind of
the Worker is conditioned by his Work, he
would have soon forgotten all about his Doubts,
which would begin to look silly and unhealthy.
Luckily Frederick's wife is a sensible woman
whose attitude towards archeology has always
tended to be that it made for attractive holidays
for herself and the children, and all she said to
Frederick was that she could hardly complain

about not going to Madeira when she had been able to get about so much. She went off to stay with a friend in Spain who has a villa, leaving Frederick in London.

And now for an interesting psychological fact ... in an account which I hope you'll agree is not short of them. Frederick forgot all about his Doubts that resulted from the African visit—this is not surprising since it happened a decade ago. But he also forgot his Doubts of last year after the Turkey excavations. Forgot completely, until just recently, after his visit to Wiltshire, when he made a deliberate effort to remember things he might have buried because they were painful. He then slid into a Euphoric, or Male Menopausal, or Manic Depressive (pay your penny and take your choice!) state of mind which he enjoyed enormously. If enjoyment is the word for such a bonus. He walked about London, and amused himself by going to museums and looking at pots and spears and stones and things and inventing theories as powerful and as convincing as currently accepted ones, about previous societies. And so now I've reached the end of what I agreed to write and tell you. If what I have said doesn't mean anything to you, then I have made a mistake, but I do find that hard to believe. I don't know why it is, but I am sure you will understand. Would you like to come and see me next time you are in London? I would be delighted, and so would Frederick and the others.

Incidentally, about Frederick's stammer, in case this is of any use to you, he has cured it by letting the "parallel stream" of ideas, or words, that inhibited him from saying the usual things, come out: he listens and then voices it. Aloud.

Either to himself, into a tape recorder, or to me. The results are surprising. . . .

I do look forward to hearing from you,

Sincerely yours,

ROSEMARY BAINES

DEAR MISS BAINES:

I don't know when I have felt so flattered. What a large result from what I am afraid I have to tell you was nothing but a routine occurrence for me. For my sins I give quite a number of lectures outside my own field. My wife says that I have too much energy for my own good. Perhaps she is right. The remarks which struck you so disproportionately—if I may be so frank!—I am afraid are one of my stock ploys. When I run dry or run out of breath, I have a few old standbys to get me started again. Yes of course I do feel that education is not what it ought to be. But few of us do not. I suppose I have to admit that what was once a crusade, a bit of a bee in the bonnet, has cooled rather. As regards your kind remarks about stammering, I am extremely grateful, of course. I have recently been overworking, or so the doctor tells me, and I developed a tendency to stammer. But I don't seem to remember doing so at that lecture. But you appear to remember it all in such very remarkable detail. Perhaps my making a joke about stammering had a prophylactic effect? I have found this the case. As regards Frederick Larson, I do seem to know the name, but that is all. I take his word for it that we have met. I think he is making too much of the stammering. Mine was relieved by remembering to speak very slowly and carefully, particularly when tired, and above all, by not forgetting to take the doctor's pills. I am sorry I have to disappoint you in replying so churlishly to your quite extraordinarily lengthy letter. But alas, I have not yet retired, with my time to myself. Which must be my excuse for not accepting your extraordinarily kind invitation to meet you and Mr. Larson. I am very seldom in London and when I am my time is taken up with interviews and visits in connection with my work.

Yours truly,
CHARLES WATKINS

DEAR DOCTOR Y:

Professor Watkins came to consult me in the spring of this year, in connection with stammering. I prescribed Librium and a holiday. I also gave him the address of a speech therapist, when the stammering did not stop. He has been on my books for five years. I took his practice over in 1964. He has not been ill in that time, except for influenza last year. He seemed to me to be in pretty good physical shape in March. He said he had lost weight. When I got your letter I asked his wife to come in and see me. I know her rather better than I know him, because I attend the children. She doesn't seem able to throw much light. But in her interests, I suggest that she see her husband pretty soon. Of course I am only that old-fashioned thing, a family doctor, and I don't know as much as I should about mental health. But Mrs. Watkins is under heavy strain.

Yours sincerely,
DOCTOR Z

Hello Charles.

You are . . .

I'm your *wife*.

Would you like to sit down? ....
....

I'm sorry, I don't know what to say.

But Charles it isn't possible that you don't know me?

I'm sorry.

But I just can't . . .

Then Felicity . . .

How do you know my name is Felicity?

They told me. They said you might come today.

You didn't ask to see me then?

No ....

Charles you sit there and tell me . . . oh, no, I just can't believe it. Oh, I'm so sorry.

Tell me then?

Tell you *what?*

For instance, how long have we been married?

Fifteen years.

....
....

The doctor says he has had other cases. I'm not the first, by a long chalk. Why are you laughing?

You always say that, just like that, "by a long chalk."

Do I? ....
....

When they told me you were coming, I hoped that if I saw you I'd remember ...

And you don't?

No. You're so angry. I didn't expect you to be angry.

Angry? Of course I'm not angry. What a funny thing to say. It's not your fault you've lost your memory. It happens to people. I'm very sorry for you. I really am.

No, you are angry.

Well, if I *were* angry ... it's so like you Charles. All the time, since I knew you had lost your memory I couldn't help thinking, That's so like Charles.

But why is it? Have I lost my memory before?

No. Well, not so far as I know. You never told me, if so. But you don't tell me things, do you?

There, I said you were angry.

Oh *no*, now I'm in the wrong again. *I simply can't believe* ....
....

Don't cry.

We've lived together for fifteen years. Fifteen years, Charles.

I'm sorry. I'm really very sorry, Felicity. And now you are angrier still.

I'm not angry but I can't help crying. Wouldn't you?

Please go. You must go away. I don't know you, you see, Felicity.

> *Patient was visited by his wife today. Visit terminated at patient's request. Wife hysterical subject, better kept away from patient for the time being, in my opinion.*
>
> DOCTOR X.

Doctor X, I simply have to see you.

Ah, Mrs. Watkins, I thought you had gone back home. Well, sit down, I'm very pleased to see you. Now, what can I do for you?

What can you do for me! Doctor X, he's been here now nearly two months.

Yes, I'm afraid he has. But he is better, we think.

How do you judge betterness, then? How? You say he didn't know who he was when he came in here. And he still doesn't. So why is he better?

He's better in himself. More rested.

Rested? Was he ill when he came in?

No, he didn't have flu, or bronchitis.

I know I am very stupid Doctor. I know that. But it doesn't help me when you are sarcastic. You say he is better. But I've never seen him look so awful. Never. He's so thin. And he seems shaky and weak.

It is very understandable that you are upset.

Oh thanks. Thanks very much.

Look at it from our point of view. Your husband was brought in here nearly two months ago, by the police, in a state of shock, having been robbed, without papers, money, or knowledge of who he was. He was talking to himself, hallucinated, he had religious delusions and he was paranoiac. We did what we could to get him better, that's all.

And you say he is better?

In my opinion he is better.

Can I see Doctor Y?

Certainly, but he isn't here today.

He wasn't here yesterday either. He wrote to me about my husband, you see.

He does two days a week at another hospital.

When will he be here?

Tomorrow.

Can I see him then?

Certainly. Tell the office on your way out that you will be back tomorrow, and ask them to make an appointment.

Oh please don't think that I want to be rude, Doctor, I don't.

Not at all. We are quite used to it Mrs. Watkins.

––––––––––––––––––––––––––––––––––––

Oh Doctor Y, I stayed over in town to see you.

And I'm very pleased that you did. How do you think your husband is?

How do I know? How can I tell? Oh, I think he looks awful, awful . . . I don't see how it is possible!

Oh, believe me, it happens.

No, no, I don't mean that. That people don't lose their memories. But . . . are you married, Doctor?

Yes, I am.

How long have you been married?

Nine years. No, ten.

Imagine you walk into your bedroom tonight when you go home, and your wife is there, and she looks at you and talks exactly as she always does and then suddenly she says she doesn't know who you are.

Yes, Mrs. Watkins, I have tried to imagine it happening. I really have tried.

But . . . I'm not complaining about that. I don't seem to be able to make myself understood. It is this—how can you say he has lost his memory then?

Now I don't understand . . . cigarette? They are bringing some tea in a minute.

If he has lost his memory, then why does he speak as he always speaks. The same phrases. Everything the same.

Ah, now I understand.

If he had lost his memory, if he really didn't know who he was, then he'd be like a—newborn baby.

In some respects I'm afraid that he is.

No, I don't think he is. If what he was before is cancelled out—washed away, then he might just as well come back to us as—oh I don't know, a South Sea Islander, or a German or a man from Mars or something.

I see your point. I do, really. Ah, here is the tea.

Thank you. So it isn't that he has lost his memory. He is still who he was. He just doesn't remember—me. And the children.

He says he doesn't remember anything at all. Not his childhood. Nor his parents. Nothing.

Yet, Doctor Y, when you say to him, Do you remember your childhood, he says, No, I don't remember my childhood. He doesn't say—oh I don't know, Gobbledegook, or Worra worra worra worra. Oh I wasn't making a joke, I assure you. I'm very far from making jokes. Oh, God, I know it is stupid to cry.

Mrs. Watkins, would you like to see him again—that is, if he agrees. It might help.

If *who* agrees?

Yes, I do see your point. But don't you see, I'm as much in the dark as you are. More. You know him well and I don't. If you talked to him again, let him get used to—and don't mind my saying this, if you try not to cry . . .

Doctor, I took his hand, and he's my husband, remember, and he looked as if—he looked like a man that a woman is flirting with and he's not sure he likes it.

Look, my dear. I'm going to make a suggestion. You have another cup of tea and a cigarette. Wash your face—there's a washbasin in there. I'm going to ask him to talk to you again. But don't come in if you can't stop yourself crying. Do you understand why? If you are very emotional, it may have the effect of blocking him—try and be easy and relaxed, and things may come back.

I'll try, doctor.

Well, Charles, I talked to Doctor Y.

Yes.

I like him.

I can see him.

See him?

Some you can't see at all.

Oh, yes ....

I didn't understand that, it's no good pretending I did. But I want to ask you something. This is hard for me Charles. Please don't be angry. . . .

I don't think I've felt anger yet. I haven't felt. But I can see emotions on your face and on the faces of the doctors and nurses.

But you asked me to go away. What did you feel then?

I felt, not that all over again, not that again.

What?

You asked me what I felt. That is what I felt—if that is feeling. I didn't want that. I don't want that, you see.

Now Charles, I'm very calm, and I'm not crying at all. But I want you to look at me, and answer me. When you see me sitting here, am I just the same to you as—oh I don't know, the nurses, or the doctors?

The same?

I mean, don't you know me any better?

I know you, I know you very well.

You *do*—oh, then. . . .

I know them too. Looking is knowing.

Oh, I see.

You are all very . . .

Very what?

You are all so—large. Very bright. Very hot and bright.
You press on my eyeballs. You press into my eyes. It is too much.

Are you afraid of me, Charles?

Your anger . . .

Charles, when you say you don't remember anything, do you mean that? Not me, nor your children, nor your home? . . . . Not your mother and your father? You were fond of your father, Charles, very fond, don't you remember? . . . .

My mind is full of memories,

Oh you *do*—but the doctors say . . .

I don't remember the things you talk about.

What do you remember then? . . . . Charles? . . . . You don't answer . . . Tell me, what you remember might link up somewhere with the truth.

Truth is a funny word, isn't it?

Oh, Charles, you never used to be philosophical!

Philosophical? What's . . .

Why is it that some words you know quite well, and others you look blank?

I'll tell you, if you like. Some words—match. A word falls out of your mouth and marches with something I know. Other words don't fit in with what I can see.

But what do you *see*? Charles? Tell me? ....

Felicity—you talk to me. Tell me what you think. Tell me what you know. You are my wife? Well then, tell me about that.

Charles! Very well, then. I'll try. We were married in London, Kensington Registry Office. In February. It was 1954. It was a very cold day. Then ... we went to a farm in Wales for our honeymoon. We didn't have very much money. We were there for three weeks. We were very happy ... Charles? Shall I go on? We went to a flat in Cambridge after that. Later we got a house. I started with Jimmy in Wales. Jimmy is our elder son. We have been very happy.

Why are you so much younger than I am?

But ... well, you fell in love with me, Charles.

And I'm not surprised.

Charles, for God's sake, don't flirt with me, I can't stand it. I'm your wife.

I'm sorry.

You were worried, you said fifteen years was too much. But I said nonsense, and I was right, it hasn't made any difference at all. I was one of your students.

Oh yes, they keep telling me I teach. Teach. That's a funny word ...

Do you want me to go on? ....
.... I think I'll go now, if you don't mind, Charles. Do you want me to come

back? I don't mean tomorrow, because Aunt Rose is
with the boys and she has to go back to stay with
Aunt Anna, because Aunt Anna isn't very well, she
has her bronchitis back again, and of course I can't
leave the boys alone, but I could come back in four or
five days if I can get Mrs. Spence to come and stay a
couple of days. . . . I'll ring the Doctor. Goodbye
Charles.

> *Mrs. Watkins spent an hour with
> patient today. She says he did not
> remember her at all. In my view the
> visit was helpful to patient and
> should be repeated soon.*
>
> DOCTOR Y.

> *I disagree. E.C.T. should be at-
> tempted.*
>
> DOCTOR X.

> *Patient had a very disturbed night
> with recurrence of hallucinations.
> Have put him back on Equanil.*
>
> DOCTOR Y.

DEAR DOCTOR Y,

You asked me in your first letter if I could
remember anything at all in my marriage that
seemed to me strange at the time. I don't think
I know any longer what strange is—not after
seeing Charles in this state. But I'm sending you,
after lying awake all night to think it over carefully, the first letter my husband sent me. I *did*
think it very strange then, because he had not
said anything about loving me before, although I
had been his pupil for seven and a half months. I
was only eighteen then. I didn't think it was
strange later, when I agreed to marry him, but

perhaps I had got used to him. I don't know if
you would think it a strange letter. The circumstances of the letter were that I had never
thought of him like that. I admired him very
much of course. One afternoon after a class he
took me to tea and he talked. I thought his
manner was rather strange, but then falling in
love is strange. When I got his letter I didn't
know what to think, particularly as I began to be
so happy and proud. And then later, when we
agreed to marry, I forgot about thinking him
strange, and even now I don't know what to
think. Please send me the letter back when you
have read it. It is one of my most precious possessions.

Yours sincerely,
FELICITY WATKINS

Oh my God Felicity, I haven't slept since I saw
you—Yesterday?—I don't know—I keep seeing your
face—your hair is too bright for my eyes. It was your
hair first—I always look for your head shining in the
dark class—You are a light in a naughty world—yes
and it is enough to look—touching too?—That would
be too much joy—And yet if I can look touching
could be too—for both of us?—How dare I think it—
and yet yesterday with you I knew differently—you
too—I didn't sleep—I am old Felicity—thirty-five.
You, eighteen? A baby! But girls have no age—they
shine in dark corners—if you could—I keep thinking
of you in a big forest somewhere with the sunlight
coming down through branches and you and your
bright shining head and you smiling at me—smiling—
will you?—oh I don't know if—I wonder if I will post
this at all—it is one thing sitting here putting words
on a paper and your thoughts rushing by fifty at least
to a word—so what is the use of sending it if I can't
send the thoughts—one in fifty—so much diluted—is

it worth your attention even?—I wonder—you could
take the word for the—I love you. Yes, that is it, I
know—you would never keep me a pig in your pen—
no, I'm sure. She had bright yellow hair and blue eyes
too, she must have had—but it is the soul that counts.
Not like that dark one, black hair and white teeth
and red lips—those are the colours for pig-keepers.
And in war time too—The light and the dark of it.
But the yellow-hair locked *him* in her pen and fed
him husks. Later a fatted calf? But I don't dare—Yes.
Would you—I've never dared, I've been alone for fear
of that. *She* died, and so could never lock me in her
stye. Must I be afraid of you? Felicity Felicity Felicity Felicity—you have a name like bright sunlight to
match your hair. If I see you smile tomorrow I'll
know. I love you. Felicity Felicity Felicity Felicity
Felicity Felicity Felicity

DEAR DOCTOR Y,

I can't say how distressed I am to hear that
Charles Watkins is ill and in hospital in your
care. Yes, of course I shall be only too glad to
help in any way I can. As it happens I heard
about his illness when I returned from Italy last
night, and my wife telephoned Felicity Watkins.

No, I don't think that Charles showed any
unusual signs of stress or strain this year but he is
not the sort of person one would take much
notice of, if he did overshoot any marks, but I
cannot, I am afraid, explain that without going
into considerable detail about our relationship.
Which is not, far from it, that I am his "superior"
—did Felicity Watkins say I was? If so, then I
regard that as painfully and sadly significant—
not because of Felicity but because of Charles.
He is, and has been since he joined us, the "star"
of our Classics Department, even when I was
nominally over him, and in theory Head of De-

partment. I hope that doesn't sound like a criticism. Letters are tricky things, and I certainly would have preferred to talk it over with you, but the term starts tomorrow and, alas, needs must.

I don't know if this sort of comment is in any way helpful, but recently I sat down to write out an account of my own life, a sort of balance sheet. It seemed a useful thing to do, at the age of fifty, well past the halfway mark. But when I came to read it over, it was more about Charles Watkins than about myself. I have always been aware of the influence Charles has had on me, but not, perhaps, quite how much. Of course, all this sort of thing is beyond me, and particularly when it gets into deep waters with mental breakdowns, that sort of thing, but the essence of the thing from my point of view is this: that I have never liked Charles. I believe that I don't admire him, or approve of him. Yet he has certainly been the biggest influence on my life.

You ask about his early life.

Our parents were friends. We were described by them as "great chums" almost from birth. I believe that Charles regards this as wryly as I do—and did then. We went to the same prep school. We were neither of us particularly distinguished. We stuck together out of homesickness—an alliance of mutual aid and defence, if you like. My view of that period does not coincide with Charles' at all, as emerges rather painfully when we ever discuss it. Briefly, I think he was rather a con. But not deliberately or consciously. However, I'll skip all that and choose a typical incident from Rugby where we both went together. The summer we were both sixteen our form master invited six of us for a summer's yachting, based on the Isle of Wight. I was one of the six. The invitations were not "personal," but issued every holidays on a sort of rota system, in quite a regular, fair way. This master was a kindly man, quite the best influence on my young life, and I daresay on Charles too. The reason why I was invited that holidays and Charles was not was simply that I was minimally older. Now, I had done a fair bit of yachting for various reasons, and my parents were better off than Charles' parents. I knew he was not looking forward to going home that holidays, and for a variety of reasons. To cut it short, I suggested to the form master that Charles should go instead of me. Again, I must ask you to take it as read that it was not possible for Charles to remain impervious to the fact that this was a real sacrifice on my part. The form master was surprised and touched. No, that is not why I did it. It was just that, given the circumstances, Charles might have been expected to show a consciousness of some kind. When Wentworth told him I had backed down in his favour, Charles simply nodded. Wentworth was so surprised that he repeated what he had said—that I had offered to back down, and Charles said, yes, thanks, I'd like to. I said nothing to him about it, when he did not mention it. Now, it was a particularly good summer, and I was stuck with a pretty boring crowd, and I am afraid I did spend far too much time thinking of that crowd down there, on the water, and of Charles' quite extraordinary attitude. I never mentioned it. I could not bring myself to, for it stung so badly. Not until years after, after the war as a matter of fact. I said to him in so many words—perhaps I was hoping to take the sting out of the memory, what I had felt throughout that summer holidays. He looked at

me and said: Well, there was no need to offer it,
was there?

And of course, there was not.

I am sure that looks a very small thing and
very petty, and it does me a great deal of
discredit to mention it at all. But you did ask me
to say what I thought and that "anything I could
tell you might be helpful."

That incident sums up something in Charles
for me.

I must say at this point that our relations were
formalised by the time we were nine in this way:
Charles was the original eccentric oddball, and
Jeremy was the solid dependable one. I've always played along with it. I'm stuck with it, as it
were. But when I say to Charles and to others
that what I admire is his originality and his dar-
ingness of thought, and so on, that is not the point
at all. For in fact there is something too careless,
almost sloppy, about his "originality." I suppose
he is a bit of an anarchist. Of course his experience has tended to make him one.

His father was in business and did badly in the
slump. Charles started work, while I went to
University. He did every variety of job, and there
was talk of his going off to the Spanish Civil
War, but he didn't. The war started and he
joined up at once. I was flying throughout the
war, and Charles was in infantry, and then with
Tanks. We met once or twice. I knew a bit of
what he was up to, through mutual friends. He
refused a commission, more than once. This was
so like him. I asked him why, and he began
roaring with laughter and said he had refused to
annoy people. I found it then, and find it now—
affected. And unconvincing. I told him so. I
could say that "this caused ill-feeling" but as I
was about to write that, I realised that it might

have caused ill-feeling in me, but I don't think in Charles. We did not quarrel, though I'll acknowledge that I would have liked to quarrel—at last.

When the war ended, Charles went back to University. This he got through well and easily. He has a not uncommon facility—a memory that is really almost photographic. For an examination he will study day and night for the month beforehand, get phenomenal marks—and will have forgotten most of it months later. He says this of himself.

Very well. By the time he was ready for a job, I had been lecturing four or five years. I was in a position to pull strings or at least put a friendly oar in. There were a dozen applicants for the post and Charles was the youngest, and least experienced. Well, he got the post and through me—but that is not the point. Which is this. In the crisis week, when things hung in the balance, he came to visit me. He was scruffy, untidy, a bit flamboyant—all this as usual. Nothing terrible—not like our present students, far from that level of exhibitionism, but pretty irritating. I told him that he had to take his appearance more seriously, and that he was putting me in a difficult position. He listened, didn't say much. Next time I saw him, he had got the post, and—he was looking like me. I must explain that. We are physically different, but I have some mannerisms. Not that I knew of them until Charles showed me them! He had equipped himself with an old jacket of mine—asked my wife for it, she was throwing it away. He had acquired a pipe, which he had never smoked before, and he got his hair cut like mine. When I first clapped my eyes on this, I thought it was a monstrous joke. But not at all. You'd expect this to be a joke between us perhaps? Or at least an issue? No, it was not men-

tioned for a long time. Yet everyone noticed it,
commented. When I came into a room, or saw
him across a street it was like seeing a monstrous
caricature of myself.

When someone did finally mention it (my
wife, as it happened), and I looked at him,
hoping for some comment, he merely nodded,
rather impatiently, but not very. With a sort of
small frown, as if to say: Oh that, what a detail.

I suppose it may strike you as a detail, too. But
I may add that now, years later, people tend to
think that it is I who have copied Charles, mod-
elled myself on him. And that fact says everything
about how we are both judged. And yes, it
rankles.

Now an episode from last summer. It so happened that my wife and I were having a stormy
patch. I had been overworking and so had she.
We had agreed to spend the summer apart. We
knew we were on the slippery slope to divorce.
We had quarrelled and talked and made scenes,
the usual sort of thing, and I daresay we were as
much emotionally worn out as anything. She decided to go to her mother in Scotland, leaving
the children with friends—as it happens, the
Watkins. Both of whom were towers of strength
throughout the whole episode. Charles drove
Nancy to her mother. Nancy was in a pretty
hysterical state, as she would be the first to admit. Now I find it rather hard to describe what
happened in a way to convey its importance. Far
from Charles behaving badly, it was the opposite. Nancy says he was kind and helpful. But
before they even reached Scotland, she was pretty upset because of his attitude—which was that
the whole thing was not very important. He took
it absolutely for granted that she would be back
with me before the year was out—but that if she

were not, what of it? Now I must mention Felicity, his wife. I have a valuable relationship with her. I've known her since she was a tiny thing. No, I'm not in love with her, nor ever have been, but we have always known that we are close, and that if neither were married elsewhere, we might well hit it off pretty well. My wife has always known of this, so has Charles, there is nothing to hide.

Before Charles left Nancy at her mother's he stayed over for two days, and in those days he behaved impeccably, supporting Nancy against her mother, who was cutting up rather, and taking her for walks and so on. But he was making her worse because of his attitude—not making light of the whole drama, on purpose, but it was implicit in his attitude. He spent a whole afternoon, she tells me, pointing out that he might have married her—and I, Felicity, and it would have been the same, and that we all were much too personal about the whole thing. Yes, "we are all much too personal about the whole thing." He was talking about marriage, after all. After all, we aren't Hottentots. Anyway, Nancy found herself half crazy, because of Charles. She describes it as feeling as if her entire life was made to look silly, and that she was not any more important than a she-cat or a bitch. Well, she *was* in a pretty emotional state anyway. In the end she screamed at him to go away and leave her. Of course she apologised afterwards, I insisted on it, for he had been wonderfully kind, as had Felicity. Afterwards my wife said to me that the real crisis that summer was not her leaving me to give us both a rest, but the four or five days in Charles' company. Any more of him and she would have cut her throat, she says, or could

have done if she had been able to believe it
mattered whether she did or not.

I've chosen this last incident because again it
illustrates something pretty fundamental in
Charles. It is that he doesn't even pay lip service
to ordinary feelings. Perhaps they aren't as important as we think. But perhaps I would respect
him more for his attitude if I believed there was
conflict involved, if he had ever *thought* it out, or
even suffered over it, instead of its being his
nature.

Now, a final incident. In spring of this year
there was an evening at our house which struck
me very unpleasantly indeed, but I suppose I am
used to being uncomfortable where Charles is
concerned. There were present myself and my
wife Nancy, Charles and Felicity, a couple of
other members of our team—as I like to call
it!—and a visitor from America. Now I don't like
to think that we have to put on a special show
for visiting firemen, but on the other hand there
is such a thing as tact. Our American visitor was
on his first visit to our country, and was hoping
to—and may even yet succeed—spend a year
with us. Charles behaved outrageously. I thought
he was drunk, though he is not a drinker. It is
simplest to say that he behaved like an undergraduate, if I may be permitted that oldfash-
ioned comparison, but *I* am not one to be proud
of flattering the youth. Charles was not even
witty, which he very often is. He was boorish,
badmannered, in a silly sort of way. The classics
were "hogwash" and the course of lectures we
had drafted together for him "a lot of pigs-swill."
And so on. I'm afraid his epithets were pretty
limited, but that is the nature of undergraduate
humour.

Now, if I were a reactionary and impervious to

new ideas it would be easier to understand, but I am not. I cannot remember ever refusing to listen to Charles or to anyone else when they have a new angle. But to say that everything taught under the heading of Classics is pigsfeed from beginning to end, and never has been anything else, and that we have never had any idea at all of what Plato or Socrates and Pythagoras were teaching—and etc. and so on, that kind of thing—well, I did cut him off short and sharp more than once during the evening, and he went home early. Felicity his wife was annoyed, and did not go home when he did.

Now, next day he came to me with a demand that he should be empowered to arrange the coming term's work according to ideas which I don't really see much point in elaborating—but suffice it to say that his point of view amounts to damning generations of scholarship out of hand. He said, what was wrong with that? That it is a historical commonplace that ideas valid for centuries can vanish overnight. I may say that Charles is very fond of talking in centuries if not millennia, always the sign of a lazy mind, to my way of thinking. However, I asked him what gave him the confidence—or did I say conceit?—to talk about the work of scholars infinitely better than himself, in such terms. Did he really have no qualms at all. He said no, that it was "perfectly obvious to an unprejudiced mind" that he was right.

I must confess we quarrelled violently. I think it was the first quarrel we have ever had—astonishingly. He was abusive and derisive. Usually of course he is rather bland, or appears to be indifferent. I was patient—I am, in fact, a patient man. He became increasingly unpleasant. You understand that all the time there was the underlying implication that it must be obvious he was in the right and that I could see it if I wasn't stupid. Finally, I asked him to leave before I lost my temper.

Next morning he rang up—as if nothing had happened. No explanation. His manner, as always, was that an unimportant incident was over. Not that he had been in the wrong, no. Not, even, that *I* was rigidly in the wrong and that he had had to force himself into my mould— though I suppose that was implicit. No, it was that nothing had occurred that was in the least bit important. Yet that was intolerable, because what in fact he had done, and in front of an American colleague who may yet be working with us, was to damn not only our team and its work, and of course our respective careers, his included, but all scholarship in our field to date. Or most of it. And, having done that, and behaved with shocking offensiveness, he was now quite casually arranging to meet me and discuss a series of public lectures which only the day before he had refused to consider at all and about which he had been exceedingly abusive. His manner was appropriate with saying: I'm sorry I was a bit off colour last night, but I had a headache.

I don't know if I am succeeding in conveying to you the flavour of this particular incident.

I don't think I can tell you more, though there is an infinite choice of such examples.

I am at this moment in the usual frame of mind when thinking about Charles—he forces me to ask myself what it means to like or dislike a person. We have always been in each other's lives. We have our friends in common. It is my considered opinion that Charles Watkins is a destructive person. Negative, perhaps, is the better word. I find him a pain in the neck, even, far too often, a bore. I conclude from all this that we do not know very much about human relationships.

Yours very truly,

JEREMY THORNE

P.S.

I do hope you will let me know if there is anything else I can do to help. It goes without saying, I hope, that I would do anything for Charles. An idea has struck me: I don't know if you have been contacted by Constance Mayne, or if her name has cropped up at all? She has been Charles' mistress, or perhaps still is. She was one of his pupils. No, I have nothing to complain of in his behaviour, as she did not become his mistress until she had ceased to be his student. And I am not a moralist. I tell you this because I believe his wife Felicity does not know of her existence. If you think it might be of assistance, let me know and I'll get hold of her address for you. She was in Birmingham when I heard last.

DEAR DOCTOR Y,

Can I "assist" you in "rehabilitating" Charles Watkins? I don't know. Yes, I do know him, very well indeed. How very tactful you are. I was his mistress. You must know that or otherwise why did you write to me? I would be interested to know who told you, but I don't expect you will. Well, now, about Charles ... he has lost his memory? He can't remember who he is? I am very sorry to hear it, but how does it concern me? No, don't think I am being dishonest. I wish it did concern me, but as it happens, I think you should ask his wife Felicity Watkins. I suppose you must have done. Did she tell you to contact me? If so, it is no more than I would expect of her. What I mean by that, specifically, is that it would be so damned high-minded and above every normal human emotion, just like Charles. I am sure these things rub off. They say married people get to resemble each other, but of course I wouldn't know.

After (believe me) due thought, I am simply sending you the enclosed letter. The letter is one I wrote to Charles. That letter was written after due thought, too. Years of it. What I mean is, I could have written that letter before I did, but I was a fool and didn't.

I sent that letter (the enclosed one) to Charles at his home address. Not out of spite, but I didn't have another address. He came posthaste. When I say posthaste, I mean, for him. About ten days went by. He came by train to Birmingham. He brought my letter with him. It was, as it might be, a goodwill visit. He stayed the night. Why not? Old habits die hard. When he left in the morning, the letter was lying on my night-table. The point is, but I don't expect you to see it as a point, he hadn't left it there on purpose, or for post-departure comment—we had after all, touched on its contents the night before. To put it mildly. No, he forgot it. It slipped totally out of his mind. So I'm taking this opportunity of returning it to him, via you. He might like to refresh his memory—when he gets it back.

Sorry I can't be of any use.

With my good wishes,
CONSTANCE MAYNE

DEAR CHARLES,

Don't be alarmed, this isn't one of those drivelling slobby *wet* letters I wrote you when you decided you'd had enough of me. No fear. I'm very far from that now. I woke up this morning and thought it was three years this June since you left me.

The thought of you
So sweet and true
For dreary years
Has been boo hoo.
Boo hoo, boo hoo, boo hoo. BOO!

It occurred to me that far from boo hoo, far from it, I was in a good old paddy, a good old rage. Fury. It occurs to me Charles Watkins that what I feel for you is not boo hoo at all, I hate you. More than that, I simply can't get over your sheer damned preposterousness.

Now let me tell you a tale.

There was once an earnest idealistic young student taking Literature and Languages, who went, God help her, to a lecture, an Introduction to Old Greece, and heard a mad professor claim that there was only one literature and one language, namely Greek, (Ancient, not Modern). And such was his persuasive force that this stupid student dropped her lovely *useful* literature and French and Spanish and Italian, and went over to Useless Old Greece, just because this professor said so. Three years passed while this stupid student sweated and got full marks all for the sake of an approving smile or two from the Mad Professor. The day she heard she had got her B.A. behold, it happens this Silly student is in London and there is the Mad Professor giving a lecture on the television about Greece, the Cradle of European Civilisation. Intellectual this and Moral that, and so it went on, but not one word about, it occurs to silly Female Student, Women, let alone Slaves in that paradise of Moral Superiority, Ancient Greece. Stupid student got into a taxi as the lecture was ending on the telly, and went to the B.B.C. and he came out of the building, looking oh so Classical and Woolly, rough tweeds, pipe, rugged charm, the lot, she said to him, In all that there was not one word about either Women or Slaves. To which the Mad Professor returned: Oh, is that you Connie? Well done! Congratulations on your results! Well, you are concerned about Women and Slaves are you? What are you doing about them? It took the Stupid Student five dazzling dizzying seconds to get his drift, and she said to him, Right, you're on. At which she refused to go back to University to get her M.A. and probably on to Ph.D. and so on ad infinitum but she went off to Birmingham, got a job in a factory, with women making plastic containers for detergents, found they were indeed Slaves while being Women, and she made scandals and fusses with the management, became a shop steward and a communist and three years later went to Cambridge to confront the Mad Professor with the news. Very well, then, I've done it, she cried, and told him the tale, three years hard, but very hard, but very very hard, slogging, hard intolerable bloody work for the plastic-detergent-container-making women of Birmingham, and he took his pipe out of his mouth and said: Well done! And then he said: Let's go to bed.

Yes I *do* know whether to laugh or to cry. This morning I am laughing and God knows it is about time.

So the love of the century begins, in Birmingham for the most part, but a busy and popular Professor of Classics with a wife and two sons hasn't all that much time left over for amusements, and the Silly Shop Steward hardly ever sees her Love. In the meantime this same Stupid

Shop Steward has a beau, a Steady, a faithful love, being the Shop Steward on the Men's Component's Floor, where Men make plastic containers for transistor radios, for since they are Men and therefore more advanced and evolved, they can put on those difficult buttons and screws and handles and things, much more tricky than detergent containers. This faithful and loving swain gets the boot from the Silly Shop Stewardess, because of the Love of the Century. Forlorn and alone she says Boo hoo, Boo hoo, marry me, and he says, the Mad Professor says, Don't be absurd. But what about your vows, your love, your passion, she cries? He says, anyone who believes a word anyone says in bed deserves what she gets.

How's that for a Professor?

But I've twice changed my whole life for you, she cries, sobbing, weeping, wailing.

No one asked you to, says he, taking the pipe out of his mouth for the purpose.

What shall I dooooooo, she wails. I've lost my true real right love, the Shop Steward, and I can't have you, my life is empty and I want a Famileee.

To which he replies, Well, what's stopping you?

You'd think the girl would have learned by now? You would, wouldn't you?

Well, now. You'll remember that bit, if you have time to remember at all, as a lot of very sloppy letters from me. But actually what was happening was that I was thinking. Well, what *is* stopping me? For as it happens I was pregnant, but only half knew it.

So I went back to Birmingham, had a fine bouncing son, eight pounds, two ounces, keeping my job more or less throughout and with the aid of some kind and loving plastic-container packers and—that was two years ago.

Boo hoo, boo hoo, all the way.

Yes, the child is two and his name is Ishmael, how do you like *that?*

No, I don't want a damned thing from you. Nothing. If you want to see the boy, fine. If you don't, fine.

I don't care.

I can manage by myself thank you very much.

It occurs to me actually, yes, it's true, and *thank you very much*, I mean it. I don't need anyone, no, not I.

I'm leaving Birmingham next month and shall spend the summer with a kindly aunt in Scotland, and I shall teach Greek to some misguided idiots who would be better employed learning Useful Italian, French and Spanish. But which, alas, I am not equipped to teach anybody, thanks a thousand times to you. No, I am not blaming you, like hell I'm not.

I heard from an old school chum yesterday that you are going about saying that the classics are a load of old rope and all current teaching absolutely ropy, and that no one understands what it was all really about. Except, of course, you.

Congratulations. Oh congratulations. I'm not surprised that you've lost your voice—so a little bird tells me? and can't utter!

I've told you, you are preposterous.

With hate. I mean it.
CONSTANCE

DEAR DOCTOR X,

I can answer your question very easily: yes, Charles Watkins did come to see me in the middle of August last. It was late one night: I think a

Wednesday, but I can't really remember, I am afraid.

Yours truly,

ROSEMARY BAINES

DEAR DOCTOR Y,

After I posted my letter—two letters, actually— I remembered something about Charles that perhaps you should know.

It is about the last war. Of course to me it is rather old hat, but almost from the start of knowing Charles really well I thought that the last war hadn't done him much good. I once met a friend of Charles (with Charles) who said that Charles once said to him that he—that is, Charles—had decided early in the war that he wouldn't survive it. He was in danger a lot. His friends, that is, the men he was fighting with, were all killed off around him, twice. He was the only one left alive in a group of buddies, twice. Once in North Africa and once in Italy. When he reached the end of the war he could not believe he was still alive. He had to learn how to believe that he was going to live, said this man. Whose name is Miles Bovey. I'll put in the address for you because perhaps you should ask him. He said that Charles had a long stretch at the end of the war when he did not want to begin living. He was drinking then. So Miles said but I have never seen Charles drink more than usually. Then Charles went back to University. Charles once said something to me that I have remembered. He said that ever since the war he couldn't believe that people really found important the things they said they found important. He said he had had to learn to "play little games." He said Miles Bovey was "the only person who ever really understood me." I asked him what little games and he said "the whole damned boiling." Needless to say, I said: Love, too? I don't remember what he said to that.

Yours sincerely,
CONSTANCE MAYNE

DEAR DOCTOR Y,

Thank you for your kind and explanatory letter. It was not possible to gather very much from Doctor X's letter.

Yes, I suppose one could say that Charles Watkins was "not himself" that evening, but you must remember my knowledge of him to that date was confined to hearing him lecture, and some remarks about him by mutual friends.

I can't tell you if that lecture was important to him. It was certainly important to me. I wrote him a long letter telling him it was important and why. Perhaps writing it was a mistake, but looking back I don't regret it. We sometimes have to take the chance of embarrassing people by claiming more than they want to give—or can. My letter was a claim. Of course I knew it was. You may ask: what did I say in it? but to answer that would mean writing the same letter. Suffice it to say that I heard him lecture, and things he said started me thinking in a new way. Or experiencing in a new way. Of course not in any dramatic exterior way. I did not get an answer to my letter. I thought once or twice of writing again, in case the first letter had not reached him, but there was no reason to suppose it had not. I concluded that my letter had been tactless, or perhaps ill-timed, and that I would not hear at all from him.

But I was sitting that evening in a little Greek restaurant in Gower Street where I go fairly often. Frederick Larson was with me—the archeologist. Suddenly Charles walked in and sat down with us saying: I thought I would find you here.

This was not nearly as odd as it looks. For one thing he knew where I lived, for he *had* received my letter, and had been to my flat to see if I was in. When he found I was not, he walked about the adjacent streets to see if I was in a pub or a restaurant. As indeed I was.

But his unconventional arrival matched the general oddness of his manner. At first both Frederick and I thought he was drunk. Then, that it might be marijuana, or worse. Then Frederick began pressing him to eat and, clued by this, I realised that his clothes had that peculiarly unconvincingly grubby stale look that grubby clothes get when they are obviously clothes that are usually kept clean. Because he is not the kind of person one would ever expect to wear clothes that have been slept in, this stopped me from seeing at first that everything he wore had a rubbing of grime, and that he had grime marks on his hands. And he had a stale tired smell.

At first he kept refusing food, or rather, seeming not to hear when he was offered it. Then he began eating some rolls on the table, and Frederick simply ordered some food for him, without asking him again, and when it came we could see he was ravenous. He was talking in a disconnected sort of way all the time. I don't really know what about. It made sense while he talked. He was chatting away as if we were both very old friends and able to pick up all his references to people and places. The thing that made this less extraordinary was that both of us indeed felt we were old friends, for we had talked of him a great deal. He was making references to some voyage he was thinking of making, and even seemed to think we would be with him. Of course by then we had understood he was not at all "himself"—as you put it.

When the meal was over we asked him back to my flat. The three of us walked. It was not more than a couple of hundred yards. In my flat he did not sit down. He was restless and walked about all the time, examining objects very carefully, examining the surfaces of walls, and so on. But I got the impression that he had forgotten or lost interest in the thing he had just examined so carefully by the time he put it down. This went on for two or three hours. He was talking about getting out of the trap, getting out of prison, of escaping—that kind of talk. And it did not seem as odd to us as perhaps you may think it should, because our own thoughts were running on similar lines—or it sounded like that, but I am sure you have often found that one may talk for hours —indeed for days, or a lifetime, with a friend, and then discover that the words you use stand for very different things.

I have no way of knowing how real to Charles that night were the prisons, the nets, the cages, the traps that he talked about. If you can call so disconnected and rambling a stream of words "talking." But I and Frederick Larson have very definite meanings for such words. But Charles? I can't say. Once when Charles was out of the room (he suddenly noticed his hands were dirty and went to wash them) we discussed whether or not to call a doctor, but decided not. He did not seem to us unable to look after himself. Perhaps we did wrong—after all, there was the evidence of his grimy clothes, and his obvious need for food, and the general strain and exhaustion. But I am one who does not believe that other people's crises should be cut short, or blanked out with drugs, or forced sleep, or a pretence that there is no crisis, or that if there is a crisis, it should be concealed or masked or made light of. I am sure that other people, and they would be those that a doctor might consider responsible, would have arranged for a doctor to come and take Charles into custody—forgive me for putting it like that. But his state of mind—as far as I could judge it—seemed not unlike my own at times in my life which I have found most illuminating and valuable.

And then, too, I wanted to go on listening to him.

While his remarks may have been scattered, there was an inner logic to them, a thread, which sounded at first like a repetition of certain words or ideas. Sometimes it seemed as if the sound, and not the meaning of a word or syllable in a sentence, gave birth to the next sentence or word. When this happened it gave the impression of superficiality, of being "scatty" or demented. But we have perhaps to begin to think of the relation of the sound of a word with its meaning. Of course poets do this, all the time. Do doctors? Sounds, the function of sounds in speech ... we have no way yet of knowing—have we?—how a verbal current may match an inner reality, sounds expressing a condition? But perhaps this sort of thought is not found useful by you.

At about midnight it was clear that the framework of ordinary life was going to make a pressure for Charles. For without it, he would not have made a move. Frederick had to go home. His decision to go brought to Charles' notice that it was in fact midnight. He went with Frederick. It was an automatic going. He might just as well have stayed. In the street, he said to Frederick: "I'll see you next time round." And walked off. And that was all we knew of Charles until I got a letter from Doctor X at your hospital.

I hope that this rather inadequate account of that evening may be of assistance. I am sorry he is so ill. I have it in me to envy him. There is a good deal in my life that I would be very happy to forget. May I visit him perhaps? I would like to, if it would be helpful.

Yours sincerely,
ROSEMARY BAINES

DEAR DOCTOR X,

I am of course only too happy to help in any way possible.

I knew Charles Watkins off and on during our schooldays. We were at different schools. When the war started we both found ourselves in North Africa. Charles saw more fighting there than I did. I was in Intelligence and at that stage less active. We met from time to time, but then I went to Yugoslavia and he went to Italy. Yes he had a hard time in the war, but more in the sense that he had a steady hard slog right through it, infantry, and then tanks. We did not see each other until the end of the war. In 1945 we met again and spent some months together. We both found ourselves pretty well shaken up and needed the company of a person who understood this. Personally I do not believe that people are "changed" by stress. In my experience certain characteristics get emphasized, or brought out. In this sense I did not find Charles Watkins "changed" by the war. But he was certainly ill after it. I would like to see Charles if it is possible. I think his C.O. may help you. He was

Major General Brent-Hampstead of Little Gilstead, Devon.

Yours sincerely,
MILES BOVEY

DEAR DOCTOR X,

Charles Watkins served under me for four years. He was satisfactory in every way, responsible and steady. He refused a commission for some time although I brought pressure to bear, because of friends he did not want to separate from. Understandable, but I was glad when he changed his mind, towards the end of the war. That was during the Italian affair. He ended up a lieutenant, I believe, but we are talking of twenty-five years ago. I am sorry to hear he is not too fit.

Yours truly,
PHILIP BRENT-HAMPSTEAD

DOCTOR Y: I'd like you to try something else, Professor. I'd like you to sit down and let yourself relax and try writing down anything that comes to you.

PATIENT: What sort of thing?

DOCTOR Y: Anything. Anything that might give us a lead in.

PATIENT: Ariadne's thread.

DOCTOR Y: Exactly so. But let's hope there is no Minotaur.

PATIENT: But perhaps he would turn out to be an old friend, too?

DOCTOR Y: Who knows? Well, will you try? A typewriter? A tape-recorder? I hear you are a very fine lecturer.

PATIENT: What a lot of talents I have that I know nothing about.

*Patient's time is up at the end of
this month. See no reason why he
should not be transferred as previously discussed to the North
Catchment.*

DOCTOR X.

*As patient is very tractable and
amenable and co-operative and will-
ing to assist with other patients I
suggest this improvement should be
consolidated by further stay here in
present conditions. There is a prec-
edent for an extension for another
three weeks.*

DOCTOR Y.

DEAR DOCTOR X,

Thank you for your letter. I am so glad that
my husband is so much better. Does he remember me and his family yet?

Yours sincerely,

FELICITY WATKINS

PATIENT: Yes, I am trying, but I don't know what to
write about.

DOCTOR Y: How about the war?

PATIENT: Which war?

DOCTOR Y: You were in the last war, in the army, in
North Africa and in Italy. You were under a Major
General Brent-Hampstead. You had a friend called
Miles Bovey.

PATIENT: Miles. Miloš? Miloš, yes, I do think I . . .
but he is dead.

DOCTOR Y: I can assure you that he is not.

PATIENT: They all of them were killed, in one way and another.

DOCTOR Y: I'd like to read about it. Will you try?

The briefing was in the C.O.'s tent. I did not know until I got there what to expect. I had been told that I had been chosen for a special mission, but not what the mission was. I certainly had no idea that it was in Yugoslavia.

The Allies had been supporting Michailovitch. There had been rumours for some months that Michailovitch was supporting Hitler and that Tito was the real opposition—which we should be giving all the aid we could. But Tito was a communist. Little was known about him. And things in Yugoslavia were confused, with ancient provincial and religious feuds being settled under the cover of the Tito-Michailovitch struggle.

The campaign to support Tito came first from the Left, which claimed that Britain was refusing to aid Tito because he was a communist, and that this was in line with the wider strategy of trying to remain the U.S.S.R.'s ally while containing or destroying local communist movements. Finally Churchill put in his oar, had gone over the heads of the "brass" to listen to better-informed left-wing advice about Yugoslavia. It had been decided to establish liaison with Tito's Partisans and to make them trust us, the Allies, particularly Britain, by convincing them that we would no longer support Michailovitch or any other Nazi-oriented movement. We would offer the Partisans arms, men, equipment. But it was not at that time known exactly where the Partisans were. It had been decided to parachute in groups of us, where Partisans were thought to be.

There were twenty of us in the C.O.'s tent that

night. We had been chosen for a miscellany of accomplishments. But we all spoke French or German or both. We could all ski, and in civilian life could be described as athletes. Mostly we were not known to each other. I sat next to a man who during the period of training became a close friend. His name was Miles Bovey.

During the next month we were put through our paces in every way, toughened up physically, taught parachuting, taught how to use radio equipment, and given an adequate knowledge of the history of the country, with particular reference to the regional and religious conflicts which we were bound to encounter.

The final briefing saw our number reduced to twelve. Two men had been killed in parachute jumps. Another had cracked up and was in the hands of the psychiatrists. There were other casualties, trivial enough, a sprained ankle, a dislocated shoulder, but sufficient to disqualify a man for the jump and the ordeal after it.

Miles Bovey and I were to be together. We were to be dropped over the Bosnian mountains, to contact the Partisans.

The final briefing was primarily to tell us how to survive if we did not immediately contact the guerrillas. Also to instruct us in the event of our capture by the Germans or by local quisling groups. These instructions were very unsophisticated compared with what we now take for granted in the way of torture, preparations to withstand torture, drugs, psychological methods. We each were given a couple of poison pills to take in the case of extreme need. But implicit in our last briefing was the idea that we were expected to resist torture if caught, to stand up to it. The idea that human beings cannot stand up to torture and psychological methods and should not be expected to, had not yet become part of general knowledge. I cannot remember this idea being expressed even by implication at any time during my war service. I would not have allowed myself to hold it, and if I had heard someone else use it I would have been shocked. And yet torture had been, was being, brought to its present height of sophistication everywhere the war had spread or might spread. We were in the condition of peasants in a technological society. We still believed in the power of heroism over any odds. I do know that men continue to resist torture against impossible odds, but frightful pressures have increased compassion: every soldier now who may have to face torture has as his property the knowledge that if he cannot stand it, if he cracks, he is not a coward and a poltroon, and that no one anywhere would think him one. Progress.

I can remember very clearly my fantasies of those few days of waiting, the daydreams that are the most useful of preparations for forthcoming stress or danger. My daydreams—or plans—might have come out of a boy's adventure story, or Beau Geste. The sordidness, the dirty-cellar nastiness, the psychological double-twisting of modern torture would have taken me completely by surprise if I had had the bad luck to be caught.

I and Miles Bovey were dropped together on a dark and very cold night into a total darkness. We might have been falling into the desert or the sea—or upwards into the nothingness of space—instead of into mountains where, we knew, were villages, and which were full of groups of fighting men, the Partisans and their opponents, the Chetniks.

Bovey dropped first. He gave me a small nod and a smile as he jumped—it was the last human contact he had. I did not even see the white of his parachute below me as I fell into the dark. The tiny gleam from the aircraft fled into the black overhead, and I swung down and down until something black came swinging up—I missed the crown of a tall pine by a few feet

and landed in a heap in a space between sharp rocks.
I hurt my leg a little. It was four in the morning, and
still night. It was cloudy: they had waited for a
cloudy night. I did not dare call out to Miles. I piled
the parachute behind a rock, where its whiteness
would be hidden, and I sat on it. It was extremely
cold. I sat on until the light came filtering down
through high conifers. I was on the side of a mountain. It was still dark under the trees when the sky
was flooded with a rosy dawn light. I saw a white
glimmer high in the air about a hundred yards away
and sat on without moving until I could determine
that it was, as I thought, Miles' parachute. But it
could have been a layer of snow on a branch.

The parachute was hanging from a high branch,
stirring and moving in the dawn wind. I emerged
from behind my rock with caution, and found, a few
feet away from the tree which held his parachute,
Miles, quite dead. He had not been shot, as I first
thought from the dark stain of blood on his forehead.
He had crashed down through the tall pine. His
parachute had caught in it. He had hung there like a
fly in a web. Trying to unhitch himself he had fallen,
and had knocked his head on a rock. The fall had not
been much more than thirty feet, and all around the
rock he had struck the forest floor was soft with old
leaf mould and littered with pine needles. It must
have happened no more than minutes before I landed. He had been as unlucky as I had been lucky.

The parachute was catching the light, making a
beacon that could be seen for miles. I had to climb
that tree and get it down. The trunk rose straight up
without a branch for twenty feet or so, but had many
sharp projecting woody bits. I went up it clinging
with my arms and legs, trying to by-pass the sharp
pieces, and trying, too, to keep a lookout for anyone
who might be coming to investigate that high patch
of glistening white. I got to the level of the first

branch, when I heard a sound that might have been a twig breaking or the crack of a rifle, and I remained quite still in indecision before thinking that nothing was more dangerous to me than that heap of stirring white. I went up the remainder of that trunk as fast as I could, and, lying face down along the projecting branch that held the parachute, wriggled out towards it. I had just grasped the silk, and was tugging and jerking it to free it from the twigs that held it, when I saw coming down over the shoulder of the mountain, five soldiers, holding their rifles pointed at me. I had no means of knowing whether they were Partisans or Chetniks. I therefore sat up on the branch like a boy caught stealing apples, and went on wriggling and jerking at the parachute to free it. I saw that the second of the soldiers was a girl. She was the most beautiful girl I have ever seen. She had thick black braids falling down her back under her cap, black oriental eyes, and a face like Aphrodite's.

I saw the Red Star on their breasts and said: I am a British soldier.

The leader said something to the others, who lowered their rifles.

He said, in French, We were expecting you.

I said: I'll just get this parachute off. As I said this, it came loose and flopped to the forest floor.

The sun had come up. The forest was infused with a reddish golden light. The birds were singing. The five under me were staring up. They were smiling. I said: But my friend has been killed.

They had not seen Miles; their attention had been on me.

The girl went straight to him, to make sure he was dead. She was a medical student who played the part of doctor for her Partisan group. I will say here that her name was Konstantina and that I loved her from that first moment, as she did me.

By the time I had slid and scrambled down the

tree, she had finished examining Miles, and now she examined my hands for scratches from the rough trunk, and saw to my leg, which was aching badly from the blow I had given it on landing. The others were already digging a grave in the forest. My first moment of meeting with the Partisans, with my love Konstantina, was a burial. They were scooping out the soft leafy soil with their hands, their belt-knives, their canteens. Before we laid Miles in the grave we took his equipment, very precious to those underequipped hand-to-mouth soldiers, and I took his poison pills from where I knew he had hidden them, in his belt.

The six of us left him there and walked down into a valley where a stream was swollen with melted snow, and across the stream and up into a mountain peak where the snow still lay thick and wintry, although the spring sun was hot enough to make us fold our great coats and carry them with our packs. There, just below the snow line, were caves, and in them the temporary headquarters of this Partisan group: they never stayed anywhere longer than a few nights.

In other countries occupied by the Nazis, there was the pattern of people fighting against them, and those who collaborated with them, out of a natural sympathy, or because of a belief that they must win. In some countries this pattern was very simple. People living in a town, a village, knew that so and so was a Nazi, and that so and so was not. Northern countries seemed more straightforward than the South. Norway for instance, or Holland. Information from occupied Holland might come that the Nazis had hanged or shot or imprisoned twelve members of the Resistance; that certain members of the Resistance had committed such and such acts of sabotage. But in Yugoslavia things were at the opposite extreme. The information was not: The Germans entered such and such a village and shot twenty Yugoslav Resistance members; but that: "The Croat collaborators entered such a Serbian village and exterminated all its inhabitants," or "Moslem troops massacred all the people in the village of ..." or, the Partisans entering such a village after sharp fighting found all the inhabitants murdered by—the Croats, or—but it was endless, with Catholics, Moslems, Montenegrins, Herzegovinians, Croats, Serbs, and so on and so on.

As I came out of the thick forest into the rock-surrounded space outside the cave, I saw a dozen or so soldiers, all of them watching our approach from where they squatted together eating their breakfast, bread and some sausage. They were all young, and some were girls. My presence was explained in a few words. I was handed a hunk of rough bread. A can of water was being passed around. For me it was a powerfully emotional moment: I was joining the famed Partisans whose exploits people were talking of everywhere. Their heroism had the simplicity of other days, a clean straightforwardness, like the heroes outside Troy. These were people like those. When I had time to look around, and examine their guns and equipment, I saw that this must be a very rough and simple fighting. If they had uniforms, they were taken from dead enemies, so that boots, caps, jackets, belts were of every sort of design. Some had no uniform, they wore anything that could serve as protection in these wild mountains, peasants' boots, students' winter knitted caps. The Red Star on their caps or on their breasts was what linked them.

This group of young soldiers contained Serbs, Croats, Montenegrins, Catholics, and Moslems. Nowhere but in these mountains, among these soldiers, these comrades, could it be possible for two people to meet, take each other's hands, call each other by name, Miro, Miloš, Konstantina, Slobo, Vido, Edvard, Vera, Mitra, Aleksa . . . take the Red Star as their bond, and forget the rest.

Now, re-creating in imagination that moment, when I came out of the forest with that group, and sat down with them all eating the peasant bread and drinking cold mountain water, I think most of all of something that I took for granted then—their extreme youth. No one was more than twenty-five. I was not myself. Among them, and among those I met in the mountains in the next few weeks were men and women who after the war became the rulers of the new Yugoslavia, a nation fought for and created by the very young.

I believe that a man who fought with those young people who now has to stand up on a platform in a big hall to lecture, or teach, must often, a quarter of a century later, look down on the upturned faces of students who are rioting and sullen and critical and undisciplined and who in every country of the world reject what their society offers them ... this man, a professor perhaps, with responsibility, a place in society, looks at those faces and thinks how young people exactly like them, "children" to their elders, fought the most vicious and terrifying army in history, Hitler's, fought short of weapons, short of warm clothes, often without food, always outnumbered—fought and won, and created a new nation.

I was with them for—I could say three months. It is only in love and in war that we escape from the sleep of necessity, the cage of ordinary life, to a state where every day is a high adventure, every moment falls sharp and clear like a snowflake drifting slowly past a dark glistening rock, or like a leaf spinning down to the forest floor. Three months of ordinary living can be not much more than the effort of turning over from one side to another in a particularly heavy uncomfortable sleep. That time in the mountains with that band of young soldiers—it is as if I remember every breath I took. Remembering that time is as if a friend's eyes rest in loving curiosity on your face, and you feel your face spread in a smile because of the warmth the two of you generate.

The band remained in numbers between twelve and thirty. A man, or a girl, would come quietly into the camp with a handshake, a smile, slide off his—or her—pack and rifle, and become one of us. Or someone would leave quietly to take a message, or to reconnoitre, or to slip back to a home village to fetch food or supplies. We stayed on that mountainside outside the caves for not more than two days. I had to be taken to the H.Q. of the Partisans, to transfer messages and to collect their messages and news to take back to North Africa. We had to move carefully, because the mountains were full not only of Chetniks but of ordinary villagers who had fled away from their homes to live the life of outlaws until the coming winter's snows would force them down again, to death, or to servitude under the Germans or Chetniks.

To stand on a high mountain's shoulder, and look down and around over hundreds of miles of mountains and valleys and rivers and hillsides: it was the wildest scene on earth, with nothing moving there in all that space but a bird hanging on the air, or, very far away, the smoke rising from a village too distant to see if it was the smoke of pillage, or from an ordinary hearth. Empty. Emptiness. The world as it was before man filled and fouled it. But, as you stood there and waited and watched, a different conviction took hold. On the slope of a mountain high on the other side of a racing mountain stream there was a flash of metal which, no matter how you stared and peered, was not repeated: the sun had caught a rifle barrel, or a knife. Trees two miles away that were painted yellow sage and viridian and blue-grey by spring had a smudge of indistinctness over them that was—a tree late-in-leaf, a green so lightly spread over the structure of bough that it seemed grey?—or was it

smoke from a Partisan's fire? The binoculars brought
the hillside opposite close into the eye, and the
smudge was indeed smoke, not new leafage, but the
people under the trees, who had made the fire, were
wearing grey indistinct clothing, and it was hard to
say whether they were villagers, Chetniks, or Partisans. Or, at night, keeping our cooking fire low
behind an earthwork or a pile of cut branches, making the flames clear and bright to forbid the sight of
smoke to an enemy on a near slope, a quick leap of
red faded out again into the dark opposite and we
knew that a mile or half a mile away another fire had
escaped the shield of banked earth or brush or branch
and had been caught and confined again—but by
whom, friend or foe? One of us would then, with a
smile and a nod, or the stern dedication of the very
young, whose duty forbids smiling and lightness, slide
away from our low circle of flamelight into the trees
and reappear an hour or five hours later with: "People from the village." Or, "Croats." Or, with him (or
her) would come in from the trees a group of soldiers
wearing the Red Star, greeting us with the handshake
that was the promise of the life we would all live
after the war, when the fighting was over.

Those vast mountains, in which we moved like
the first people on earth, discovering riches at every
opening of the forest, flowers, fruit, flocks of pigeons,
deer, streams of running splashing water full of fish,
these mountains were host to a hundred, no, a thousand groups, all moving quietly, beneath the great
trees, eyes always on the alert for enemies, people
who slept with their hands on their rifles, and who
were skilled to know a friend as much by an instant
recognition of comradeship and optimistic heroism as
by the Red Star.

When this war was over, we all knew, and our
trusting hands, our smiles, our dedication promised
this—this land that was so rich and so beautiful

would flower into a loving harmony that was as much a memory as a dream for the future. It was as if every one of us had lived so, once upon a time, at another time, in a country like this, with sharp sweet-smelling air and giant uncut trees, among people descended from a natural royalty, those to whom harmfulness and hate were alien. We were all bound in together by another time, another air. Anything petty and ignoble was an outlaw. We could remember only nobility.

If I say all this and put my love in a sound place it was because it was a love that flowered from the time and the place. No, of course I don't mean that if I had met her in an ordinary way, in peace, we would not have recognised each other. But our love in those weeks was an aspect of the fine high comradeship of the group, whose individuals did not matter, because an individual could only be important insofar as he or she was a pledge for the future, and where individuals came and went and were always the same, being by shared nature high and fine and foreign to the consciousness of ugliness of race or region or a hostile religiosity. Our love was carried, or contained by the group, a flower of it, and this although some comrades did not approve of it, thought and said that a war of this kind was no place for love. But such criticisms were made within the spirit of comradeship, with a simple frankness, without spite or need to hurt. There was nothing we could not say to each other. There was no criticism we could not make and which, thought over, and followed or resisted, did not become of a conscious growth which—this was assumed by every one of us, was the greatest of our contributions to this war which was a war not only against the bad in our own nation (while I was with them I felt with them, felt Yugoslav), collaborators, Chetniks, the selfish rich, but against all the evil in the world. In those high mountains we fought against

Evil, and were sure to win, for the stars in their courses were on our side, whose victory would be at last when the poor and meek and the humble had inherited the earth, and the lion would lie down with the lamb, and a loving harmony would prevail over the earth. We knew all this because—it was as if we remembered it. And besides, did we not live like this now, loving each other and the world? With rifles in our hands, grenades in our pockets, gelignite in our packs, moving as silently as thieves among the towering trees of those magnificent forests, we knew ourselves to be pledges for the future, and utterly unimportant in ourselves, because as individuals we could have no importance, and besides, we were already as good as dead. Of the men and women I lived with, fought with, during those months, very many were killed, the majority—as they knew they would be. It did not matter. What was spilt could not be lost, because at last love had come to birth in man, communism and its Red Star of hope shone out for all the working poor, for all the suffering everywhere, to see and to follow. Within that general Love, I and the Partisan girl loved each other. We hardly spoke of it, were seldom alone, were soldiers, thinking soldiers' thoughts. When we did find ourselves together and alone, it was not because it had been planned by us. An accident of our group life had sent us off to forage for food in an abandoned village, or we were put together on guard duty. But we *were* on duty and so had to be responsible. I do not remember when I kissed her first, but I remember our jokes that it had taken us so long to kiss. We slept together once in the frenzy of sorrow after I was told that in a week I would be finished with my mission and with Yugoslavia—and with Konstantina.

That was after I had been taken to Tito's headquarters, had given and taken information—had done what I had come to do. It was then a question of how

I could get away again. That could not be by air. It was dangerous enough dropping men in, but at that stage impossible for aircraft to land. I had to make my way to the coast, from where I was taken in a small boat by fishermen to an island where I met up with others who had been on missions in Greece and Yugoslavia. And how we got back to North Africa from there is another story.

The weeks before I made liaison with the guide who was to take me to the coast were full of dangerous fighting. Our group blew up a railway, destroyed a couple of bridges, fought two bloody battles with groups of Chetniks much larger than ours. After these battles we were weakened and depleted. Some of us were wounded. Vido, the leader, was dead, and Miloš, who was an old school-friend of Konstantina's, became group leader. She became his second-in-command, and was even more busy than she had been. For there was much more to do, and many fewer people to do it all. But new people kept coming in. I remember one evening we were on a mountain flank above a village which we knew to be occupied by German and Croat troops. It was a village where Miloš had friends—or rather, had had friends. He was talking of how, next day, he might slip down, with one of the girls, to the village, in disguise. It was a question of getting hold of an ordinary peasant dress and kerchief. Vera, one of the girls, had had such an outfit, but it had been lost in recent fighting. As we sat there that night, talking in whispers, huddled in together, very hungry and cold because we did not dare light a fire, we saw two people move out of the bushes towards us. Rifles flew up, but Miloš shouted out, *No*—and it was just in time. Two boys ran forward silently over the grass, smiling. Miloš embraced them. They were from the village, had heard of our presence near them in the mountains, had come to join us. They were brothers, sixteen, and

seventeen. Neither had so much as held a rifle before.
They had brought with them two old revolvers from
the 1914 war. Also some bread and sausage—even
more welcome than the revolvers. That night we began training them in the art of guerrilla warfare and
in a couple of weeks these two boys were as skilled
and resourceful as any one of us. If memories of
wartime are frighteningly precious, the main reason is
that in wartime we learn again that peacetime should
never allow to be forgotten. That "every cook can
learn to govern the state." In wartime every little
clerk, every confined housewife, learns what he or she
is capable of. In peacetime these two schoolboys
would have become what the pettiness of village life
would have allowed them to become. In England
boys of that age, or certainly middle-class boys, are
spoiled children. In war, in our guerrilla group, they
were trackers, crack shots, brilliant spies, thieves and
pilferers, able to march twenty-four hours at a stretch
remaining lively and alert, able to find berries,
mushrooms, edible roots, able to track down a deer or
a pheasant and kill it silently without wasting precious ammunition. What could possibly happen to
them in the life after the war—to them and the
millions like them in the countries where guerrillas
and partisans and the underground operated—to
match up to what they were given in war? That is,
unless they went to prison (where many still are) and
learned a different kind of skilled endurance. In the
less than a month that I was with the two boys, I had
learned again what I had already understood in my
first day with the Partisans—that any human being
anywhere will blossom into a hundred unexpected
talents and capacities simply by being given the opportunity to use them. Both those boys survived the
war. Both are now high in the government of their
country. They had their education with the guerrillas
in the mountains and the forests.

They were not the only ones to come secretly from the villages. By such recruitment, our group went up again to nearly thirty, seeming always to get younger and younger. The "old ones" would joke about "the children." Miloš was "the old man." He was twenty-four.

Although it was summer, we were always short of food, and our medical supplies were low. Konstantina was reduced to a few bandages and ointment. It was decided that she and I would go to a village where her aunt lived, to try and get supplies. The plan was for us to move up to the edge of a field above the village, where the women would be at work among the maize. Konstantina knew the village well, and the habits of the people. She knew they were sympathetic to us, and hated the occupying Croats. The women would bring a skirt, a blouse, a kerchief. Konstantina would put them on, join the working women, return with them to the village at midday, and go to her aunt's house. There she would get her aunt to find bandages, disinfectants, medicines, and food. There was only one point of danger that we could foresee, which was that at this time of the year the women often did not return to their homes for the midday meal, but took it in the fields as they worked. But one of them could run back to the village and fetch Konstantina's aunt to us in the forest. Or, if all this was too dangerous, if the occupying troops were too alert, then we would have to stay at the edge of the field above the village, and one of the women would take the message down to the aunt, and the supplies could be brought to where we were.

But it all went off very simply. We left our friends early, before the sun was up, and had reached the village by mid-morning. We slid on our stomachs to the edge of the field. Often fields were guarded. But it was apparently a pleasant peaceful scene. The women were hoeing among the tall maize plants, talking and laughing. Konstantina called out to a woman who looked up, startled, and who then showed how well she had been taught by war—she took in the situation at once, gave us a single gesture, "I understand, keep quiet," and worked her way slowly towards us, while keeping up her chat with another woman ten yards away. When she reached us, she and Konstantina talked in low voices, one from the field, the other from thick bushes at the edge of it. The woman's lips scarcely moved. In this and in her quickness and her caution we could see very well the state of that village under its occupying troops. She said that with the women in the fields was the wife of a man known to be sympathetic to the Germans. It was necessary to think of a plan to get rid of her. But luck was with us. After we had lain hidden in the bushes for not more than an hour, watching the lively women working, this dangerous woman of her own accord went back to her house. She said she had bread to be baked. After that it went fast. One of the women slipped back to her house, and fetched a bundle of clothes, which was thrown into the bushes where we lay. In a few moments Konstantina had changed from a soldier to a young girl. She walked out in a full blue skirt and a white blouse and white kerchief from the trees, and joined with the women, bending and making the movements of someone who held and used a hoe. In a few minutes all the women went off together to the village, Konstantina among them.

The field that sloped down to the village was quite empty. The maize plants were a full strong glossy green. All the trees and bushes around the field were in the lush fullness of early summer. The sky was deep and blue. It was rather hot. The maize plants were at that stage when they have reached their full growth, but still seem as if the push of the sap is sending them up. They were very straight and the stems were as crisp as sugarcane. The tassel on each plant had turned white, but only just. The acres of tall green plants were topped with waving white braided tassels, but they were a greenish white still. The cobs pushing out heavily from the stems were not filled out yet, and the soft silk that fell from the end of each cob was fresh and new. None had dried. Each cob had its tongue of gleaming ruddy silk, a welling of soft red. That morning it had rained. The tips of the arched leaves and the dangling red floss dripped great glistening raindrops. The earth smelled sweet and fresh. A lively steam went up off the field. Everything in that field was at a peak of young but mature liveliness. Even a week later, the curve would have turned, and begun to sink, with the arching leaves just tingeing yellow, the crests on the plants very hard and white, the dark red of the tassels drying and clotting. It was like looking at a wave just before it turns over and breaks.

Down in the village some smoke went up into the blue. There was no one to be seen. It was absolutely silent. Yet the village was occupied, and we knew that two weeks ago a dozen people had been shot in the main street. They had sent supplies to the Partisans, and for this adventure today, people might be killed, if we bungled it. But things continued to go well.

Soon a dozen women came up from the village into the field, taking their time about it. They picked up their hoes where they had dropped them. Konstantina now had a hoe and worked with the rest. I could have sworn that she was working for the pleasure of it, remembering peace and village life. She slowly hoed her way to the edge of the field, and in a moment had dropped the hoe and rolled in beside me. Under her full skirts were suspended parcels of bread, meat, sausage, even eggs. Her aunt went past, her hoe rising and falling; a package flew into the

bush where we lay hidden, and I reached up to grab
the precious medical supplies off the branches, like a
fruit. By then Konstantina was out of her peasant
woman's garb and was a soldier again. She threw the
bundle of clothes back into the field; and after a swift
good-bye, good-bye, between her and the woman
hoeing not six feet away, we were off and away. The
raid was a success. There were no consequences to
the villagers. And before that winter our people
routed the enemy and the village became itself again.

We stowed the goods carefully about us. We
were now heavily laden, and it was hard to walk
lightly, as we had to. We had about ten miles to go
before meeting up with our group, which we knew to
be making its way to a peak which we could see
straight in front of us. But between us and this peak
were lower mountains, rivers, valleys. It was not an
easy ten miles.

When we had gone about half way, we stopped
on the flank of a mountain before the one we were
making for. It was now midafternoon. The sun was in
front of us and shining into our eyes. The sky was still
cloudless, and it was all a glitter and a dazzle of light
off sky, leaves, grass, rocks. We decided to rest for a
few minutes. It was not that we were prepared to
relax our guard, or to become careless. But we had
finished our task, and we believed that we had not
endangered our allies in the village. We sat with our
backs to a big rock, and held hands like children. In
front of us was a glade that opened out among very
large old trees down the hillside. At one side of the
glade were some low rocks, where the yellow light lay
broken and dappled. A small tree at the foot of the
glade was a cloud of creamy pink blossom on which
butterflies clustered. It was very silent.

Into this scene of perfect sylvan peace came a
deer. Or rather, it was a question of realising that the
deer had been there, looking at us, for some time. It

stood about twenty yards away, near the pile of rocks. It was because the light lay broken over rock and plants and deer that we had not seen the animal. Now it was hard to understand why we had not seen it. It was a pretty sight, a golden beast, with its fur warm and rich and sunny, and its little sharp forward-pointing horns black and glossy. We stood up. I was thinking that if we had so easily overlooked a deer that stood so close, we might equally have overlooked an enemy. Probably she was thinking the same. Now I wondered for a moment if I should shoot the beast, and carry it back to camp with us. But it was always dangerous to shoot. We did not know who else was on that mountain slope—perhaps watching us, just as the deer had done, before we saw it. And we were very heavily loaded. The thought of shooting it faded. I was pleased to let it go. For it looked so very delightful standing there, its head slightly lowered, looking at us rather sideways out of its eyes. It was a small deer, not much higher than Konstantina's waist. I was suddenly incredibly happy. This appearance of the beautiful animal seemed to me a crown to that successful day. I looked at Konstantina, to share the pleasure, but she was not smiling. She was serious, severe. There was a small frown between her brows that I knew well: it showed when she was puzzled, in doubt. She was looking doubtfully at this deer. The beast was much closer. I remember thinking that perhaps we had moved forward towards it without knowing we had, just as we had stood up automatically after seeing it—alerted by it, as if it were in fact an enemy. I thought that the deer's pretty sidling prancing movements were too slight and delicate to have advanced it so fast. Then the deer was very close. It kept making the same movement, a light shaking semi-circular movement with its horns, and I felt I had to watch this movement, it was so graceful. And then, as the thought came into my mind that this small pretty beast might be dangerous, Konstantina made a sharp exclamatory warning noise, and moved in front of me, as the beast took a jump forward and sliced out with its sharp black horns.

And then nothing happened. The deer stood there, blood dripping from its horns which now were lowered, immediately in front of Konstantina, who was standing between me and it. Then she began to slide downwards. It was as if she had decided to let herself sag at the knees. I caught her, my hands under her armpits.

I said, "Konstantina," in wonder, or even admonishment. I still had not quite understood that this charming creature had wounded her.

Then her weight dragged her down to the forest floor, and I turned her face up and I saw that her eyes were closed and that blood poured from her stomach. She was greenish white.

And now I did understand. There followed minutes of impotent anguished incompetence. In a package that lay two feet away from her were medical supplies, but there was nothing there that could staunch such a wound. Later I understood that it did not matter, that she was not saveable. I pulled up her jacket, pulled down her soldier's trousers, exposed her stomach. The deer's horn, sharp as a surgeon's knife, had cut straight across her entrails. I did not think she would open her eyes again. I believed she would die at once, for her pulse had already nearly gone and her face had shrunk with death. I looked for my poison pill, for I did not want her to suffer the pain of that terrible wound, but before I had found it, she opened her eyes, smiled, closed them again and was dead.

I laid her on the forest floor. I saw that the deer had retreated a little; it was standing near the rocks where I had seen it first. Again I wondered if I should shoot it, and this time knew if I did it would be in revenge. It did not occur to me that it might still be dangerous. It had killed Konstantina because she had stepped in front of me to save me from the slicing horns. It might again come close and kill me. But I did not think of it. I forgot the deer.

I knew I had to bury Konstantina. I had nothing to dig a grave with. But by then I had assisted in many forest burials. I knelt down and began scooping up leaves with my hands. The light was very heavy and yellow and strong. It laid a yellow patina over Konstantina's face.

I went on digging. It was very easy. The leaf mould was many autumns' work. The rich sweet-smelling crumbling soil which was the flesh of the forest leaves came up in great double handfuls. I worked on and on steadily and methodically, trying to get it done fast and well. For I knew that if I and Konstantina did not appear by ten that night, our people would send out search parties to look for us. They knew we would be slower and more vulnerable than usual—and what we carried was precious.

It would be evening very soon ... Then it was evening. By then I had dug a pit from the leaf mould about five feet deep and three wide. I slid her into the pit, so that she lay straight in it, and I lay on my stomach on the edge of the pit, and covered her face with some fresh green leaves. I laid her hands on her breast. I threw the leaf mould back over her. I was swearing and crying all the time, but silently: later I discovered I had bitten my lips through. Quite soon the place where she lay in the forest was shown only by a roughing of the surface of last autumn's leaves. I could not mark her grave then. Standing by it I picked out three trees whose intersecting lines met here. I cut big chips of bark out of the trees, and then rubbed earth into the white gashes so that an enemy might not notice them.

When the war was over I took a plane to Belgrade, a train to the village we had visited that day, and walked with a friend into the mountains. The friend was now a government official, and he had been a member of our group—but after I left it. We met in London. Together we found that place on the mountainside by the by now old scars on the three trees. We put up a simple headstone. On it was this inscription:

KONSTANTINA RIBAR

PARTISAN

SHE GAVE HER LIFE FOR HUMANITY

And of course, for me.

By the time she was buried, the setting sun was straight above the peak I had to reach before moonrise. The glade was now flooded with yellow evening light. And as I picked up the packets and parcels of food and medicaments, trying to make two peoples' burdens into a convenient load for one, I realised that all this time, two or three hours, or more, that deer had stood there, twenty paces away, among the rocks. I believe it was the sound of its hooves clicking on a stone that made me look up. It was still facing me, and its head again began to make the delicate sidling movements as I took a few steps nearer to pass it. On one of its horns was a stain—Konstantina's blood, that might very easily have been mine. I stood still, looking at the beast. I did not understand. I could not understand why, having attacked and killed, it did not simply run away. That it should have stood there, watching me during my labour of digging out the forest floor, and then burying Konstantina, without coming nearer and making itself felt at all—I did not understand it. By now I had slid into that detached, dreamy state that follows an excess of emotion. That glowing little beast standing there, with its elegant horns lowered, apparently waiting, for no reason at all, only added to the sharp unfocus of the scene.

I stood opposite the beast and stared at it. I was about fifteen paces away. This time I saw that the beast was a doe. And that it had a loose staggering look to it—exhaustion. I saw that it had lately given birth. Then I saw the fawn.

The little creature lay beside the rocks facing towards the setting sun. Its softly glowing coat was full of health. Over it, as if standing on guard, was a tall plant, with clear bright leaves, that fanned and sprayed out all around the fawn, so that it lay under a fountain. The fawn was perfect, a triumph, too dazzlingly so, as if those vast mountains and forests had elected this baby animal in the sunny glade to represent them, but the scene was overcharged with meaning and with beauty.

Then I saw that on its hide lay some dried threads of the birth liquor, and on its creamy stomach lolled the fat red birth cord, fresh and glistening. Three or four days later, the cord would be withered and gone, the fawn's coat licked and clean, the fawn, like a human child, or like the maize plants I had seen that morning, at a crest of promise and perfection. But to witness a birth is to be admitted into Nature's workshop, and there life and death work together. The sight of the cord, the still unlicked coat, rescued the creature from pathos, restored it to its real vulnerability, its terrible weakness. Yet its eyes regarded me quietly, without fear. For between it and me stood its mother. I think that the fawn had not yet clambered to its feet. Probably the two soldiers, coming into the glade, had interrupted the birth scene, had in some way upset the mother and baby in the ritual they had to accomplish, had thrown things out of balance. And there stood the deer, and it was only now that I saw it was standing shakily, for its back legs trembled with weakness where they were planted on the soft grass.

I walked at a careful distance around the mother and her baby, keeping my eyes on the exhausted beast who slowly moved about to keep her lowered horns pointing at me. Behind her, the fawn lay presented in the glowing light under the plant, which was probably a fennel, or a dill.

I could only move slowly. I was carrying something like two hundred pounds of food and medicaments. When I reached the bottom of the glade, I looked back and saw that the fawn was in the act of struggling up on to its long slender fragile stalklike legs. The deer still watched me. And so I left the glade with its new grave, where the mother deer had one blood-dulled horn pointed at me, and the little fawn stood upright under its shining green fountain.

DEAR DOCTOR Y,

No, I am very sure that Charles Watkins was not at any time in Yugoslavia. I am unable to account for his insistence that he was there during the war. When I got back from the war, I was in fairly bad shape. This is what Charles and I had in common. We spent some months together in a cottage I had in Cornwall. We both talked a good deal about our experiences. This probably cured us both. Even after this lapse of time I could give you a pretty detailed account of Charles' war, which is almost as vivid to me as "my" war. I find my memories of my two descents into Yugoslavia the most vivid of my life. If I were to forget those months, I would be forgetting events and people who formed me more fundamentally than any other. I suppose I could be regarded as lucky. I know that Charles thinks—or thought—that I was. "My" war was very different from his. I couldn't say that I enjoyed "my" war, but it was certainly like being in a highly coloured dream, whereas I am afraid Charles' war must have been like a long tedious nightmare. He had very much more than his fair share of boring repetitious slog, if you can agree that danger can be boring.

If I may intrude a personal note that is probably beyond what you asked for from me, I find the current scene frightening because yet again great numbers of young people, whether for or against war, whether they would welcome conscription or not, don't know that the worst thing about war is that it can be so boring. I would never have believed that such a very short space of time—twenty-five years—would have again made it possible to see war as glamorous. The point is, you see, that "my" war was, rather, or for some of the time. Whereas Charles used to say that "his" war's fortunes were maximum hard routine work, maximum physical discomfort, maximum boredom, and pretty steady doses of danger and death. This wasn't necessarily true for all the men who got dealt his particular hand— Dunkirk, North Africa, Italy, Second Front. Some had quite extensive patches of respite and even enjoyment. But Charles' luck was different. In fact it was a bit of a joke between us, when we traced his course of events, how he always seemed to have missed out on possible leave, or a lucky transfer to somewhere easier. We used to say that he had been fighting a modern war, for five years—I mean, of course, modern for then, he was fighting the Second World War—but that I had regressed to a much earlier style of war. Of course that is a pretty unsatisfactory generalisation when you think of the contribution guerrilla fighting made to our winning the war.

If Charles believes that I am dead, perhaps it might help to see that I am not?

Sincerely,
MILES BOVEY

DEAR DOCTOR X,

I am only too happy to come and see Charles any time it will help him. But I don't want to bring James and Philip to see their father. I don't think they ought to have that inflicted on them. I must say that I am surprised you suggest it at all. I know Charles is ill, but other people in the family are as important as he is. Of course it does not matter that it is painful for me to see Charles as he is now, but the boys are fifteen and fourteen years old and should be spared such things at their age. So I am afraid I am refusing to bring them.

Yours sincerely,
FELICITY WATKINS

DEAR DOCTOR Y,

Of course I am ready at any time to have my husband home. It will be very painful for us all, but I would do anything to help him get well again if you think it will help. I am sure that once he is in his own home and with his family and his own things around him he will remember who he is.

Yours sincerely,
FELICITY WATKINS

It was ten in the morning. In a large public room on the first floor, which overlooked a formal pattern of flowerbeds now dug over and left exposed to catch the first frosts, a couple of beeches in their end-of-year colouring, and some late-flowering roses, sat, or lounged, about forty or fifty people. None looked out of the windows. They were of any age, size, type and of both sexes. But the middle-aged predominated, and particularly, middle-aged women. Some watched television, or rather, since the programme had not yet started, were looking at the test picture, of some water rushing down over some rocks, under spring trees in full flower. Some knitted. Some chatted. It would be easy to think that one had walked into the lounge of a second-rate or provincial hotel, except for the characteristic smell of drugs.

There were tables as well as easy chairs dotted about the room, and at a table in full centre, which was spread all over with a particularly complicated game of patience, sat a young girl, all by herself. She was a brunette, of a Mediterranean type. She had smooth dark hair, large black eyes, olive skin. She was slender, but rounded, but not excessively the latter, thus conforming both to current ideas about beauty in women, and that moment's fashion. She wore a black crepe dress that fitted her smoothly over her breasts and hips. The sleeves were long and tight. The neck was high and close. The dress had simple white linen cuffs and a round white collar. These were slightly grubby. This dress would have been appropriate for a housekeeper, a perfect secretary, or a Victorian young lady spending a morning with her accounts, if it had not ended four inches below the top of the thigh. In other words, it was a particularly lopped mini-dress. It would be hard to imagine a type of dress more startling as a mini-dress. The contrast between its severity, its formality, and the long naked legs was particularly shocking: it shocked. The girl's legs were not quite bare. She wore extremely fine pale grey tights. But she did not wear any panties. She sat with her legs sprawled apart in a way that suggested that she had forgotten about them, or that she had enough to do to control and manage the top half of her, without all the trouble of remembering her legs and her sex as well. Her private parts were evident as a moist dark fuzzy patch, and their exposure gave her a naïve, touching, appealing look.

There were two female nurses sitting among the patients. Both were poor women, badly paid, working class, and were only here because their husbands were not paid enough to keep a family according to the standards which television promises the nation as its right. These women looked at the young girl more often than at any other patient. It was with a resentment that ten times the wage they earned would not have been enough to assuage.

Both had female children, adolescents; and both were familiar with fights over makeup and dresses. One woman liked her daughter in very short dresses and plenty of makeup, and the other did not, but this difference between them had vanished under the pressure of a profounder disquiet. It was because of the violent battles both had with this girl, Violet, whose mini-dresses were shorter even than fashion demanded, and which both thought disgusting, even without the fact that she refused to wear panties. And her accusations of them, the nurses (mother-and-authority-figures, as both had been trained to understand very well) that they were old-fashioned, girl-hating, sex-hating, *old*, and so forth, were exactly the same, but exactly, word for word as both had during their fights with their own daughters. The fact that Violet was crazy, and that she used their own daughters' arguments for not wearing panties, so that she always looked provocative and was a source of trouble with already unstable male patients, was seditious of the framework of ordinary morality. Of course, one nurse's framework was very much more liberal—the one who was happy to let her daughter wear mini-skirts and make up her eyes with false lashes and loads of coloured grease—than the other's; but to both of them the thought was brought home several times a day, that these stands, liberal, and old-fashioned, stands on which both women prided themselves, were made to look irrelevant and even ridiculous by Miss Violet Stoke's sitting there with her legs apart showing everything she had got. And on principle. In the name of freedom, the rights of youth, and the advancement of womanhood. Both women had confessed to themselves, to each other, and to doctors that of all the patients in their charge, Violet made it hardest to maintain self-control. They were prepared to say that they hated her, an attitude which some of the doctors in authority deplored, as lacking in insight and control, and others applauded, as showing a releasing honesty and frankness—releasing to the patient as much as to themselves. They both knew quite well that her way of sitting there, dressed in a parody of a housekeeper's dress with her sex on view was a challenge to their sanity. Besides, she was not washing as much as she ought (a very familiar sign of her illness) and she smelled, apart from smelling sickly from the drugs.

She was also beautiful, and in an exotic and un-British way.

She sat alone, for she knew she had always been alone. She was playing patience because it is a game that is played alone. All around her, if only people had the eyes to see it, was a space where flickered and darted flames of hatred, a baleful fire. She was isolated by this aura of hatred, which only she knew about. She was aware that the two middle-aged women observed her more than they did the others, but she did not see them as they were, poor women doing an unpleasant job because they were not qualified for better paid jobs. She saw them three times lifesize, arbitrarily powerful, dangerous, frightening. She hated them wholeheartedly because they were middle-aged, dowdy, tired, suburban, poor, and because that morning and for the last week of mornings they had told her she must put on panties as well as tights, and that she looked disgusting, and that their task was difficult enough without having men getting excited on her account, and that she was selfish, antisocial, disobedient.

When she looked at them, she was possessed by a young person's terror that she was looking at her own future, for it so happened that her life had taught her very early that it was easy, and indeed, common, to be young and very pretty and gay, and then soon afterwards, to be middle-aged, tired and disregarded.

In some of Goya's earlier pictures, not those that describe war or madness, but the gay and gallant pictures, there is something that disturbs, but you don't know what it is. Not at first. It is because of any group of those people, the charming, the formal, the pastoral, the essentially civilised, there is always one that looks straight out of the group, out of the canvas, into the eyes of the person who is looking at the picture. This person who refuses to conform to the conventions of the picture the artist has set him in, questions and, in fact, destroys the convention. It is as if the artist said to himself: I suppose I've got to paint this kind of picture, it is expected of me—*but I'll show them*. As you stand and gaze in, all the rest of the picture fades away, the charmers in their smiles and flounces, the young heroes, the civilisation, all these dissolve away because of that long straight gaze from the one who looks back out of the canvas and says silently that he or she knows it is all a load of old socks. He is there to tell you that he thinks so.

The eyes of Violet Stoke had the same effect, that of negating the rest of her appearance—and perhaps of saying the same thing.

As if it were all not enough of a challenge, the shocking contrast between formal black dress and the lower nakedness, the smooth dancer's hair and the sad moist patch below, the social position of "the cardplayer" and the isolation spread around her by her fear and hatred, as if these were not enough (to which must be added the social and possibly less important comment made by the expensiveness of her dress, shoes, handbag, any of which was a week's salary for the poor nurses) there was this other contrast. The girl's black eyes looked directly out of the picture, and if you followed that gaze, let yourself slide inwards, so that you slid into her head, what you became part of was not the violence of hatred, but a puddle of tears, and a little girl's tears at that: Oh love me, hold me, forgive me, and never let me go, don't make me grow up. What she was feeling inside that façade of upsetting contrasts, was what a very small girl feels when she has been beaten or illtreated by a powerful parent, and she knows quite well it will happen again next time the parent is angry or drunk or frightened himself—or herself. She was all victim, betrayed, tormented, vulnerable, and a sponge for love.

She had been sitting there, playing patience in a way which was the cry: *Why do you all make me stay alone like this?* when into the public room came a tall good-looking man of about fifty. He had wavy dark grey hair that had been black, he had blue eyes, he had a good smile.

Unlike others who had come in while she sat there, saying silently: *I dare you to come and sit with me*, and had gone to sit elsewhere, he went straight towards her, sat down, and immediately pulled a pipe out of his pocket and started on the business of filling and lighting it. He wore a casual jacket, and a dark blue sweater under it. He looked like a man who had been an amateur athlete.

He was Professor Charles Watkins and he and Violet were friends.

Now, without asking him, she swept her cards together and began dealing for a poker game which was a favourite of theirs, which meant that each played three hands, seven cards a hand, with four cards wild, and high-low into the bargain. She nearly always won these games, not because she was brighter than the Professor, but because she cared more.

"Threes, fives, sevens, Jacks wild," she announced, in a companionable girl's voice.

They played. She won.

She shuffled and said: "Did you see him today?"

"Yes, Doctor X is away."

"What did he say?"

"He says I've got to be moved somewhere. I can't go on here the way I am."

"Why, why can't you? Oh, it is too much!"

"He just keeps saying that this is a reception hospital and he can't bend the rules any more."

"Don't you let them send you to the North Catchment then, whatever else."

"Don't worry, I won't."

She dealt.

"Twos and sixes and Queens wild," she said.

They played in silence. She won.

"Haven't you got any money at all?" she cried, a petulant and wilful child, as it were demanding a new doll, or dress.

"The Professor is quite loaded, so they tell me," he said. "But that doesn't help me much, does it?"

"I could get a job and earn, I have had jobs. Never for long though."

"I'm sure I could too. I'm very handy around the wards, after all. I could wash up in a restaurant or work in a bar?"

"Would we earn enough to live on?"

"We could try."

"Oh do let's. Oh please."

"Yes ... we wouldn't—force each other. We wouldn't—impose."

"No. We'd help each other, I'm sure of that."

She dealt. It was for five cards.

"We'll play it straight, cool and classical," she said.

They played. She won.

"Aren't you cheating at all?" he enquired.

This meant, was she identifying more than was inevitable with one or other of the hands she was playing, for in this personal version of poker they had evolved, the different hands stood for aspects of themselves. They might or might not know what each other's different hands stood for. But he knew now that when she dealt for the classic game, this meant she was feeling calmer and more in control of her different selves than when she dealt three hands each and with so many cards wild. And so on.

Yesterday morning, she had let him win the first game, making it clear that it was because she knew he had had a bad night.

"Was I cheating? Did it look as if I was? I was trying not to."

"Well perhaps I was too, a little."

"But I *won*," she claimed fiercely. "*I* won, didn't I?"

"Yes, you did, Violet. You always do."

"Yes, I do, don't I?"

She dealt again, three hands each, five cards.

They played, she won.

"Are your sons coming to see you?"

"No. She won't bring them."

"Don't mind. Oh please don't. I'll go and make you some tea. Would you like some?"

"I'd like some tea, yes, but I don't mind that they aren't coming. What I mind is, that I don't mind, when *they* are so sure that I ought to. Who are *they*, though? I know you. I suppose you are my daughter. They say I haven't had a daughter?"

"Oh I wish I was your daughter. Oh I do so wish I were. But you'd be like the rest, I suppose."

"Perhaps I would. How do I know I am a good father to my sons? But that is *then*. You are now. I am good for you, Vi? Am I?"

"Yes. But you like me, you see. My families don't."

"Yes, I do like you Violet. Very much."

She went off to the little kitchen used by patients to make themselves tea, cocoa, toast, sandwiches. When she returned with two cups of tea, a woman patient had sat herself near the handsome and distinguished Professor, but at Violet's killing black glances, she hastily withdrew.

"I heard Doctor X say that Doctor Y favoured you unfairly."

"Yes, Doctor Y told me that too."

"And Doctor X said to Nurse Black that he thought it was possible you are shamming."

"That I do remember?"

"That you remember more than you let on."

"What I remember they won't have at any price, that's my trouble."

"Doctor X said there was a case last year when a man went on pretending he couldn't remember his wife, but then Doctor X caught him out and he had to go home."

"I don't remember my wife or my mistress. I am very attractive to women, that's clear enough. They both hate my guts."

"I don't think that is very funny, if you do."

"I'm sorry."

"I don't hate you."

"No, but you aren't a woman."

"No. Oh no, I'm not. Oh no, no."

"You look very like my girl, the one that was killed in Yugoslavia."

"You never were in Yugoslavia."

"But I—oh very well. I don't see why you should mind that."

"But I *do* mind. They *know* you weren't in Yugoslavia."

"All the same, you do look like her."

"Perhaps I am the first person that belongs to your new memory. I mean, the people in the ward and me and Doctor Y and Doctor X, we are what you've made your new memory out of?"

"Not Doctor X!"

"Oh, I don't know, I suppose he's not as bad as that. I mean, why do we all hate Doctor X? They aren't all that different, are they?"

"Yes. Oh yes, they *are*."

"Well all right. I'm sorry, oh, please don't get upset."

"All right."

"But when you do start remembering all the people in your life, what will happen to me? I mean, I was thinking last night, now I'm an important person in your mind . . ."

"You are, you are, I promise you, Violet."

"But when it all comes back, I'll be one of—hundreds?"

"Perhaps it won't come back."

"When it does, will you want to be my friend?"

"I am sure I will."

"But *she* won't."

"Are you sure of that?"

"Yes. I saw her both of the times she came to see you. I was the one who took her in to you, and showed her the way and everything. That was when I was being co-operative and amenable."

"She is very attractive. He has good taste, the Professor has."

"Is she what you would choose now, do you think?"

"I wouldn't mind. I wouldn't mind at all if I could just go off with her as if I had just met her."

"But you have only just met her."

"I know when I'm with her that she is telling me the truth. She hates me, you see."

"Yes, she does. But it's not you she hates so much. She hates her life."

"Are you sure of that?"

"Yes. I saw her face. I took a good close look, both times. I knew what she was feeling."

"Tell me then."

"She's like my mother."

"But perhaps everyone is?"

"No. Because if that is true it means you are like my father, and you aren't, you aren't, you aren't."

"Don't cry then."

"I don't cry. *Never.* Or if I do, it isn't me that's crying. I can watch myself cry—it's not worth anything, not like real sorrow ... *she* was crying like anything last time."

"They say I lost my memory because I feel guilty."

"Do you?"

"I think I feel guilty because I lost my memory. I do feel very deeply indeed that it is irresponsible to lose one's memory."

"If you feel that, you haven't lost your memory, but you have only lost some facts, some events."

"Oh yes, I do tell myself that. But there's something else. Yes. There's something I *have* to remember. I *have* to."

"But don't get excited, it makes it worse."

"I've been here over two months, Violet."

"Don't let them send you to that place. Don't."

"But if I refuse to go, they say I'll have to have shock."

Both of them, the middle-aged man and the pretty girl, turned to look at a person, a woman, who sat in a chair a few feet away, watching the television. The programme had at last started. Then they looked at another person, a middle-aged man, and then at another, and so on, around the room. The people their glances were isolating in this way had had shock treatments, or were in the course of having them.

There was no method of treatment that caused more emotion in the wards, more fear. Yet of the people in that room, more than half had had the electric current switched through their brains. Although some of the new drugs that were being used were as powerful as electric shocks, and although as little was known about their effects as was known about shock treatment, these new drugs did not provoke nearly as much fearful comment and speculation.

"Brian Smith says he knows to a week when he is going to have to come in and have another set of shocks," she said.

"Mrs. Jones told me she couldn't bear the thought of living without them," he agreed.

There was a considerable silence.

"Roger is going out next week," she said at last. "He says he will be looking for a flat to share. He says we can go and live with him if we like, until we find a place of our own."

"Oh good. That's very kind. Yes, I'm sure that would be the best thing for both of us."

Well now Professor.

Well now Doctor Y?

I've got you another two weeks. But it wasn't easy and I am afraid it's the last extension possible. It would be so much easier if you didn't show your dislike of Doctor X so strongly. It is quite irrational you know. I understand that among the patients I'm a goody and he is a baddy. It's like schoolchildren.

I don't dislike him.

But you never say a word to him.

There is nothing I can say. He's not there.

Well, well.

Doctor Y, have you thought at all of what I suggested?

Oh, come now, Professor!

I'd look after her. You don't imagine ... I understand her. All she needs is to be allowed to behave like a little girl.

You fancy yourself as a nursery maid?

Or as her father.

It doesn't matter what I think, anyway. It wouldn't be possible. She has two fathers, two mothers, three sisters and a brother. As I know to my sorrow.

But it's not illegal?

No. But you'd find the whole lot buzzing around you day and night. No, it's better she stays here where she is allowed to be a little girl without the benefit of her relations.

It is very strange to me, Doctor Y. You say you'd be delighted if I went to stay with Miles Bovey. Or with Rosemary Baines.

Both have said they'd be happy to have you stay with them as long as it would help. Mr. Bovey has a cottage in Wales, he says. It would be quiet for you.

And Miss Baines sounds a reasonable type of woman.

And yet I don't know either of them.

You said you did remember wandering around by yourself that night when you got to Miss Baines?

A little. Not much. It isn't the wandering around that is the point. No. The point is—there was something I had to remember. Have to remember. I know that. I was looking for something. Somebody.

Yourself?

Words. That's a word. To you that means one thing, but it's different to me.

You think you'll remember if you share a flat with Violet.

I don't know. But you see, she's *now*—do you understand? She's not like a person in a dream. She can't suddenly turn into something else—*and make up a past for me.*

I don't think either Miles Bovey or Miss Baines would make up a past for you. And above all, it wouldn't be an emotional pressure, as it might be if you went home too soon.

I don't know why I can never make you understand. I can get Violet to understand everything I say.

Are you sure she's not behaving as a small girl would—playing at grownups?

I am sure sometimes, yes. But she is not just a small girl, Doctor Y. Emotionally yes, of course. But in other ways she understands things you don't.

Well, I'm sorry. What do you want me to do? I can say to you that I agree it might help both you

and Violet to spend a period of convalescence together. I could say that. But I am sure there would be
other opinions. Not least from her parents. All four of
them.

She's twenty-one.

Legally.

So that's that.

If you and Violet left tomorrow and set up a
ménage together you wouldn't be stopped physically. But I guarantee she'd come running back to us
inside a week.

To be protected from me?

From her feelings about you, first of all. And
mostly because of her family.

But why should they know?

It's extremely easy to find out where people are
these days. There is an industry to do just that.

All right Doctor. Then I have one choice the less.
And the one that I'll end up with is my wife and
family.

In the end, yes. Because that's where you belong.

Tell me, was there a point in your life that was a
real turning point? You could have chosen to do
something else?

No, I think my life has been pretty mapped out
for me by circumstances.

But when you think of yourself, you don't think
of yourself as your circumstances, surely.

I could have done other things, of course. But
I've been the same person.

Then why do I *have* to be Professor Thingabob?
And I'm not Felicity's husband and the father of
James and Philip. Suppose I had gone back to Yugoslavia after the war and married Vera? She was Konstantina's close friend.

Look Professor, whether I understand you or not
doesn't make any difference, you know. There are
certain roads open to you. I want to list them again—
right?

Why don't you *see?*

You can go home. Your wife says she'll be happy,
any time you decide to go home. We think this would
be a mistake as you are now. We don't know but we
think it is possible that your home or your wife or
your children set you off in the first place.

It was nothing to do with Felicity. It was to do
with . . .

Go on, catch it—to do with what?

It went. How can I not remember? How? It's just
there, always, I feel I could catch it by suddenly
turning my head, it's so close. Like a shadow out of
the corner of my eye.

And it is not your wife or your home?

No. I know the nature of it very well. I keep
telling you that. The kind of thing it is—I know that.
But not exactly what. There's something else I ought
to be doing. Something different. I know that, and I
have to . . .

I'm going on with the alternatives. The second
one is that you could stay with a friend, either Miles
Bovey or Rosemary Baines, since they have both
offered . . .

But you say I don't know Rosemary Baines, I met her once at a public meeting, and she wrote me that letter you showed me. Sometimes I do think that there is something there for me. Last time I read her letter yes, I did think—but how can I be sure? It is so easy to be trapped. I'm trapped here. I might find that another trap and . . .

I'm going on. But that is my advice—try a friend for a short time. They are less exacting than families and . . .

Friends. Friends, yes. Real friends. Friends are not for comforting, and licking each other's muzzles and saying how nice you are, how kind. Friends are for fighting, they are for . . .

I am going on. If you decide not to go home, and decide not to stay with a friend, there's the North Catchment Hospital in two weeks from now. And there you would find the same conditions as here . . .

Everyone says much worse.

The same, I mean, for your choices. Because if you wanted to leave there, you'd be in the same position exactly as you are now. The same alternatives.

It's not a question of alternatives. It's a question of remembering.

I'm going on. Or you can agree to have shock therapy. I've already gone into the pros and cons pretty thoroughly. It has to be shock, because you haven't responded to the alternative drugs.

Tell me.

The essence of it in my opinion is that I don't think it would do you any harm, and it may have the effect of making you remember.

Remember what, that's the point!

Or it may leave you exactly as you are now.

When you give people electric shock treatment you don't know, not really, what it does.

No. But we do know there are thousands, probably millions by now, of people who would be too depressed to go on living without it.

I'm not depressed, Doctor. I am not.

Well, well.

And if you were in my place, you'd have the electric shock treatment?

Yes I would. You'll probably come to that in the end. That's my view. It is also the view of Doctor X. You have had the drugs we use instead of shock. None has worked with you. Nothing has worked. You had lost your memory when you came in, and you still have no memory. So what shall we do?

But I have two weeks more here?

Yes.

Of course I might remember in that time.

Yes, you might. Would you like to try writing things down again? A tape-recorder?

My room in college looks out into a small court. The court is square and has white walls. There are various plants in tubs and pots. The wall opposite my door is the retaining wall of the garden above it. Honeysuckle dangles down over this wall from that garden. Last summer the honeysuckle let down two long tendrils side by side, but separated from each other by about a yard. The two green dangling sprays look attractive on the white wall. It is the nature of honeysuckle to look for a support, a wall or a trellis or another plant. There is nothing on that wall for it to fasten itself to. But there is a camellia in a pot in the corner. I noticed that the strand of honeysuckle nearer the camellia was swaying back and forth in wider sweeps than the strand further away. At first I thought that for some reason the wind or a breeze was reaching this strand to make it move more than the other—though this seemed unlikely because it was the strand on the outer side of the wall nearer the entrance which was more vulnerable to wind or air passing. Or at least it would be reasonable to think so. But there was no doubt that it was the inner strand which moved faster and in wider sweeps, in its efforts to reach and fasten itself on to the camellia. I sat there last summer a good deal, watching. It was really a remarkable sight. After watching for a few minutes, the faster moving strand began to seem like an arm or a part of some sea animal, as it swayed back and forth, trying to reach the camellia. Day after day passed, but no matter how hard the honeysuckle tendril tried, it could not reach the camellia. Then I moved the pot with the camellia in it inwards a few inches, and sat to watch how the honeysuckle finally managed to latch itself on, helped by a small breeze.

Then I moved the camellia back again, into its corner, though by now I was so involved with the efforts of the honeysuckle to find a support it was like taking away food from a creature. I marked the length of the honeysuckle on the wall with chalk. But it had become autumn, and the plant had stopped lengthening itself for that year.

One afternoon I looked up from my desk and saw that the honeysuckle had swung itself far enough to lay a tight tendril around a branch of the camellia.

It had been a stormy night. And the tendril or arm of the honeysuckle that was farther away had been swung up by the wind past the camellia-loving tendril to lay hold of a trellis high on the wall. So now both tendrils were fastened and made pretty loops of green on the wall. But then in a few days there was another strong wind, and the outer trendril lost its hold on the trellis and fell down. Now, hanging down by itself, it began a slow determined swinging to reach its sister tendril that was hanging down on the wall, but curving away, since this inner one was fastened to the camellia. As I watched one afternoon, I saw how a small breeze took this outer strand to hook on to the inner one, but the combined weight of the two was too much for the still tentative clasp of the tendril on the camellia, and now both sprays fell back and dangled down the wall.

We were all back where we started.

Both again started their slow aspiring swinging back and forth, back and forth, more or less, according to whether there was a wind. But they were never entirely still. Even on a windless day, the sprays would be in perpetual light movement, the one closer to the camellia moving more than the other.

I used to sit and watch and I asked myself if the honeysuckle sprays "remembered" how one of them had been able to reach the high trellis on the night of the strong wind, and the other how it had found a host in the camellia. After all, the genus honeysuckle "remembers" that it must hold fast on to something or other, and it knows how it must swing back and forth inside the attraction of another plant which becomes its host. And what of the camellia? Does it lean over as far as it can to help the honeysuckle to reach it? Surely the camellia cannot be indifferent to the efforts of the honeysuckle?

By the time the autumn ended, the honeysuckle

spray had several times reached the camellia, with the aid of light breezes, and had several times been pulled away again, either by too strong a breeze, or because of its sister strand adding its weight to it.

And all the times between, when the inner strand was not attached to the camellia, it hung there, lightly quivering, always in subtle movement, waiting as it swung for the wind, as a surfer adjusts the balance of his body for an expected wave.

Sometimes, watching, I could feel the process on that wall as a unity: the movement of the honeysuckle spray, the waiting camellia, and the breeze which was not visible at all, except as it lifted the honeysuckle spray up and close to the camellia.

It was not: The honeysuckle spray swings and reaches the camellia.

It was not: The wind blows the spray on to its host.

The two things are the same.

Not until the spring came, when the honeysuckle spray lengthened its growth, and achieved a wider swing, was it certain of a really solid grasp of the camellia.

Now I see a third part of the process.

Not only: The movement of the spray made it reach the camellia,

Or: The wind blew it so it could reach the camellia,

But: The further growth of the honeysuckle made it possible to reach the camellia.

But the element in which this process exists is— Time.

Time is the whole point. Timing.

The surfer on the wave. The plant swinging in the wind. And it's just the same with—well, everything, and that's what I have to say, Doctor. Why can't you see that?

It was ten at night in a ward or room shared by the Professor and three other men. The ward was cosy, with its pink curtains drawn. The Professor was reading that day's *Times*. Outside was a wild night, noisy with wind.

Of the other three patients, two were already asleep, their bedside lights off, and one was listening to the radio through headphones.

A girl came into the ward. She wore flowered little-girl pyjamas, and a white fluffy dressing gown. Her señorita's hair was now loosed from the formal bun, but she had pulled it back and tied it at the nape of her neck, making it a brown bush caught neatly by a pink ribbon bow. She was everything that was proper and right, but poor girl, she could not help herself and now the shock inherent in Miss Violet Stoke's presence was because the little girl had a sad, knowledgeable woman's face. She sat on the Professor's bed and lowered her voice to say furiously: "Is it true?"

"Yes, I suppose so."

"But *why?* Don't. Please don't. Oh please please don't."

That day the whisper had gone around that Professor Charles Watkins had voluntarily agreed to have electric shock treatment. Some of the patients were indifferent, but not many. Most were agitated by the news. He had become a bit of a symbol. For the Professor, unlike most of them, had had a choice. He had not been given shock treatment when many would have had it, because Doctor Y opposed it, in his case. But now, when he was himself again (except for the fact that he still could not agree that his past was what they said it was) he had said to Doctor Y, and to Doctor X, that he would try it.

He was going to have his first shock the following morning.

Some of the patients reacted as if they were in a prison and one of their number had offered to be electrocuted.

The Professor, an agreeable, smiling, middle-aged man with distinguished greying hair and kindly blue eyes, took the girl's hand in his, and said: "I'm sorry if you are upset. But I do feel a bit at a loss. For one thing, they won't hear of our sharing a flat. But I suppose it was unrealistic."

"It was only unrealistic because we didn't insist on it. What am I going to do now? Where shall I go? I don't have anybody."

"Well, if as I hope I do remember, then I'll be well and you can come and stay a while with Felicity and myself and the children."

There was a furious silence.

Then he said: "I'm sorry. I know that that is dishonest. Or it could be. But I suppose if I am Professor Thingabob and I have a home then I can have people to stay?"

"You've settled for that. Why, why, why?"

The Professor examined the two sleeping men in the beds opposite him, and then the man on the same side of the room as himself who sat straight up in bed, smiling with pleasure, and sometimes laughing a little out loud, as he listened to the radio programme.

The Professor said: "There's only one thing they all seem to agree on. It is that the electric shock might jolt me into remembering."

"Yes and it might not. You know as well as I do what some of them get like. They're like shadows. They're like zombies. It isn't as if you haven't seen what happens."

"But some are perfectly all right and they improve."

"But you are taking the chance."

Feet were coming along the passage to this room, and a cheerful voice was saying Goodnight, Goodnight, Goodnight, and lights were going out in the wards off the passage.

"But supposing I remember what I want to re-remember? They take it for granted that I'll remember what they want me to remember. And it's desperately urgent that I should remember, I do know that. It's all timing, you see. I know that, too. It's the stars in their courses. The time and the place. I was thinking and thinking . . . I lay awake last night and the night before that and the night before that . . . I was working something out. Why do I have this sense of urgency? It's familiar. It's not something I've had only since I lost my memory. No. I had it before. Now I think I know what it is. And not only that. There are lots of things in our ordinary life that are—shadows. Like coincidences, or dreaming, the kinds of things that are an angle to ordinary life, do you follow me, Violet?"

She nodded. Her sad woman's eyes were looking towards the door, where the nurse would stand in a few moments. This was the last ward of this set of wards.

"The important thing is this—to remember that some things reach out to us from that level of living, to here. Anxiety is one. The sense of urgency. Oh, they make an illness of it, they charm it away with their magic drugs. But it isn't for nothing. It isn't un-connected. *They* say, "an anxiety state," as they say, paranoia, but all these things, they have a meaning, they are reflections from that other part of ourselves, and that part of ourselves knows things we don't know."

"Well now," said the nurse, arriving, and seeing the man and the girl in bedtime chat. "It's time you were in bed and asleep Miss Stoke."

"I'm just going," said Violet, instantly transformed into a sulking three-year-old.

The nurse was turning off the ward's central lights.

"My sense of urgency is very simple," said the Professor. "I've remembered that much. It's because what I have to remember has to do with time running out. And that's what anxiety is, in a lot of people. They know they have to do something, they should be doing something else, not just living hand to mouth, putting paint on their faces and decorating their caves and playing nasty tricks on their rivals. No. They have to do something else before they die—and so the mental hospitals are full and the chemists flourishing."

"Would you like a sleeping pill, Professor?"

"No thank you, Nurse."

"And I must remind you not to eat anything in the morning, please. You'll have your breakfast after your treatment."

"I'll turn out the light in just a minute. Can I?" demanded the girl peremptorily, all flashing eyes and pouting lips, trying out her three-year-old powers.

"All right, Miss Stoke. But please, the Professor needs his sleep tonight, and so do you, dear."

She went out. "Dear yourself," muttered the girl.

The two now sat close, in a half dark. The man sitting up listening to the radio laughed out loud, held his breath in anticipation of an expected joke, and laughed again.

"So that's why, you see, Violet. The shock might shock me into remembering what it is that I know is there, the shadow I can see out of the corner of my eye."

"But it might turn out to be just that—you are Professor Charles Watkins?"

"I know I am taking a chance. I know that very well. Perhaps the shock will make me forget what I already know. That I should be living quite differently."

"Yes, but how, we all say that, we do keep saying that, I know that is the point of everything, but how?"

"There's something I have to reach. I have to tell people. People don't know it but it is as if they are living in a poisoned air. They are not awake. They've been knocked on the head, long ago, and they don't know that is why they are living like zombies and killing each other."

"Like Eliza Frensham after a shock."

"Or like me, tomorrow, after mine. Yes I know."

"But how can we be different? How can we get out? If you find out, will you come and take me with you?"

"It's all timing, you see. Sometimes it is easier for us to get out than other times. . . ."

"Miss Stoke!" said the nurse from the door.

"Coming," said the girl. "I said I was coming and I am. Right?"

She slipped off the bed and stood close to the elderly man's pillow.

"There are people in the world all the time who know," the Professor said. "But they keep quiet. They just move about quietly, saving the people who know they are in the trap. And then, for the ones who have got out, it's like coming around from chloroform. They realise that all their lives they've been asleep and dreaming. And then it's their turn to learn the rules and the timing. And they become the ones to live quietly in the world, just as human beings might if there were only a few human beings on a planet that had monkeys on it for inhabitants, but the monkeys had the possibility of learning to think like human beings. But in the poor sad monkeys' damaged brains there's a knowledge half buried. They sometimes think that if they only knew how, if only they could remember properly, then they could get out of the trap, they could stop being zombies. It's something like that Violet. And I've got to take the chance."

"I'll be thinking of you tomorrow morning."

"Goodnight my dear."

"Goodnight Charles."

"Goodnight Professor."

"Goodnight Nurse."

OH MY DEAR DEAR CHARLES,

Doctor Y telephoned me to say you are yourself again. I'm coming up to fetch you on Thursday. Oh my dear dear dear dearest darling Charles. And the boys are so happy and so looking forward. I can't write . . . this is just to say I'll be there on Thursday at four with the car.

FELICITY

DEAR CHARLES,

Felicity tells me you are restored to yourself. It goes without saying that I'm delighted. I had planned to give the series of lectures you had engaged for this term—as well as holding the fort for you in various other directions. But I'm only too delighted to hand back the responsibility to you. The first is The Homeric Epithet, Part I, The Iliad. It is on Monday week. If you don't feel up to it, never mind. Please let me know.

JEREMY

DEAR JEREMY,

Thank you for everything. I'm sorry I've been such a bore. I seem to be in full possession of my faculties again. I do remember all about the lecture series. I feel quite well enough to undertake them.

Yours,
CHARLES

DEAR MILES,

I have to thank you for your very kind interest while I was ill. But I am better again. Are you thinking of coming up to London at all this winter? If so we could have a meal? Do let me know if you are. Or a family weekend in Cambridge?

Yours,

CHARLES

DEAR MISS BAINES,

I am sure you will be pleased to hear that I am fully recovered again, and so expect not to be such a burden on your continuing kind interest. Incidentally, I have to thank you for your patience on the night when I inflicted myself on you in what was an unforgivable way. Please apologise on my behalf to Mr. Larson. As I shall be back in Cambridge and extremely busy I am afraid I shall not be able to accept your very kind invitation to dinner.

Yours sincerely,

CHARLES WATKINS

AFTERWORD, OR END-PAPER

A SMALL, RELEVANT REMINISCENCE

Some years ago I wrote a story for a film. This story was the result of a close friendship with a man whose senses were different from the normal person's.

BLAKE ASKS:
How do you know but every Bird that cuts the airy way,
Is an immense world of delight, closed by your senses five?

To know very well, and for a long time, a person who experiences everything differently from "normal" people, poses the same question.

The point of this film was that the hero's or protagonist's extra sensitivity and perception must be a handicap in a society organised as ours is, to favour the conforming, the average, the obedient.

The script was shown to various film-makers, several of whom toyed lengthily with the idea of doing it—as is the way of that industry, but they all asked the same question: What is wrong with the man in the film?

Now, it had not occurred to me to think of that before, partly because to my mind the way I had written the thing made the question irrelevant, and partly because, in life, the original of the hero, or main character, had been diagnosed by the medical profession so variously and contradictorily for so many years, that thinking on these lines seemed unhelpful.

Also, one has to be particularly trained to believe that to put a label on a feeling, a state of mind, a thing—to find a set of words or a phrase; in short, to describe it—is the same as understanding and experiencing it. Such a training is the education obligatory in our schools, the larger part of which education is devoted to teaching children how to use labels, to choose words, to define.

I thought of something to do. I sent the script to two doctors. One was the Consultant Psychiatrist at a teaching hospital attached to a large university—a man who trained future doctors and who treated patients. The other was a neurologist working at a large London teaching hospital, who had a Harley Street practice.

In short, these were men at the head of their profession.

I asked them to read the script and to tell me what was wrong with the man, as dispassionately as if he were a patient coming to their consulting rooms or outpatient departments.

They were kind enough to do so, taking trouble over it, and time.

But their skilled and compassionate diagnoses, while authoritative, were quite different from each other's. They agreed about nothing at all.

ABOUT THE AUTHOR

DORIS LESSING was born of British parents in Persia in 1919, and moved, with her family, to Southern Rhodesia when she was five years old. She went to England in 1949, and has lived there ever since. She has written more than a dozen books—novels, stories, reportage, poems and plays.

READ TOMORROW'S LITERATURE—TODAY

The best of today's writing bound for tomorrow's classics.

☐	V. Thomas Pynchon	4203 •	$1.25
☐	ONE DAY IN THE LIFE OF IVAN DENISOVICH Alexander Solzhenitsyn	4639 •	.95
☐	THE ELECTRIC KOOL-AID ACID TEST Tom Wolfe	4717 •	$1.25
☐	THE END OF THE ROAD John Barth	4775 •	.95
☐	PORTNOY'S COMPLAINT Philip Roth	4899 •	$1.50
☐	SNOW WHITE Donald Barthelme	7116 •	$1.25
☐	BEING THERE Jerzy Kosinski	7275 •	$1.25
☐	THE PAINTED BIRD Jerzy Kosinski	7443 •	$1.25
☐	AUGUST 1914 Alexander Solzhenitsyn	7677 •	$2.25
☐	THE BREAST Philip Roth	7700 •	$1.25
☐	MUMBO JUMBO Ishmael Reed	7715 •	$1.50
☐	THE GOLDEN NOTEBOOK Doris Lessing	7747 •	$1.95
☐	DOCTOR BRODIE'S REPORT Jorge Luis Borges	7765 •	$1.95
☐	AMERICAN REVIEW #20 Theodore Solotaroff, ed.	7920 •	$1.95
☐	THE SOT-WEED FACTOR John Barth	8068 •	$1.95
☐	GRAVITY'S RAINBOW Thomas Pynchon	8099 •	$2.50
☐	THE SUMMER BEFORE THE DARK Doris Lessing	8360 •	$1.75
☐	NINETY-TWO IN THE SHADE Thomas McGuane	8421 •	$1.50

Buy them at your local bookstore or use this handy coupon for ordering:

Bantam Books, Inc., Dept. EDO, 414 East Golf Road, Des Plaines, Ill. 60016

Please send me the books I have checked above. I am enclosing $_____ (please add 35¢ to cover postage and handling). Send check or money order—no cash or C.O.D.'s please.

Mr/Mrs/Miss_____

Address_____

City_____State/Zip_____

EDO—7/74

Please allow three weeks for delivery. This offer expires 7/75.

READ THE WOMEN
WHO TAKE STANDS
AND ACT ON THEM

THE NAMES THAT SPELL GREAT LITERATURE

Choose from today's most renowned world authors—every one an important addition to your personal library.

Hermann Hesse

☐	MAGISTER LUDI	5555	• $1.50
☐	BENEATH THE WHEEL	5859	• $1.25
☐	NARCISSUS AND GOLDMUND	5868	• $1.50
☐	THE JOURNEY TO THE EAST	7362	• $1.50
☐	ROSSHALDE	7370	• $1.50
☐	DEMIAM	7734	• $1.50
☐	GERTRUDE	7767	• $1.50
☐	STEPPENWOLF	7979	• $1.50
☐	SIDDHARTHA	8819	• $1.50

Alexander Solzhenitsyn

☐	ONE DAY IN THE LIFE OF IVAN DENISOVICH	4639	• $ .95
☐	THE LOVE-GIRL AND THE INNOCENT	6600	• $ .95
☐	THE FIRST CIRCLE	7074	• $1.50
☐	STORIES AND PROSE POEMS	7409	• $1.50
☐	CANCER WARD	7843	• $1.50
☐	AUGUST 1914	7677	• $2.25

Jerzy Kosinski

☐	BEING THERE	7275	• $1.25
☐	THE PAINTED BIRD	7443	• $1.25
☐	THE DEVIL TREE	7865	• $1.50
☐	STEPS	8709	• $1.25

Jorge Luis Borges

☐	THE ALELPH AND OTHER STORIES, 1939-1969	7117	• $1.95
☐	DOCTOR BRODIE'S REPORT	7765	• $1.95

André Schwarz-Bart

☐	THE LAST OF THE JUST	7708	• $1.50
☐	A WOMAN NAMED SOLITUDE	7880	• $1.75

Buy them at your local bookstore or use this handy coupon for ordering:

Bantam Books, Inc., Dept. EDG, 414 East Golf Road, Des Plaines, Ill. 60016

Please send me the book I have checked above. I am enclosing $_____ (please add 35¢ to cover postage and handling). Send check or money order—no cash or C.O.D.'s please.

Mr/Mrs/Miss_____

Address_____

City_____State/Zip_____

EDG—10/74

Please allow three weeks for delivery. This offer expires 10/75.